② Lost Lords of Pembrook

2012

"A kiss."

She spun back around to face him. "Pardon?"

"A kiss. That's what I want you to barter for passage on my ship."

Slowly he prowled over the thick carpet, until he was standing before her, his gaze smoldering as it dipped to her lips. Then he was looking into her eyes, holding her captive as easily as if he'd bounded her with silk.

"A long, slow, leisurely kiss," he whispered in a velvety smooth voice that sent a shiver of something that resembled pleasure scurrying along her spine. "On my ship, the moment of my choosing."

"A... kiss," she repeated. "That can't be all you want."

"No, it's not all I want, but it's what I'll be content to take. Anything more, you must be willing to give..."

Romances *by* Lorraine Heath

LORD OF
TEMPTATION

LORRAINE HEATH

AVON

An Imprint of HarperCollinsPublishers

AVON BOOKS
An Imprint of HarperCollins*Publishers*
10 East 53rd Street
New York, New York 10022-5299

To Matt, Sienna, Shelby, Shannon,
Dr. Ratna Sajja and the staff at North Dallas
Radiation Oncology Center,
and to Dr. William C. Mitchell and staff.

For your calm, your kindness, your devotion to
healing,
your ability to make us believe that everything would
be all right . . .
And then for making it so.

This one is dedicated from my family and me
With our heartfelt gratitude

Prologue

LIBRARY I LAURI

*Yorkshire
Winter 1844*

They were running for their lives.

At fourteen, Tristan Easton was well aware of that fact as he scampered behind his twin brother along the creaking docks. They wouldn't be together much longer. It was far too dangerous. They were matching bookends with pale blue eyes— "Ghost Eyes" the gypsies called them—that made them easily identifiable as the lords belonging to Pembrook. And when they were within each other's shadow, they became an easy target for the one who wished them harm.

Through the midnight haze, barely illuminated by the occasional lantern or torch, Sebastian led the way because he was the older by twenty-two minutes. As such he was the eighth Duke of Keswick, now that their father was dead—murdered, no doubt, by their vile uncle who yearned to gain the titles and properties. But three lads stood in his way. Tristan was of a mind to see that it remained that way.

Even though his heart was galloping madly at the sight of the monstrous ship looming ahead of them, rocking on the water, fog swirling ominously around it. Bitter bile rose in his throat as the stench of brine mingled with decaying fish assaulted his nostrils.

Sebastian staggered to a stop, swung around—his black hair flopping into his eyes—and grabbed Tristan's shoulders. "You understand that I have no choice. We must do this."

He'd said the same words to their younger brother, Rafe, when he delivered him to a workhouse. But Rafe hadn't understood. Not really. Four years their junior, he'd reacted the way he usually did when the twins formed plans that didn't include him: he whined, blubbered, and begged not to be left behind. What a sniveling little pup!

Tristan was above putting on a similar disgusting performance, even though he could barely breathe with the dread of what awaited him churning in his gut, even though he had to clamp his teeth together so they didn't betray that he was shaking with fear. Tiny chilled tremors that somehow seemed far worse than outright trembling. But he wouldn't add to Sebastian's burdens. He'd be a man about this, prove his worth.

He wished Sebastian hadn't stopped, hadn't given him time to think about what was happening. Their uncle, Lord David Easton, had locked them in the cold dark tower at Pembrook as soon as all the mourners had left following their father's funeral. Their mother was long dead. They were in their uncle's care now, and it seemed he intended to rid himself of them.

They'd still be shivering in that prison if Mary, their neighbor's daughter, hadn't helped them to escape. Tristan had wanted to use the opportunity to slay their uncle then and there, be done with the troublesome bastard, but Sebastian favored waiting until they were men, better able to command the situation. Unfortunately that plan involved going into hiding. Where better than far from England's shores?

Tristan gave a brisk nod in response to his brother's earlier words. He clenched his hands into balled fists to keep them from reaching out and clutching Sebastian's shirt in a last vain attempt to avoid the impending separation.

Sebastian's fingers tightened, digging painfully into Tristan's shoulders. "Remember, ten years from now, on the night we escaped, we meet at the old abbey ruins. We'll get our revenge, I swear to you upon mother's and father's graves."

He nodded once again.

"All right then."

Sebastian continued along the dock until they came to the hulking ship. It groaned in the darkness of the night. A large man stood near the plank that led onto the ship. His greatcoat barely stirred in the breeze coming off the water. A scar along the left side of his face brought the corner of his mouth up into a mockery of a smile. His eyes were as black as sin.

A shiver skittered down Tristan's spine. He wanted to turn on his heel and head to the stable where they'd tethered their horses. He wanted to climb onto Molly and gallop away, never stopping. Instead he forced himself to stand beside his brother as he faced the captain to whom Sebastian had spoken in a tavern earlier.

"Have you the coins?" Sebastian asked.

"Aye." The captain tossed a leather pouch into the air, caught it. The coins jingled. "You sure you be wanting this, lad? To be me cabin boy?"

Tristan nodded.

"Hard life on a ship. Neither of you look like boys accustomed to a hard life."

Tristan fought to find his voice—

"He's not afraid," Sebastian announced confidently.

Tristan was grateful for his brother's words, glad he was successfully hiding that he was truly terrified.

"All right then." The captain tossed the pouch to Sebastian, who caught it with both hands, as though it weighed far more than it did, as though it carried the burden of his conscience. "Let's get aboard."

The captain turned and began to walk up the gangway. Tristan took a step—

Sebastian grabbed him, hugged him tightly. "Be strong."

Tristan's eyes burned. Dammit. He wasn't going to cry. He wasn't going to be a baby like Rafe. With a nod he slapped Sebastian on the back, broke free, and ran up the ship's corridor. He leaped onto the deck.

When he looked back all he saw was Sebastian's retreating shadow disappearing into the darkness. Tristan wanted to go with him. He didn't want to be here. He didn't want this.

The captain's huge paw of a hand landed on his shoulder with enough weight to jar him.

"I'm called Marlow. Have you a name, lad?"

"Lo—" He stopped. He couldn't tell anyone that he was Lord Tristan Easton, second in line for the dukedom of Keswick. Until they reclaimed their birthright he was only a commoner. He cleared his throat. "Tristan."

"Well, Lo Tristan, who you be running from?"

Tristan pressed his lips tightly together. The captain had caught his mistake, was mocking him. He would never be so careless again. If he was to be nothing else, he would become a master keeper of secrets.

"So be it," the captain said. "I'll call you Jack."

Tristan jerked his gaze up to the towering man. "Why?"

"When you're seeking to hide, lad, you hide everything."

Tristan looked back toward the looming black void into which his brother had vanished. He could do that. He could deeply bury everything about himself. He could become someone else. He *would* become someone else.

He only hoped that when the time was right, he could find himself once again.

Chapter 1

I had always heard that the eyes were a window into one's soul. As I stared into his, I could not determine if they were merely shuttered or if the rumors about him were true: that he possessed no soul to speak of because he'd traded it to the devil for immortality. By all accounts, the life he pursued was one that should have led him to an early grave. Yet, there he sat, his ghostly blue gaze unwavering, challenging . . . dangerous. A time would come when I would question the wisdom in not walking away, but I longed for more than I possessed and so I stood my ground, refusing to be put off. I often look back on that stormy night and wonder how different my life might be now had I realized that the journey he would take me on was one that

I would soon discover I had little desire to travel.

—The Secret Memoirs of an Adventurous Lady

London
April 1858

He didn't look at all like a hero.

Lady Anne Hayworth had expected him to be . . . well, at least tidy. She'd never seen a man so unkempt, with three buttons on his shirt undone to reveal a narrowing V of chest that to her surprise seemed as bronzed as his hands. He sat alone at a table in the corner of the tavern as though he owned the establishment, although she was well aware that he didn't. Or at least she didn't think he did. The particulars about him were as difficult to find as the man himself.

Standing before him she was sorely tempted to take a pair of sharp shears to the ebony hair that hung to his shoulders and a razor to the stubble darkening his jaw.

She was accustomed to gentlemen rising when she approached. Instead, he continued to slouch in his chair, leisurely trailing one long thick finger up and down his mug, his gaze fastened on her as though he were imagining what it might be like to stroke that finger along her throat. It was an absurd thought, and she had no idea from whence it had sprung. She was not used to men openly looking at her as though they were contemplating doing wicked things with her.

No, no, this man wasn't hero material at all.

Perhaps the gentleman at the door, the one she'd questioned, had directed her to this man as a cruel prank. If so, she would demand he return the sovereign she'd paid him for his assistance. Still, on the off chance . . .

She cleared her throat and said, "I'm searching for Captain Jack Crimson."

"Crimson Jack. And you found him."

"I see. Captain Crimson Jack, the adventurer?"

One side of his mouth curled up slowly into a mocking smile. "Depends. What sort of adventure are you looking for, Princess?"

"I'm not a princess. My father is an earl, not a prince or a king. He—" She halted. The particulars of her heritage—of anything at all actually—were none of his concern. "I was told you are a man who could help me."

As he raked his insolent gaze over her, her stomach quivered, and she balled her white-gloved hands into fists at her side to stop them from trembling.

"Depends on what sort of help you're needing," he said. "If it's an adventure between the sheets—"

"Definitely not!" she snapped at the arrogant cad.

"Pity."

Pity? Obviously the man had no standards. She

knew she was not a beauty. She lacked color. Her hair was a ghastly white, her eyes silver. Her nose too small, her lips too plump. She knew she should seek help elsewhere, but he had come so highly recommended. Instead, she heard herself ask, "May I sit?"

The chair in front of her wobbled a bit, and she realized that he'd nudged it with his booted foot. *Mannerless jackanapes.* Still, she could not discount the fact that she had been assured that he was a man she could trust not only with her life, but with her virtue. He wasn't in the habit of forcing women, but then based on his handsome features alone—not to mention that wicked smile—she suspected women stumbled over themselves clambering into his bed. She, however, would not be one of them. She pulled out the chair farther and sat. "I am Lady Anne." She halted there. Her father and brothers would not approve of her plans, which was the very reason that she'd chosen to be secretive. "I wish to hire you to take me to Scutari."

"Not a very nice place for a holiday. What say I take you to Brighton instead?"

"My fiancé isn't in Brighton," she snapped. She squeezed shut her eyes as they began to sting. Her family had told her it was a bad idea to go to the place where so many soldiers had died during the Crimean War, to visit the hospital and grounds where Florence Nightingale had fought to save so many lives. But it wasn't so much that she *wanted* to go there. It was quite simply that she *had* to.

She opened her eyes to the expressionless man

sitting across from her. If he thought anything at all about her outburst, he didn't show it.

"You don't need me to get you to Scutari. You can purchase passage—"

"I wish to journey on my schedule. I want to get there quickly. I don't intend to stay long, but it's imperative that I—" Damn the tears that once again threatened. She was stronger than this. She *would* be stronger than this. She swallowed. "—visit with my fiancé and return home before the Season begins."

A handkerchief, surprisingly white and pressed, appeared before her, held in a large roughened hand. She took the offering and dabbed gently at her eyes. "Thank you." She looked down at the scarred table, then lifted her gaze. "I didn't expect this part to be so incredibly difficult."

"How long has it been since you saw him?"

"Four years, almost to the day. I saw him off at the railway station on the morning that he and so many others in service of the Queen began the journey to the Crimea. He looked so incredibly dashing, so confident. Promised to be home in time to go pheasant hunting . . ." She cleared her throat. "I'm frightfully sorry. I'm not sure why I'm telling you all this."

Especially when his eyes held no compassion, no warmth. She didn't know why he'd bothered to offer her the handkerchief unless it was simply that he couldn't abide tears.

"Have you ever been separated from anything, anyone you held dear?" she asked.

He clenched his jaw, and she quickly shook her head. "I'm sorry. That was a silly question. You're a seaman. I'm certain your life is filled with separations."

"Where I'm concerned, don't be certain of anything, Princess."

"I told you that I'm not—"

She saw triumph light his eyes. He'd baited her, and her anger had shoved her sorrow aside. What sort of man was he? Compassionate one moment, distant the next?

Very primly, she folded the handkerchief and extended it toward him.

"Keep it."

She shook her head. "I'm sorry. I've not handled this encounter at all well. As I said earlier, I wish to hire you to take me to Scutari. I've heard you have a remarkably fast ship and you are an exceptional captain."

"True on both counts. But I transport cargo, not people."

"I'm willing to pay handsomely for your ship and services: two hundred pounds."

She'd shocked him. She could tell by the way that he slowly trailed his gaze over her, without insolence, but with a new measure of respect, as though truly seeing her for the first time.

"That's a good deal of money," he finally said.

"Enough to make you go to Scutari, Captain—" She shook her head. "What is your last name, if not Crimson?"

"Jack will suffice."

"I couldn't be so informal."

He plopped his arm down on the table, palm up. "Give me your hand," he ordered.

"Beg pardon?"

"Your hand."

His eyes held a challenge that she couldn't mistake. She saw no harm in doing as he asked. She was wearing gloves after all. Taking a deep steadying breath she placed her hand in his.

Before she could blink he curled his long fingers around her wrist. Then slowly, ever so slowly, he began releasing the buttons on her glove with his other hand.

"Captain—"

"Shh."

She watched in horrified fascination as he leisurely peeled off her glove and set it aside. With no request for permission, he lightly trailed his fingers over hers, then circled them around her palm, following the various lines as though he expected them to guide him somewhere. His fingers were callused, rough, scarred. She doubted he ever wore gloves.

"Your skin is like silk. Your fiancé is a very fortunate man," he said, his voice scratchier, rougher than it had been moments earlier.

"Not as fortunate as you might think."

He didn't question her further, but rather he seemed enthralled by her hand, by the lines that traversed her palm. "There is very little room on my ship for formality," he said, returning to her earlier comment regarding how she was to address him. "You would have to sleep in my cabin."

"But surely you would not be there."

With no rush, he lifted his hooded gaze to hers. Her heart was pounding so hard that she wondered if he could feel it in the throbbing of her pulse at her wrist. "Not always, no. But I would eat my meals there. Study my charts there." A heartbeat of silence. "Bathe there."

She swallowed hard. She could be on deck when he was bathing. Besides, how many baths would the man need in the week or so it would take to reach their destination? "I'm sure we could work out a suitable arrangement."

A corner of his mouth lifted. "It's bad luck to have a woman onboard. My men would not be particularly pleased by your presence. You would have to remain very close to me so that I could offer you protection."

He was striving to manipulate her now, seeking to intimidate, to make her wary. She had four brothers. She knew how the game was played. "I sought you out because I'd heard that you were somewhat of a hero—"

He tightened his jaw, narrowed his eyes, and she realized he wasn't at all pleased with that characterization.

"—although the particulars regarding your heroics were not forthcoming. But I was assured you had excellent command of your men. Surely if you tell them to behave, they will behave."

"For the chance at one of your kisses, I suspect they'd be willing to risk the bite of a cat-o-nine."

"I don't give my kisses freely."

"And I have no need of your two hundred pounds. So tell me, Princess, what else are you willing to barter?"

Lord Tristan Easton, more commonly known along the waterfront as Crimson Jack, couldn't stop his smile from widening as she released a small gasp and snatched her lovely hand free of his grip. He wasn't certain he'd ever encountered such silkiness before. Or such fire in a woman's eyes. But then he wasn't in the habit of taunting women. Yet something about her called to the devil in him.

"You're a cur," she snapped.

"I never claimed otherwise." And he'd hang from the nearest yardarm whichever of his men was spouting tales that he was a hero. He wasn't. Not like his brother Sebastian who'd fought in the bloodiest of battles and barely survived to tell the tale. "You're asking me to go someplace that I have no desire to go. It needs to be worth my while to be so inconvenienced."

Although presently he had no commitments other than lifting tankards of ale and doing as he pleased.

"Obviously the tales I've heard of you are untrue—you're not a man of honor."

He refused to acknowledge how her words bit into his soul. He'd long ago stopped caring how anyone judged him, so why the devil did he give a fig what she thought?

She rose elegantly to her feet. "I'm sorry to have

wasted your time and mine. Good night to you, sir."

With an indignant swish of her skirts, she pivoted on her heel and marched toward the door. Someone jumped forward to open it for her, and then she was gone into the storm.

Pity.

Tristan shifted his gaze over to the nearby table where a lad of sixteen was trying to entice a serving girl onto his lap. "Mouse," he barked.

The boy immediately snapped to attention. "Aye, Cap'n?"

He gave a quick nod toward the door. "I want to know where she goes."

Without delay or complaint the nimble lad took off. If anyone could follow her, he could.

Tristan caught the eye of the disappointed maid and signaled another tankard be brought to him. When it arrived he took a long swig of the thick dark ale and leaned back his chair until it bumped against the wall. His thinking pose.

He'd grown remarkably bored of late. Two years ago he and his brothers had finally made good on their promise—a bit tardy, but still they'd returned to London, routed their uncle, and reclaimed their birthright as the lords of Pembrook.

But London Society had not been so quick to welcome the lords back into the fold. Once Sebastian's position as the Duke of Keswick was secured and their uncle dead, Tristan had returned to the love that had usurped Pembrook in his heart: the sea.

But after nearly twenty months of fighting tempests and gales, he was back on England's shores, feeling untethered, as though he'd somehow broken free of his moorings. He had no desire to return to the tedious London ballrooms. While there, he discovered women aplenty to warm his bed, but they were all cut of the same cloth: satin and silk and lace. They were drawn to the danger he represented. He had only to smile and they fell into his arms. They presented no challenge.

The lady who'd been sitting before him was different. She'd stepped through the door as though she owned the night, had called down the rain, had commanded the thunder to rumble. With the most gracious movements he'd ever seen, she'd reached up and moved aside the wet hood of her pelisse.

He'd felt a quick, almost brutal tightening of his body in response to the exquisiteness of the face revealed. High cheekbones, flawless skin. Her hair, piled on top of her head, was not quite blond, not quite white. The palest of shades.

She'd spoken to a man standing nearby, and Tristan—who had never been jealous of any man—was envious. When the lady began wending her way toward him, he'd anticipated her arrival as he'd anticipated little of late. He'd made a wager with himself regarding the shade of her eyes. Green, he'd thought. But he lost the wager. They were a faint silver, haunting. They'd known tragedy. Of that he was certain.

But they'd not been conquered and he was suddenly of a mind to do so. Her fiancé was a fool of the highest order to go off and play at war when he had her here to warm his bed.

Sebastian had fought in the Crimea. He'd left half his face on the battlefield, perhaps even a portion of his soul, until Mary had come back into his life and made him whole again. So Tristan had no love for that area of the world, for the trouble it had caused his brother, but the notion of having Lady Anne on his ship intrigued him. Although he didn't quite fancy the idea of delivering her to another man. Rather he wanted her for himself. For a time anyway. For a bit of sport, a bit of fun.

He wasn't surprised that she'd not recognized him. He wasn't decked out like a gentleman. It was also possible, since she was betrothed, that she'd not attended the two balls where he and his brothers had made their scandalous appearances after returning to London. *The nerve of them to actually be alive and not devoured by wolves.* While Sebastian might be frequenting those circles now, it would take a keen eye to recognize the similarities between the two men. Most people didn't see beyond his brother's disfigurement.

Tristan liked that she didn't know how he fit into her world—quite uncomfortably if the truth were known. He'd hid it well with quick smiles, laughter, and teasing. But he had little desire to return to the maze of London Society. Rafe had the right of it. Better to stay in the shadows where they were comfortable. They'd been too long without politeness. It was a tight shroud, one he didn't enjoy wearing.

He had a keen insight when it came to discovering buried treasure. He wanted this Lady Anne who'd dared approach him and offer him money. He could have taken it and then wooed her once she was on his ship, but that would have made it all too easy.

He stroked her discarded glove where it remained on the table. In her haste to leave, she'd forgotten it. He yearned for a challenge.

He was fairly certain that she would provide him with one—one he was likely to never forget.

Chapter 2

"**W**ell?" Martha asked as soon as Anne was comfortably settled in the carriage and they were on their way.

"Your brother was unfortunately mistaken," she said succinctly to her lady's maid. "He has not the makings of a hero at all, and he is most certainly not an honorable man."

"Are you certain you spoke with the correct person?"

"Quite."

"I don't understand. Johnny sailed with him, spoke so highly of him—"

"Yes, well, I assure you that he is a man with whom I have no wish to associate." She balled her hand into a fist. Blast it! She'd left her glove behind. Her hand was still so warm from the journey his fingers had taken over it that she'd not even thought about the silly glove. She'd never known such a sensuous touch. It was dangerous. So very dangerous. "Please, speak with your brother and ask him for another recommendation."

"Would it not be better to simply book passage—"

"I will if I must but I'd rather not." She didn't want a long sojourn. She simply required a little bit of time with Walter to say good-bye. But when she had mentioned this to her father and brothers, they'd thought it an awful idea to go there. They didn't understand, but then how could they? She loved Walter, but during their last night together before he left, she'd hurt him with words and deed. Perhaps if she hadn't, he would have come home. She needed to apologize, to ask for his forgiveness.

He'd sent her his wages every month. It wasn't a great deal, but she invested the funds for them, for their future. It was those funds that she would now use to visit him. She would leave a note for her father to find after she was gone. She feared that her departure being at the mercy of schedules and other passengers would result in her family being able to find her more easily, prevent her from leaving.

But a ship at her beck and call—they would leave during the dark of night and be well out to sea before her family discovered she was gone.

She gazed out the window and strove not to think about how Crimson Jack quite possibly ruled the night as easily as he did the sea. He no doubt was accustomed to women fawning over him, crawling into his bed with no compunction what-soever. A naughty part of her that she didn't wish to acknowledge could hardly blame them.

He was devastatingly handsome and something about him was regal in bearing. He'd ruined the illusion, though, when he'd turned down her offer for passage in exchange for money and asked what else she might barter. His smoldering gaze had revealed exactly what he had in mind.

She'd not given it to Walter. She certainly wasn't going to give it to a crude sea captain, even if he did cause images of them tumbling between the sheets to invade her thoughts with little more than the tip of a finger caressing her skin. It was only because he was earthy and rough. A heathen. A man for whom lust was common. He was interested in the conquest, but his interest would wane once a lady was conquered.

She had no interest in being conquered.

She would find a more suitable captain. An old one with more experience. A hideous one who did not cause her heart to flutter. A poor one who had need of coins.

Captain Crimson Jack might believe he was tempting—and she had to reluctantly admit that he might be a delicious morsel of manhood—but she was made of sturdier stuff and was not going to be lured by smoky eyes or the promise of passion they held. She had denied Walter, after all, while loving him with all of her young heart. Every day, every night, she lived with regret over their parting. She needed to go to Scutari so she could assuage her guilt, so she could find happiness—if not with him, then with someone else.

"**W**hat do you know of the Earl of Blackwood?" Tristan asked, standing in the doorway. The clocks had only just tolled midnight, and he'd known he would find his brother in his office. After all, vice dens were busiest when decent people slept.

Rafe gazed up from his ledgers and glared. "I've not seen you in two years and you can't even bother with a proper greeting?"

"Hello," Tristan said laconically before wandering into the room and glancing around. His brother had added a new globe to his collection since Tristan had been here. Interesting. He wondered why his brother fancied them.

"How long have you been in London?" Rafe asked.

"A month, give or take a week. Blackwood?" Bless Mouse and his eagerness to prove his worth to Tristan for providing him with a place aboard his ship. He'd not only followed the lady home, but he'd managed to speak with a servant in order to acquire the particulars regarding the household. The earl had four sons and a daughter.

Studying him intently, Rafe leaned back in his chair and rubbed a thumb over his smooth chin, making Tristan wish he'd tidied up a bit; on the docks the rougher one looked, the tougher he was thought to be. Although Tristan had obtained a reputation for being incredibly tough. He suspected he could prance around in lacy shirts and no one would mess with him. At least not with Crimson Jack.

"Does Sebastian know you're back?"

With a sigh Tristan dropped into a chair across from Rafe. "I've not alerted him to my return."

"He has an heir now, you know."

He waited as Rafe poured whiskey into a tumbler and set it before him. He downed the amber liquid in one long swallow before saying, "I hadn't heard, but I'm relieved. Takes the pressure off me."

"You've no desire to be a duke?"

"None whatsoever."

"You're not going to follow in uncle's footsteps and try to take the dukedom?"

"Uncle's actions would indicate that he was mad, I believe. I'm not. His demise was welcome." Especially as his last act was an attempt to kill Mary. Attacking the brothers was one thing, but to turn his bloodlust on sweet Mary—

"Sebastian and Mary should be arriving for the Season soon," Rafe said.

Tristan tried not to look taken aback. "I assumed they would forever stay at Pembrook."

"I think Mary convinced him that he must be accepted by Society for the sake of his heir, and any other children that come their way."

They could be of assistance in his quest to entice Lady Anne into his arms, but he didn't want to wait until she returned from sailing on another ship.

"So—Blackwood. What do you know of him?" Tristan prodded, wanting to get the conversation back to his purpose for being there.

"He doesn't belong to my club. His two youngest sons do. Mine is not quite as posh as other clubs, so it appeals more to younger men who are not so keen about keeping up appearances."

"And his daughter? What do you know of her?"

Rafe arched a brow. "I don't believe she's a member of my club."

"Aren't you quite the hilarious one? I see you've not grown more communicative in the months I've been away."

"Why do you care about her?"

"She sought to hire me to take her to Scutari."

"Why? The war is over. Nightingale is no longer there to lure nurses."

"She wishes to visit with her fiancé."

"Are you taking her?"

"Only if she's willing to pay my price."

"And that would be?"

He grinned wolfishly. "Between the lady and me."

Rafe scowled. "I see *you've* not grown more communicative either. But if she is betrothed and a lady, you would be unwise to seek a dalliance. Especially as she has four strapping brothers. You could very well find yourself in a bit of bother."

"I'm not certain she has shared with them her desire to make this trip."

"Why would you think that?"

"She has an air of mystery about her, and she is almost as tight-lipped as you. I sensed there was a good deal she had no wish to share. I rather enjoy unraveling mysteries."

"Let her go, Brother."

"Why?"

"My gut tells me that nothing except trouble awaits if you pursue this path."

"You're no doubt correct."

But in his experience trouble was seldom boring.

It was a week before she returned to the tavern. He'd known sooner or later she'd seek him out. What surprised him was how quickly the sight of her inflamed his desire. He knew, as a gentleman, he should stand as she approached but then all would know how badly he wanted her. So he stayed as he was, lounging in his chair, stroking the dew from his tankard as lazily as he'd like to caress her damp skin after a rousing session in his bed.

She marched across the room with the force of a summer gale, purpose in every stride. Fire ignited those silver eyes, turning them pewter. He could see the pulse at her throat fluttering with her anger. Her high cheekbones carried a red hue. Her lips were pursed tightly. How he dearly wanted to part them, dart his tongue between them, and taste the honeyed nectar of her mouth.

He'd never in his life had such a strong reaction to a woman he barely knew. He wanted her, he couldn't deny that. But it was more than the physical that appealed to him. What sort of woman would risk life and reputation to journey toward a man she'd not seen in four years?

He was not a great believer in love, could not claim to have ever loved a woman enough to risk all for her. Love was the domain of poets . . . and perhaps Sebastian. The last time Tristan had seen him, he'd claimed to love Mary. While Tristan held a fondness for her, he wouldn't change his life for her. He didn't understand emotions that ran so deeply.

"You cur!" Lady Anne spat.

Tristan arched an eyebrow and lifted a corner of his mouth in a mocking smile. "Good evening to you as well, Lady Anne."

"I've approached five captains, seeking passage on their ships. They've each turned me away."

"I told you: women on a ship is considered bad luck. Sailors are a suspicious sort. I doubt you'll find any willing to risk it."

"Not when you're paying double what I offer to those who turn me down."

He fought not to show surprise that she'd managed to uncover that little fact.

She took a step nearer, gripped the back of the chair in her gloved hands, and leaned forward, confusion marring her brow. "Why? Why would you seek to undermine my efforts? Why would you care?"

"Because I want you on my ship." Damnation. He'd meant to toy with her a bit longer, like reeling in a fish. His bitter confession was prompted by her eyes. The sorrow there that he didn't understand, the pain that he wanted to ease.

"But you won't take my money."

"No."

"You want me to give you something else."

"Yes."

"I know exactly what you want and you shall never have it."

He tilted his head slightly. "Careful, Princess. That sounded like a challenge. And I've never walked away from a challenge . . . or lost one."

"Rot in hell."

She spun on her heel and stormed from the tavern with the magnificence of the fiercest tempest he'd ever encountered. Dear God, he should accept her offer, take her money, anything to have her on his ship. Once on the sea, she couldn't walk away.

Once on the sea, he would have her.

Anne was furious, so furious that she could pull out her hair. No, no, that would not do at all. It was ridiculous to cause harm to herself. She was angry enough to yank out *his* hair. That's what she should have done: simply reached across the table and jerked out a clump of those long ebony strands. That would show him that she was not a lady to be trifled with.

"I don't understand," Martha murmured meekly as though she feared Anne would turn her fury on her. "My brother speaks so highly of the captain—"

"Yes, well, how he treats his men is quite obviously very different from the manner in which he treats ladies." But why? To ensure captains wouldn't accept her offer, why would he pay double what she would pay them? He could have any woman he wanted, of that she was certain. Why her? Why did he want her on his ship? So he could lift her skirts? He'd damned well discover that where she was concerned, they'd be made of lead. "Tell your brother to find me one more captain. I shall offer to pay him five hundred pounds."

"My lady," Martha gasped. "This goes too far."

Anne didn't bother to inform Martha that she'd overstepped her bounds. They'd been together too long for her to chastise the maid, especially when she knew she was right. "We'll see how Captain Crimson Jack likes paying a thousand."

Martha reached across and took her hand. "Talk to your father again, explain why you need to make this journey. Surely he'll arrange it."

"It will take longer to journey on someone else's schedule."

"Not that much longer."

She released a defeated sigh. "No, not that much longer. I'm being stubborn, I know." But this captain had made her angry, and to go by other means now would make her feel as though he'd somehow won.

"It would be safer," Martha added.

Would it? A woman traveling alone with only her maid? She might run across someone she knew and tongues might wag. She didn't want anyone to know. That was the thing of it. It was her business and hers alone. "I just want to make this sojourn in my own way."

"Lord Walter won't care."

With the tears stinging her eyes, she said quietly more to the night than to her maid, "No, he won't."

Her fury dissipated into sadness. They spoke no more as their carriage journeyed through the fog-shrouded London streets. Dear Walter. She longed to see him once more, to hear his laugh, to have him tease her, to have him hold her in his arms as he swept her over a ballroom floor in time to the music. Ever since he left, she'd avoided the balls, soirees, dinners. She'd devoted her time, along with Florence Nightingale's sister, to gathering the much-needed supplies for the hospitals in the Crimea. She'd visited the returning soldiers in hospital, bringing them what comfort she could. And then she'd gone into mourning when she received word that Walter had died. Any chance for forgiveness had died with him.

Two years. Two years of being dead as well. Of feeling nothing. Of walking around like a silent wraith. She lost weight. She took joy in so little. Even her favorite pastime of reading brought no pleasure. She would reach the end of the book with no memory of any of the words, of the tale. Yet she had dutifully turned pages, thought she had been concentrating on the task. She forgot things so easily.

Then a month ago her father had barked that she needed to snap out of this melancholy mood, as though she was a pea that could be snapped in half and the shell of her life discarded, while the soul remained. He wanted her to return to Society, to find another husband before she grew much older.

She was all of three and twenty. So difficult to look back and realize how very young she'd been when Walter left.

Now she felt so remarkably old.

She knew her father was right. She needed to get on with her life. She knew Walter was not returning home to her, but she wanted the opportunity to say good-bye to him on her schedule, in her way.

Dear Lord, but she missed him. So much. Even after all this time.

She didn't want to admit that the fury tonight felt good. So good. It had been so long since she'd felt anything other than grief. Well, except for the night when she'd met Crimson Jack and felt a slight stirring of—dare she admit it?—desire. When he removed her glove, when he touched her. Afterward she'd been glad that he declined her offer. She couldn't imagine being enclosed on a tiny ship with him. Martha would be with her, of course. Perhaps even a second maid. The sensuality that oozed off the man would require an entire army of maids to protect her.

And here she was thinking about him again, the blackguard. He'd begun invading her dreams, her waking moments. She still seemed incapable of reading a book and absorbing the story. She would find herself drifting off with thoughts of *him*. She didn't think of the old sea captain or the scarred one or the toothless one she'd approach about passage. She didn't even think of the fair handsome one who had sat with a buxom redhead on his lap during their meeting. He had a boisterous laugh and a ready smile, but it wasn't him she thought of. It was the captain with icy blue eyes that seemed to melt the longer they spoke. The one who made her wonder what it would feel like to trail her fingers over that unshaven jaw.

Walter had never been in her presence with stubble shadowing his face. All of his buttons were always properly done up. Not a single strand of his wheat-golden hair was ever out of place. The two men were complete opposites. The captain was not the sort to appeal to her in the least, so why did he plague her so?

She had no answer to that question as the carriage drew to a halt outside the manor. Suddenly she was incredibly weary. It seemed she only managed to attain any sort of energy when she was facing an encounter with Crimson Jack.

A footman handed her down from the carriage and she trudged up the stone steps, each one more laborious to reach than the one before. Once inside she felt the oppressive weight of despair. She would talk with her father. She didn't want to enter the London Season. Not this year. Perhaps next.

"Martha, please give me a half hour or so of solitude and then bring me some warm milk with cocoa," she ordered.

"Yes, m'lady."

Grabbing the banister, Anne dragged herself up the stairs. The melancholy could overtake her without warning or invitation. It just seemed to slam into her of its own will. She didn't like it, she didn't want it. She needed Walter to conquer it. Her father didn't understand that. He'd never needed anyone, not even her mother. Theirs had been an arranged marriage. They'd been content, but when her mother had passed away from influenza three years ago, her father had carried on.

Anne wanted to be that strong, but it seemed love made her weak, left her floundering when the one who held her affections departed this world.

She walked down the long hallway toward the corner room that was hers. Lamps were lit, but no sounds greeted her. Not a snore or a bed creaking or whispers. They were out, her brothers. Her father as well, no doubt. Why did men have places to go at night and women didn't?

Going into her bedchamber, she closed the door behind her. After removing her pelisse and tossing it on a nearby chair, she began tugging off her gloves, refusing to remember how lovely it had felt as the captain had removed one. Fortunately she owned several pairs, but still she didn't like that she had left one behind. When she was done she tossed them onto her pelisse and strolled to her mahogany wardrobe. The door released a quick snick as she opened it and reached into the back for the brandy she'd pilfered from her father's collection. She knew ladies didn't drink spirits, but she'd been so cold after Walter's death that she'd been desperate for warmth. She'd found it one night in her father's liquor cabinet.

She set a snifter on her vanity and poured herself a generous portion.

"I'll join you."

With a startled gasp she spun around, the decanter slipping from her fingers. It didn't hit the floor and shatter into a thousand shards because Crimson Jack was close enough to snag it on its journey to extinction. Breathing harshly, she stared at him. "What are you doing here?"

Leaning slightly past her, he set the decanter on the vanity. Then he held up a hand before her face. Over it was draped her glove, the one she'd left at the tavern that awful night, the one he'd removed with such care.

"I came to return your glove."

"How did you get in here?"

His gaze wandered over her features and she suddenly felt bared to his inspection. She desperately wanted to step back but she didn't want him to view her as a coward.

"A tree grows outside your window. For a man accustomed to climbing sail rigging during a storm, a few branches offer no challenge."

"If I were to scream, my father and brothers—"

"Are at their clubs. I doubt they'll hear you."

"The servants—"

"By the time they arrive, I'll be gone."

"Which is exactly what I want. Step back."

With a slight bow he did as she asked. She could breathe a little easier now that she wasn't inhaling his fragrance. Strangely his scent was sharp and clean. Tangy. Like an orange.

"You should not be here," she said, wondering if she should in fact scream, not certain why she hadn't as of yet.

"I do a good many things that I shouldn't."

He held up her glove again and she snatched it from him. "Thank you. You can be on your way now."

"I thought to discuss your journey to Scutari."

"As I shan't be hiring you, I see no need."

"You won't find a captain willing to take you."

She angled her head haughtily. "Not even for five hundred pounds?"

Seeing a momentary flicker of admiration, she knew she'd gained the upper hand. The next captain she approached—

"Not even for five thousand," he said.

Oh, now would be a very good time to yank out his hair. Instead, she heard herself ask, "Why?"

"I told you. I want you on my ship."

"Yes, and in your bed, I'm bloody well sure. Well it won't happen. Ever. You disgust me with your suggestion that I barter away to you the one thing I hold dear."

"Your fiancé doesn't hold that place?"

The crack of her palm hitting his cheek echoed around them. He hadn't tried to stop her, although after seeing the speed with which he'd caught the brandy, she was fairly certain he could have. His reflexes were sharp and quick. So why did he just stand there and take it? Why didn't he step away or grab her wrist or shove her aside?

She stumbled back until she hit the wardrobe. "Please go."

She hated the pleading rasp of her voice. But he was right. Walter should have been more dear than her virginity. He'd wanted it, the night before he left, and she'd been too damned proper to give it to him. Now she would never know his touch—and worse, he died never knowing hers.

The captain just stood there, studying her as though he could decipher every thought that rampaged through her mind. She hated him at that moment, hated him desperately.

She straightened her shoulders. "I'm calling the servants now."

Tossing the glove onto the vanity, spinning on her heel, she headed for the door.

"A kiss."

She spun back around to face him. "Pardon?"

"A kiss. That's what I want you to barter for passage on my ship."

"A kiss? That's all? *A* kiss?" Surely she'd misunderstood.

Slowly he prowled over the thick carpet, silent as a wraith, until he was standing before her, his gaze smoldering as it dipped to her lips briefly. Then he was looking into her eyes, holding her captive as easily as if he'd bounded her with silk.

"A long, slow, leisurely kiss," he whispered in a velvety smooth voice that sent a shiver of something that resembled pleasure scurrying along her spine. She suddenly felt so remarkably alive, so engaged. "On my ship, the moment of my choosing. If you draw back, then I get another until I am the one who ends it."

"A . . . kiss," she repeated. "That can't be all you want."

"No, it's not all I want, but it's what I'll be content to take. Anything more, you must be willing to give."

She shook her head. "You speak flattering words, designed to lure me, but I know you expect me in your bed."

He touched his finger to her lips. "No. I expect nothing more than a kiss."

"So why not take it now? Be done with the bargain?"

"Because I want to torment you as you do me."

She couldn't miss the hint of glee that jumped through her at his admission. "I torment you?"

"From the moment you walked through the door of the tavern on that stormy night. I don't know why. I only know that you do."

"Because you can't have me."

"Perhaps."

She shook her head. "How do I know that once aboard your ship, you won't force me?"

"Bring your lady's maid, bring a dozen. In spite of my behavior, I assure you that when it comes to the ladies, I'm a man of honor. I could have stopped you from slapping me. I didn't, because I deserved it. The words were uncalled for." He shifted and suddenly a shining dagger was in her field of vision. "Carry this with you. If you decide it should be plunged into my heart, I won't stop you."

"That's easy enough for you to say now."

"A kiss, Princess, that's all I require to take you to your fiancé in Scutari."

She was probably a fool to trust him, and yet—

"When would we leave?" she asked.

"When would you like to?"

"Tomorrow. Midnight."

"It shall be done."

If he'd given her a cocky smile, a triumphant sneer, she would have left him waiting on the docks. Instead he merely extended a slip of paper toward her. "Instructions for locating my ship at the wharves."

"You were rather confident that I would accept your terms."

"Not at all, but I believe in being prepared." He turned and in long strides headed for the window.

"Captain?"

He stopped and glanced back over his shoulder at her.

"You could use the front door," she told him.

He grinned, a devastatingly sensual grin that brought out the glimmer in his eyes. "Where's the challenge in that?"

Then he was out the window.

She scurried over to it, leaned out, and watched as he scampered down the towering oak like a monkey she'd observed at the zoological gardens.

She heard a knock on her door and glanced over her shoulder to see Martha bringing in her warm cocoa.

"Is everything all right, my lady?" the maid asked, and Anne wondered what her face must show.

Perhaps a hint of excitement, of anticipation.

"Begin packing our things, Martha. We're going to Scutari."

Chapter 3

The following evening Tristan stood outside Easton House, his older brother's residence. He didn't have time for such nonsense. He had a ship to ready. But after visiting with Anne the night before, he'd gone to the docks to alert his men they'd be setting sail at midnight tonight. Upon arriving at his ship he'd found a note from Sebastian, inviting—a polite word for commanding—Tristan to join his family for dinner. Obviously going to see Rafe had been a mistake. His younger brother had no doubt alerted the older of Tristan's presence in London.

He supposed he could ignore the summons, but during their youth they'd gone far too many years without contact. What was a couple of hours of inconvenience when they had the opportunity to be together?

He remembered a time when he would have simply walked into the house, but Sebastian had been a bachelor then and the house had seemed to belong to all three brothers. Now Tristan was more a guest, and his brother's marriage to Mary had changed the dynamics somewhat.

He lifted the heavy knocker and released it. Just as he anticipated, a footman quickly opened the door and ushered him in. As Tristan was handing his hat, gloves, and coat to the servant, the aging butler appeared.

"My lord Tristan, welcome home."

"Thomas, you're looking well."

"Couldn't be better, sir. Thank you."

"I assume the duke is in the library." Making use of his well-stocked liquor cabinet if he were smart.

"Yes, m'lord. Shall I announce your arrival?"

"No need for such formality." He strode through the familiar hallways, noting an empty spot or two where their father's portrait had once hung. Their uncle had destroyed a good many of them. Tristan felt the familiar fury rise with memories of the vile man who'd sent them scurrying for their lives. His death brought no satisfaction.

As Tristan neared the library a footman bowed and opened the door. Tristan went through without slowing. This room had been his father's domain. It brought a bit of solace but the sight of his brother standing near the fireplace brought more.

"Tristan." The right side of Sebastian's mouth lifted in welcome, the left side too badly scarred to do much of anything. His brother set aside his tumbler and was soon giving Tristan a bear hug and a solid slap on the back.

Then his brother released his hold and went to

the liquor cabinet as though embarrassed by his warm welcome, one that was no doubt a result of Mary's influence. "Why didn't you send word when you returned to London?"

"I hadn't quite decided what my plans were," he said as he took the tumbler filled with amber that Sebastian offered.

"And now?"

"I set sail tonight."

"So soon?" a feminine voice asked softly.

He spun around and grinned at the slender red-haired woman who had slipped into the room. "Now, aren't you a sight for sore eyes?"

He returned the tumbler to Sebastian, crossed the distance in three long strides, and lifted Mary into his arms, spinning her as her laughter pealed around them. Dear God, she almost made him feel as though he'd finally come home. By the time he eventually set her down, he was chuckling and they were both breathless.

"I hear you did your duty magnificently and provided my brother with his heir."

She slapped teasingly at his arm. "It wasn't a duty. And he's already asleep, but we shall look in on him before you leave."

"I'd like that." He realized he'd been remiss in bringing a gift for the lad. He'd remedy that situation the next time he visited.

"Do tell us everything." She sat in a large plush chair and Sebastian joined her, sitting on the arm, placing his hand on her nape as though he needed to touch her simply because she was near.

Tristan took his tumbler and a nearby chair. "Not much to tell." Glancing up, he noticed the portrait over the fireplace. It was his brother, his damaged side partially hidden by shadows as he looked at his wife. "Nice portrait."

"We were pleased with it. If you were staying longer, I'd have one done of Sebastian with you and Rafe."

"Yes, I'm quite sure you'd have no trouble at all getting Rafe to agree to that," he said wryly. He couldn't imagine him agreeing to it. "Speaking of our younger brother, will he be joining us this evening?"

"No," Sebastian said. "Unfortunately our relationship remains strained, and he declines our invitations."

"But he sent word to you that I was here."

"Yes. Don't know if he knew you were leaving so quickly. Where are you going?"

He wasn't certain how Sebastian would feel about Tristan's journey to a place where so much blood—so much of his blood—had been shed. The last thing he wanted was to bring nightmares back into his brother's life. "I'd rather not say. It's a private charter."

"I didn't know you did private charters."

"When the payment is right, I do anything."

"Nothing illegal, I hope," Mary said.

He winked at her. "Payment is everything."

She scowled.

"Not to worry," he assured her. "No danger awaits us on this trip." But even as he said the words, he wasn't convinced they were quite true. It *was* bad luck to have a woman on board a ship, even one as lovely as Lady Anne. He decided to take a risk. "Mary, are you familiar with the Earl of Blackwood's daughter? Lady Anne?"

She shook her head. "I'm sorry, I spent far too much of my life in the nunnery. I don't believe we've crossed paths. Why?"

"No particular reason."

"When do you ever ask questions that serve no purpose?" Sebastian asked.

He grinned. "Obviously tonight."

At Sebastian's narrowing gaze, Tristan stood. "I say, I'm quite famished. Any chance we can get this dinner under way?"

Neither his brother nor his sister-by-marriage moved a muscle.

"Does Lady Hermione know you're here?" Mary finally asked, and he wondered what the devil had prompted that question.

"Why should she?" She'd flirted with him two years ago when he and his brothers had first returned to Society.

"She's written me from time to time asking after you," Mary answered.

"Surely she's married by now."

"I fear not. Apparently she is holding out hope that you would return for her."

"It was innocent flirtation. I never once declared any feelings for her."

"Be that as it may, I think she was quite smitten."

"She's a child."

"Old enough to marry."

"Not me, by God. I have no intentions of ever being shackled—" He cut off his diatribe as Mary angled her chin defiantly.

"Well thank you for that," she stated tartly.

"You're an exception," he reassured her.

"I should hope so." She studied him for a moment, making him uncomfortable with her perusal. "Do you plan to ever return to Society?"

He shook his head. "It's not for me. I'm happier on the sea." Or at least he had been. He wasn't quite certain why this last voyage had left him so unsettled.

"But you worked so hard to see that Sebastian regained his place—"

"My love," Sebastian said quietly, "my brothers have their own paths to travel."

"Except that I truly believe all of you should be where you would have been had your uncle not sought to kill you."

But he had, and they were forever changed. Tristan wanted to get off this maudlin topic. He quirked an eyebrow. "Still famished here."

Mary laughed, a bit of forcing behind the sound, giving him what she knew he wanted. Bless her. Sebastian was a most fortunate man. Tristan doubted he'd ever find a love such as these two shared. It was a rare thing.

In her haste to finally see the beginning of her quest, Anne had neglected to take into account that she had selected the one night of the week when her father insisted that all his children join him for dinner. If he and her brothers followed their usual habit, they would all head to their various clubs shortly after dessert was served, but still she was so distracted by her own plans that she wished she could have avoided this situation.

She loved her family, she truly did, but the preponderance of male virility could be quite claustrophobic at times, especially as they believed that because she was female she required constant looking after, their opinions mattered more than hers, and the slightest upset could cause her to swoon—even though she'd never swooned in her life. Not even when she received word of Walter's passing. She'd put up a stoic front and shed her tears only in private. He'd have been proud of her performance—because that was what it had been. Appearances. Everything was always about blasted appearances.

She wondered how her family would perform once they learned of her plans. She was going to leave them a letter so they would not worry, but they would not discover it until sometime tomorrow when they were all sober again. The trick, of course, would be slipping out of the residence without servants raising an alarm. Fortunately, only she and Martha were aware of the small packed trunk in her bedchamber. She would require trusted footmen—

"Keswick has returned to London," Viscount Jameson, her eldest brother, said. All of her brothers were fair, but their hair contained various shades of gold that she'd always envied.

Each of them set aside their utensils at Jameson's announcement and took a sip of wine as though he'd declared that he spotted Mary Shelley's Frankenstein wandering about, and they were having a difficult time comprehending what it might mean. She loved her brothers dearly but they were, by far, the worst gossips London had ever produced.

"For what purpose?" Stephan asked.

"To reenter Society, I suspect. I've been told he has an heir now."

"That didn't take long," Phillip murmured.

"What of his brothers?" Edward asked.

"If it goes as before, they'll be right on his heels, won't they?" Jameson answered.

"Can't have that," their father muttered.

"Why not?" Anne asked.

They all looked at her as though she'd sprouted horns. She was tempted to touch her forehead to ensure herself she hadn't.

"You were in mourning when the lords of Pembrook returned to London two years ago," Jameson told her. "Rough lot. No manners to speak of. They were raised outside the confines of Society. Quite barbaric."

She envisioned them prancing around the ballrooms without any clothing. "I thought they were dead. Wolves had eaten them or something."

"Yes, quite, that's what we all thought," Stephan informed her. "But apparently they ran off. Thought their uncle wished them harm so he could inherit the dukedom."

"Did he?" she asked pointedly.

Her brother shrugged. "Was never proven."

"Fanciful tales," her father said. "Men do not kill to obtain titles."

"I should hope not," Jameson said. "I rather fancy a long life."

Her father laughed. "As do I." He sobered. "Anne, if these lords of Pembrook do make an appearance in the ballrooms, you're to avoid them. I believe the Marquess of Chetwyn may have set his cap on you."

"Walter's brother? Why would you think that?"

Her father took a slow sip of his red wine as though she wasn't waiting with bated breath for the answer. "Oh, just something I heard at the club."

"Has it been wagered on?" Her brothers wagered on everything. They'd lost a small fortune because they'd expected her to marry Chetwyn rather than Walter. But she hadn't loved the marquess. It was Walter who had stolen her heart.

"Might have seen something scribbled in the book at White's," Jameson said.

"Don't look so devastated, sweetheart," her father said. "It's as I've said, you've far exceeded Society's expectations with this mourning business. It's not as though you're a widow."

"I don't believe Society should dictate how long I mourn," she said hotly. This had been a sore point between them. "That is a function of my heart."

"Yes, well, it's time for your heart to move on. And Chetwyn would make a jolly good match."

"It would be almost like marrying Walter," Edward said. He was her youngest brother, a year older than she, and apparently a numbskull.

"That's disgusting. He's nothing at all like Walter."

"I should say not. He's alive."

She tossed her wine on her idiot brother, causing him to yelp, jerk back, and send his chair and himself to the floor. With him still sputtering, "See here now! It's my favorite waistcoat!" she came to her feet amid the stares of those who remained at the table. "I'm trying to move on, and you all are making it extremely difficult. If you'll excuse me, I feel a headache coming on."

She flung her napkin to the table, turned—

"Anne," her father barked in his not-to-be-ignored voice.

Grinding her back teeth, she faced him with her chin held so high that her neck was beginning to ache.

"We want what is best for you. You're approaching an age when you'll no longer be considered marriageable. It is my responsibility to see you with a husband so you are not a burden to your brothers."

Yes, three and twenty was so terribly old. Perhaps rather than return from the voyage, she'd simply ask Crimson Jack to drop her off on a secluded rock somewhere. That had to be better than enduring such idiocy disguised as caring.

"I'll be fine," she said. "And see to my duty this Season and secure myself a husband."

Her father smiled. "That's my girl."

"I do love you all," she added, "and know you have my best interests at heart. However, I'm going to retire now, so please enjoy your evening."

And please, please, please, go to your clubs as soon as possible so I may make my escape from this madness.

Chapter 4

She was late, dammit. Tristan checked his watch again. Three whole bloody minutes late. He fought not to pace the deck, not to give the impression that he cared one whit that his passenger might have changed her mind. He should have borrowed Sebastian's coach and stopped by her residence to provide assistance if needed.

The fog was rolling in. It distorted sounds, gave everything an ominous feel. The ship's lanterns were lit, but they would not hold the encroaching gray at bay. He wondered if the weather had turned her back, but she hadn't struck him as one who was easily intimidated. He wasn't usually a poor judge of character, so why wasn't she here?

Because she'd come to her senses and realized that he would take advantage of her. He wouldn't force her, but by God, he'd certainly work to seduce her. Although he suspected a woman who had been loyal to a man for four years would not succumb easily to his charms. She obviously loved the scapegrace. What sort of man could stay away from her and still hold her heart?

Someone far better than you, mate, more worthy. It didn't bear thinking about. She'd struck a bargain. That was all that mattered. Or so he'd thought.

Damnation. He should have taken the kiss from her when he was in her bedchamber. He was a merchant, a trader. He knew better than to set sail without payment in hand. Payment first, services second. It had been his motto from the moment he'd begun to barter his skills. Always money first. Then if someone decided to back out on the bargain, he still had his gain.

Now, he had nothing to show—

Not exactly true. He removed her glove from his pocket and stroked it through his fingers before bringing it to his nose. After she turned toward the door, he'd stolen it from where she tossed it. He didn't know what had possessed him, except that he'd wanted it and he wasn't accustomed to not taking what he wanted. Her scent of lavender with a hint of citrus wafted around him. He suspected it was a perfume made especially for her. If not, it should be. He couldn't recall ever smelling it on another woman.

What was this insane obsession with her? Why should he care if she had shown herself to be a coward, if she had decided not to make the journey?

He glanced at his watch again. Five blasted minutes. She wasn't coming. His men were waiting for his order to set sail. What was he to do now in order not to look like an absolute fool?

He could leave, decide later exactly where they would go. Or he could tell his crew to stand down, while he disembarked, hired a hackney, and confronted the treacherous—

Through the thickening fog came the unmistakable sound of rapid footsteps, determined, a steady cadence echoing over the wooden planks of the docks. A woman's steps. A slight woman. Seven stones' worth. Others followed, more distant.

He fought back the jubilation as she became visible. He wasn't going to give her the upper hand in this encounter. She was fortunate that he hadn't already cast off. Stuffing the glove back into his pocket, he strolled nonchalantly across the quarterdeck and descended the steps to the main deck. Then he sauntered down the gangway to the dock just as she came to a stop, breathing heavily. Even in the dim light, he could see she was flushed. She would be even more so when he claimed his kiss.

"You're late," he said in as flat a voice as he could muster.

Her silvery eyes widened. "I daresay, not even ten minutes."

"Ships run on a schedule, my lady."

She angled her chin. "Yes, well, as I'm paying for this voyage, I expect it to run on my schedule. If you didn't understand that was my purpose in hiring you, then perhaps I should look elsewhere."

He couldn't stop the smile this time. He should have known she'd not apologize. "Unfortunately, any schedule involving a ship is subject to tides and winds."

"Oh, my dear. Will we not be able to leave tonight?"

He wondered at the urgency, but didn't comment on it because it worked to his advantage for them to be under way as soon as possible.

"I think we can manage." A dark-haired woman who didn't seem to be much older than Anne was standing slightly behind her, her eyes blinking continuously as though she couldn't quite believe she was here. Her maid, her chaperone no doubt. He nodded toward the two men carrying her trunk. "Are they coming with you?"

"No, only the trunk."

"Peterson! Get the lady's trunk on board."

"Aye, Captain."

Peterson was a big brute of a man. He took the trunk from the liveried footmen as though it contained little more than feathers. As he passed back by, Tristan said quietly, "My cabin, Peterson."

"Yes, sir." He trudged up the gangway.

"He doesn't sound pleased," Lady Anne said.

"He's a grumbler. You'll get used to it. The men who are on board are there because they choose to be. Those ruled by superstition are remaining behind."

"Will that cause a hardship for you?"

"For you, Princess, I'd suffer any hardship."

She laughed, a sweet sound that wove around him, and he wondered if she were descended from Sirens. He thought he might gladly crash upon rocks just to hear that clear pure tinkling. "You're not going to wait until we're at least on the ship before beginning your absurd flirtation?"

She wasn't going to fall easily, but then he'd known all along that she wouldn't. "Your words are like a dagger through my heart."

"I doubt you can be so easily wounded, Captain." She spoke briefly with the men who had accompanied her. When they left, she indicated the woman who remained. "This is Martha, my lady's maid. She comes with us, of course."

"Of course. Allow me the honor of escorting you aboard." He called out for Jenkins and when the young man joined them, instructed him to escort Martha up the gangway. Tristan extended his arm to Anne.

She wrapped her hand around the crook of his elbow and allowed him to lead her up the corridor. He'd thought Lady Anne might tremble, if not with his nearness, then with the anticipation of the journey. Instead, she seemed to become almost somber as she stepped onto the deck.

"Peterson, get us under way."

"Aye aye, Captain."

While Peterson began shouting commands and men began scurrying around the ship, Tristan said, "I'll show you to your cabin."

"I'd rather stay out here while we leave."

"As you wish, but let's get you out of harm's way. Up the steps there."

She did as he bid, and he followed her up, his eyes level with her swaying hips. Once up top, she crossed over to the railing. Joining her there, he realized that the maid was right behind him. She was going to be an inconvenience, but he could work around her.

"Why *Revenge*?" Lady Anne asked quietly.

"Pardon?"

"Why did you name your ship *Revenge*?"

Planting his elbows on the railing, he clasped his hands together and stared at the black water beneath them. He'd done similarly the first time the ship on which Sebastian had left him had drawn away from the harbor. He'd thought the sea mirrored his soul. The next morning it had been a brilliant blue that had given him hope once again. "For a good many years the need for revenge gave purpose to my life. It seemed an appropriate name for a ship that would bring me untold wealth."

"It's bad form to speak of money."

"You asked." He shifted his gaze over to her. She, too, was looking out, and he wondered if she was imagining her meeting with her fiancé.

"Whom did you wish revenge against?" she asked.

"I don't know you well enough to share that tale with you."

She did glance over at him then. "I suspect you're a very complicated man, Captain."

"Not really. I see something I want and I take it. It doesn't get much simpler than that."

She looked back out as the ship gave several creaks and moans. A sudden lurch and it was moving slowly through the water.

"I was under the impression you had a fast ship," she said.

"Not when we're in the harbor. We have little moon by which to see. You could have hardly picked a worse night. A daytime departure would have been better."

"Yet you didn't try to convince me to hold off for a better time. Why ever not?"

"Because, Princess, I'm not certain you've been quite honest with me, and you required a midnight departure for a reason."

He was studying her with such concentration that she was surprised her heart still managed to beat. "I've never lied to you."

"That doesn't mean you've been completely honest."

She could say the same about him. She'd nearly spun on her heel and headed in the other direction when she'd watched him swagger down the gangway. His face no longer sported a shadow of stubble. She'd thought him handsome before, but cleanly shaven he was devastating. His hair was pulled back, tied in place with leather, and she dearly wanted to set it free. The light breeze billowed his loose white shirt, somehow making him appear more masculine.

She couldn't remember the last time she'd looked at the male form and appreciated it. Not since Walter had left. To gaze upon any man with even a hint of lust would have been betrayal to her betrothed. She couldn't claim what she felt now was lust, but it was definitely awareness. Acute awareness that was unsettling in its intensity. Her stomach quivered, and she had a strong urge to sit. Instead, she stood her ground. "As you so succinctly said, I don't know you well enough to tell you everything. But I swear to you that there is no danger."

"Pity. I thrive on danger."

"Yes, I quite imagine you do."

They were moving farther from the docks. More shadows were weaving among them and fog swirled about, challenging the ship's lanterns to hold it at bay. Water slapped against the hull. A peacefulness claimed the night. She wasn't certain how much he contributed to her serenity. Somehow she knew he had the strength and skills to protect her from any peril that might come their way.

She heard flapping and glanced back to see a sail unfurl. Soon the ship was gliding faster. Closing her eyes, she leaned into the wind.

"M'lady."

"I'm all right, Martha."

"Do you swim?" he asked.

"No, but I suspect you do. And you'd jump in to save me, wouldn't you?"

"If the price was right."

Opening her eyes, she looked over at him. He was smiling at her as though he enjoyed the movement of the ship as much as she did. "I don't think you're quite the mercenary you claim to be."

"I never do anything without payment."

"But if I drown, you won't get that kiss, will you?"

"Perhaps I should go ahead and take it."

Her mouth went dry. She'd known he'd want it of course, that he would exact payment from her. She simply hadn't expected it to be so soon. "I'd like to see my cabin now."

"As you wish."

Once again he offered her his arm, and while she wanted to ignore it, she wasn't quite certain she could move about the rocking ship without tumbling. Just as before, she acknowledged the strength in his arm, the sturdiness of his movements. He had no trouble at all making his way about the ship.

She tried to think of something to say, something to ease the tension that was suddenly mounting. She knew where he was taking her and she didn't want to think about it. He wouldn't be sleeping there, but he once had. She would lie in the bed where he had lain.

But her mind would bring forth nothing inconsequential to utter as the enormity of this undertaking was settling around her. Her father would have her head if he knew what she was about. Fortunately, the coach driver and the footman had sworn not to reveal the name of the ship she'd boarded. Not that she thought her father could catch up with them.

They took the stairs down a level from the main deck. The captain opened a door. She took a deep breath to still her thundering heart as she stepped through into the small quarters. Two pieces of furniture dominated the space. His bed. She wasn't surprised it was large. A man of his height and breadth would require a generous area in which to move about as he slept.

The other massive piece was a desk. Behind it were shelves. Books were lined perfectly along them. Dickens. Cooper. Shelley.

Martha joined her, and only then did he step inside. The room seemed to shrink with his presence.

"You read," she said inanely.

"Boredom can easily find a home on a ship."

"Yes, I can imagine." Only she couldn't. She'd thought he'd have little time for her, that he'd be steering the vessel, but obviously he had others to handle such matters.

"The room next to this one is where my first mate sleeps. It's available to your maid."

Anne spun around to face him. "There was no need to go to such bother. I'd planned on her staying with me."

His eyes glittered. "If you wish."

"I do."

He gave a curt nod. "Is there anything else you need before I leave you to your dreams?"

She nodded, swallowed hard. "Martha, leave us for a moment."

Martha opened her mouth, and Anne gave her a pointed glare. She'd tolerate no mutiny. Martha snapped her mouth closed and walked toward the hallway.

"Shut the door after you."

She slammed it.

"She doesn't approve of this journey," he said.

"She's just protective." Removing her pelisse, she set it carefully over the desk. She met and held his gaze. "I thought you might like your payment before we're too far out to sea."

"Did you now?" In two long strides, he was near enough that his breath mingled with hers and she had to tilt her head back to continue to gaze into his icy blue eyes. He rested his curled fingers in the curve of her cheek, his thumb stroking her lower lip.

Her tongue slipped out on its own accord to lick where he touched and she could have sworn she tasted the saltiness of his skin. His eyes darkened. He had such incredibly long lashes. Their ebony shade made the blue of his eyes seem that much fairer, like the sky on a bright summer day.

He leaned in.

She held her breath.

His gaze dropped to her lips.

They tingled.

He lifted his eyes to hers.

She waited, waited . . .

He came nearer. Her eyes began closing—

"The moment is of my choosing, Princess. And this isn't it. Sleep well."

Grinning, he tweaked her nose, spun on his heel, and strode from the room.

If she could have drawn in a breath past her

fury, she'd have shrieked at him. Martha rushed in. "Oh, dear God, what did he do?"

"Nothing." *He tweaked my nose!* She wasn't about to admit that. Didn't he want to kiss her? Had he changed his mind? She dropped onto the edge of the bed and stared at the closed door. She popped back up. "He told me to sleep well. I'll show him. I shall accomplish that with remarkable success."

As they prepared for bed, they were both surprised to find warm water in the basin. Obviously the captain had someone prepare the room before they came down. The bedding was crisp, freshly laundered, but when Anne climbed onto the bed, the spicy scent of Crimson Jack rose around her.

Martha blew out the lamp and crawled in beside her, but they had enough room between them that they didn't touch. Anne didn't want to consider that the bed had been specially designed to accommodate for the captain's size and a woman lying in his arms.

"I think my brother might have been mistaken," Martha whispered. "I think this captain might be a very dangerous man."

"If he were dangerous, he'd have locked that door, and he—not you—would be in this bed with me."

In the darkness, Anne listened to the creaking of the ship. But she didn't sleep. Instead, she wondered why he could so easily resist kissing her. And why she wished he'd just get it over with.

Standing at the helm, Tristan gripped the wheel so tightly that his hands were beginning to ache. Walking away from her without tasting those succulent red lips had been one of the hardest things he'd ever done. When he touched his knuckles to her cheek, skimmed his thumb over that pouting bottom lip, inhaled her scent . . .

When her breath hitched and her eyes began to close . . .

One kiss. That was all he'd demanded in payment. Stupid fool. He'd never in his life made a bargain in which he came out at the short end. He should have demanded one kiss every day. Instead he had only one for the entire journey. He had to make her want it so badly that she would willingly give him more. Because once he had his kiss, she had to initiate the next one. Unfortunately his wooing was on a schedule. He had to claim his kiss before they reached Scutari because once she visited with her fiancé, her love for him would be renewed and she would return to considering a kiss to Tristan as nothing more than a payment.

With any luck, the winds would die and their arrival at their destination would be delayed. Perhaps he'd take a wrong turn, go down around the Cape of Good Hope, then across the Indian Ocean to tropical islands. Perhaps he could even convince her to embrace local customs and strut about in very little clothing. That thought brought a smile. She could very well be in little clothing now as she snuggled in his bed.

His sheets, his cabin would smell of her when she left. No woman had ever been inside his domain. His men thought he was a bit mad to make this journey with two women in tow, but those who remained were being paid well enough for their services not to grumble.

The unrelenting fog curled around him in the same manner as he wanted to curl around her—all encompassing, leaving nothing untouched. He wondered how far she would allow him to take the kiss. Not nearly as far as he wanted to take it, he was certain.

Would her fiancé be returning with them? That was a disappointing thought that hadn't occurred to him before. Not that it mattered. He didn't want her for any longer than the voyage. As with all things in his life, the constancy of something bored him. He needed new adventures, new women, new challenges. But conquering her would be his greatest triumph.

He would taunt her with that kiss until she was willing to give him everything.

Chapter 5

Anne awoke to a gentle rocking and sunlight peering through mullioned windows. She was on the ship, on her way to Walter at last—and yet it was not visions of him that had filled her dreams. Rather it was one very dark blue-eyed devil whose nearness caused her skin to tingle with the need to be touched. She'd never experienced this sort of longing, wasn't quite certain what to make of it. He wasn't like anyone she'd ever met before. He was a curiosity. That was all. If she but touched his bristly jaw, felt his lips pressed to hers, then her interest in him would be satisfied.

Obviously her father was correct: it was time to leave her mourning behind. During the Season she was bound to meet someone who appealed with equal fervor. She was a young woman with needs. She'd been lonely for far too long. That's all these strange yearnings signified: that she was not only receptive to a man's attentions but in need of them.

Captain Crimson Jack was simply very skilled at setting a woman's blood to simmering.

After nudging Martha awake, she dressed in the same clothes she'd worn the night before. She'd brought a special dress for her visit to Scutari, and a couple of other dresses to see her through the journey there and back. But she hadn't set her cap on the captain so it mattered little if he saw her in the same clothes. In fact, it was probably better that she not go to much trouble in preparing for the day. She had no wish for him to think she had the slightest bit of interest in him. The ballrooms of London had no place for men of his roughened ilk.

When Anne was ready, she allowed Martha to return to bed while she ventured out. When she reached the main deck, she squinted at the bright sunlight. She couldn't recall it ever being so harsh in London. The men were about, all seemingly busy, but they each took a moment to doff their caps if they were wearing one or to touch two fingers to their brows if they weren't. No one leered, no one made her feel as the captain did—as though he knew exactly what she looked like beneath her skirts.

"Ye'll find the cap'n up top," a man said, and she remembered him from last night.

"Thank you, Mr. Jenkins."

Quietly, she made her way up the stairs. If he was busy, she didn't wish to disturb him. Nor did she want to startle him, although he didn't seem a man prone to being caught unaware.

She halted at the top of steps. Leaning back in a chair, with one booted foot propped on the railing, he was meticulously whittling on a small piece of wood. A lad, whom she judged to be around five and ten or so in years, sat cross-legged on the floor, hunched over a book, reading aloud. He stuttered out the more difficult words and when it was clear that he could go no further, the captain provided the answer. She wondered if he'd memorized the story that she soon recognized: *A Christmas Carol.*

She didn't realize she made a sound, but the captain looked back over his shoulder before leisurely straightening and coming to his feet. The boy ceased his reading.

"Lady Anne, I trust you slept well," the captain said.

"You have a most comfortable bed." She wished she hadn't mentioned that particular bit of furniture when he gave her a once-over as though he could clearly imagine her tangled in those sheets. "I fear, however, that my maid is feeling a bit queasy this morning."

"Hopefully it'll pass once she gets her sea legs beneath her. Are you hungry?"

"Famished."

He grinned. "The sea air can do that. Mouse, fetch her breakfast."

"Aye aye, Cap'n." The lad carefully set the book on a small table as though it were the greatest of treasures before scampering with a noticeable limp past her.

She eased nearer to the towering man with the powerful shoulders. "He's a cripple."

"Hardly," he bit out sharply. "His leg's merely bent, but I suspect he can climb rigging faster than you."

"Yes, of course. I meant no insult."

He indicated a chair on the opposite side of the table from his.

"In a moment," she said before walking to the railing, turning, and leaning against it. Her breath caught at the white cliffs in the distance. "What a magnificent sight. I thought we'd be beyond view of it by now."

"The fog required slower travel."

The breeze was again toying with his shirt and the same three buttons were undone. She didn't know whether to button them so he'd looked more proper or loosen the ones that were fastened so he'd appear less proper. Why did she care at all about the state of his buttons?

To hide the weakness that had suddenly settled in her legs, she took the chair he offered earlier. Her knees became jelly because she was on the water, not because of him. Like Martha, she'd yet to gain her sea legs.

"Why Mouse?" she asked. "The lad. Why did his parents name him Mouse? Have you any idea?"

"I've no idea what they named him. But we found him hiding in the hold, quiet as a mouse. The name stuck."

"He's a stowaway then?"

"In a manner of speaking. Now he's part of my crew."

"His job is to read to you?"

He grinned. "Among other things."

The boy returned with a tray that was far more appetizing than she'd expected. Eggs, ham, bread, oranges, and a lovely pot of tea. Once he set the tray before her, he disappeared without the captain giving any orders, and she suspected the captain had already discussed the matter of privacy with Mouse before she ever woke up.

"Will you be sharing the meal with me?" she asked, because she couldn't possibly eat the entire abundance of offerings.

"I've already eaten."

"Tea then?"

"No."

She settled the napkin on her lap. She couldn't deny that something was very appealing about sitting out here enjoying her breakfast. "Must you watch? Your intense perusal threatens to upset my digestion."

"It's difficult to look away from something so lovely."

"False flattery, Captain, will get you nowhere."

"I have no need to use false words." Still, he did return to his whittling while she slathered butter on her bread.

"You'd not struck me as a man who would apply knife to wood," she said.

"As I mentioned last night, boredom can easily overtake one on a ship. We have days, weeks, months of nothing punctuated, with a few seconds of excitement now and then. Idle hands and all that. Although I can think of more pleasurable ways to use my hands."

She jerked up her gaze to find his wicked smile aimed at her.

"Yes, well, you shall have to be content with thinking about it. A kiss involves lips, not hands."

"Ah, you are obviously not well tutored in the art of kissing, Princess."

She felt as though the winds had unexpectedly risen up from the bowels of hell, she grew so warm. Her throat knotted with the implication that the kiss they shared might be more than she'd thought she was agreeing to. She was grateful she'd not begun chewing. She'd no doubt choke. Best to change the course of their topic. "What are you carving?" she asked.

He chuckled darkly as though he understood her strategy, and she feared he'd continue on with his innuendoes. Instead, he said, "A toy ship for my nephew."

"You have family?"

"You sound surprised. Did you think I'd sprung fully formed from Satan's forehead?"

She laughed lightly. "I did on occasion suspect that might have been the case." She couldn't envision him with a family. "You seem more a lone wolf than part of a pack. Have you a wife then?"

"I wouldn't be bartering for kisses if I did."

"Yes, of course, I'm sorry. I'm having a very difficult time categorizing you."

"As I explained that first night, where I'm concerned, you shouldn't expect anything."

"I suppose." She took a bite of ham before saying, "So tell me about your family."

"Why?"

"Because I suspect you know everything about mine." He knew where she lived after all.

He grinned. "Servants will talk."

"So you know I have a father and four brothers. What of you?"

"Two brothers."

"Older? Younger?"

"One older. One younger."

"You don't like speaking about them. Why is that?"

He placed an elbow on the table, leaned forward, and tucked behind her ear several strands of hair that had come loose and begun whipping around her face. "Because they don't interest me as you do. I'd rather talk about you."

Her lips tingled and she wondered if he would kiss her now. But he only perused her features as though every line and curve were a fascinating oddity. She suspected in his travels he'd encountered the most exotic of women. How plain she must be compared with them.

She drew back, needing the distance. Reaching for the orange, she began to peel it with slightly trembling fingers, hoping he wouldn't notice that he could set her nerves to dancing with so little effort. "Have you traveled the entire world?"

"Most of it."

"Did your brothers choose a life at sea?"

"We didn't choose anything. Life presented opportunities and we took them."

She separated off a section of orange and bit into it, startled by the abundance of juice that shot into her mouth, dribbled down her chin. Before she could snatch up her napkin, he was gliding his finger below her lips, wiping away the succulent nectar. Then holding her gaze, slowly, ever so slowly, he sucked on his fingers, the light blue of his eyes darkening.

Her chest ached as she fought to draw in breath. How could something so ill-mannered be so erotic? She felt as though the sun had traveled closer and was scorching her skin. She was vaguely aware of him taking the fruit from her, tearing off a section, biting it in half before offering her the remains.

"I couldn't possibly—"

"It won't make quite the mess, and you must admit that it's frightfully good. And you don't want to get scurvy."

It was delicious, yes. She took the offering and popped it into her mouth. "I thought scurvy happened only on long voyages."

"Who knows?" He tore off another segment, ate half, and extended what was left. It didn't seem quite so wicked this time when she took it. "Maybe we'll decide not to return to England. We'll simply sail around the world."

"Oh, that sounds lovely." The words were out of her mouth before she realized her mistake in saying them. He'd grown still, the partially eaten orange seemingly forgotten. She released a self-conscious laugh. "I was only teasing. I have far too many responsibilities to go wherever the wind blows."

"Who hurt you, Princess?"

"Don't be ridiculous."

"I sense sadness in you."

She shook her head. She couldn't confide in him. She barely knew him. Her heart was only just beginning to heal. She would not, could not, risk it becoming bruised again. Perhaps she would marry Walter's brother. She would never love him, and therefore she could never again be hurt—or worse, cause hurt.

Tears pricked her eyes. She angled back her head and pointed. "What is it like to view the world from the crow's nest? It must be marvelous to see so far, to be able to see everything."

"You can't see everything. You never can."

"It's like life then, isn't it? Because if you could see everything, if you knew what would stretch out before you, you might say or do things that wouldn't leave you with regrets."

She looked to the sea, needing not to see the sympathy in his eyes. She didn't want him to be kind. She simply wanted him to get her to Scutari so she could ask Walter for forgiveness. "Walter always wanted to sail the sea. Spoke of one day purchasing a sailboat."

"Walter?"

The word came out like the crack of a whip.

"My fiancé. It's the reason he arranged for his earnings to be sent to me. His brother is a marquess, and Walter feared the money would go into the family coffers. He was going to use it as our nest egg."

"Is that what you were using to finance this voyage?" His voice was a bit more relaxed, but flat, the way the sea looked in the distance, as though nothing at all disturbed for good or ill.

"Yes." She dared to look back at him. "Why did you agree to take me on the journey for something as paltry as a kiss? I'm sure you're no stranger to kisses."

"Kisses and I are well acquainted, and so I know their value. Every woman's kiss is different. Some lips are chapped, others I could swear had been woven together from threads of silk. Some mouths are dry, others wet. Some women taste of garlic and some"—he touched his fingers to his lips, made a smacking sound before unfurling them like a flower—"are as rich as fine vintage wine. Some women make not a sound as they kiss. Others sigh a sweet melody that teases the ear and remains vibrant in memory long after she is no longer there. A kiss can be all things. It can be profound." He shrugged. "Or it can be forgettable."

She couldn't imagine that a kiss bestowed by him could ever be forgettable. Would he forget hers?

"And if you discover that my kiss isn't worth the trouble of the voyage?"

"I don't think there's a chance in hell of that happening." With a wide grin he got to his feet, towering over her, and set what remained of the orange on her plate. "I have to check my charts, see to my duties. It's my hope that you'll dine with me this evening in my cabin." He tilted his head slightly. "Your cabin."

"Yes, of course."

"Until later then." He gave a brusque nod and strode away.

She rose and walked to the railing where nothing blocked the breeze from cooling her skin. Walter had kissed her, but she could not remember the flavor or the texture or the warmth of it. One more thing to add to her guilt: she'd not savored every kiss as though it might be their last.

At the bottom of the steps, Tristan nearly ran into her maid. She was carrying a parasol, and a quick glance told him that it was finely made. For her lady, then.

For the first time, he gave the maid a closer inspection. She wasn't a beauty, not like her mistress, but she possessed a prettiness that he suspected drew attention. And something else about her niggled at his mind. "Have we met before?"

"My brother, John Harper, served under you. He recommended your ship for the journey."

"And me along with it, I suppose."

Her blush enhanced the sparkle in her eyes. "He vowed you would not take advantage of my lady."

"His vow is not mine to keep."

"But you won't take advantage, will you?" she asked with a stubborn set to her lips.

"You're both safe from unwanted advances while aboard my ship."

She smiled, and he realized she was prettier than he initially thought.

"John's married now," she informed him, as though of a sudden they were friends.

"Yes, so he mentioned when he informed me that he would no longer be serving me. Seems his wife wanted to chain him to port."

"They wanted to be together. I don't think that's so awful. He's happy."

As well as a marvelous teller of tales with a tendency toward exaggeration. Tristan now had an idea of who might have told Anne that he was a hero. John didn't believe in allowing facts to ruin a good story.

"He's employed by a merchant now, has a respectable income, and is quite settled," Martha continued on.

Tristan fought not to shudder. He hired only unmarried men—not hard to find on the docks. During a storm, he didn't want a man worrying that he might be leaving behind a widow. Women didn't understand wanderlust. In his experience, marriage and a life at sea were a volatile combination, leaving everyone unhappy. He certainly intended to never take a wife.

His uncle had forced him to run. No one was ever going to force him into anything again.

When he reached his cabin, the first thing he noticed was that it already smelled of her, of Anne. Lavender and citrus mingling about. Everything was tidy, her trunk closed. He was tempted to riffle through it, see what he could discover about her. It seemed only fair.

Everything about him was visible to her. The books he enjoyed. The sturdy furniture he preferred. The liquor he favored. The wooden chest set he'd carved with his own hands. Even the globe for Rafe that he'd made during his last voyage—a gift he hadn't yet given to his brother because he wasn't certain how it would be received. Besides it wasn't exactly perfectly round. Rather it was a lopsided view of the world that tended to roll until the north and south poles were east and west poles. He needed to make a proper stand for it. He would address that during his next voyage.

He spent an hour attempting to study his charts before returning topside. He wanted to see her again, but according to Jenkins, the breeze proved too much for her parasol. She and her maid had retreated below deck, to the cabin he'd had prepared for the servant. He was disappointed. He should have ensured that she understood she was always welcome in his cabin, even when he was there. He imagined what it would be like to look up from his desk and see her sitting in a chair near one of the windows. Domestic. He shook off the thought. There was no room for domesticity aboard a ship.

He made his way to the quarterdeck. Mouse had cleared away all evidence that she'd been with him for breakfast. The lad was good at keeping things neat and tidy. Tristan wondered if she'd finished eating the orange. He thought he might never taste another without recalling the joy of her laughter as the juice burst forth, surprising her with its abundance.

He leaned back against the railing and crossed his arms over his chest. They had a strong wind filling the sails. They were making good time. England was no longer visible. They would reach the Mediterranean within a few days. He was tempted to cause some damage to the ship that would require they head to the nearest port for repairs. He wanted to walk through foreign cities with her, through crowded streets.

He wanted to wipe away whatever it was that was causing the sadness reflected in her eyes.

She's missing her fiancé, you dolt.

Not that much if she agreed to give me a kiss.

So much that she was willing to kiss you in order to get to him.

If he were an honorable man, he would take her there without claiming the kiss—all in the name of true love. Mary would expect it of him. Which was the reason he hadn't told her more about his journey. She wouldn't approve. Not that he cared for her approval.

He suspected he might be a very different man if he'd not been forced to leave his home, to leave Pembrook . . . to leave England. He grew to manhood very quickly.

He'd tried to return to what had been—to being a lord, to living within Society, among peers. But he didn't belong there, any more than Rafe did. Sebastian had no choice. He held the title, but Tristan was free to return to the life he loved, to the sea. And he did love it. The smell of the briny water, the rocking of the ship, the tickling of the wind. He enjoyed the camaraderie among his men. He would die for them and yet something was still missing.

He shifted his gaze over to Peterson as he came to stand beside him.

"You're going to a lot of trouble to get beneath a woman's skirts," Peterson said.

"I'm paying you well enough not to complain about it."

"She's different. You could hurt her."

"I'm not going to hurt her."

"Not intentionally maybe, but it can still happen."

"When did you become a bloody philosopher?"

"Your mistake in teaching me to read."

Tristan grinned. He taught any man who wanted to learn. Mouse was his latest pupil, making great progress.

"You know the maid is Johnny's sister," Peterson murmured.

"So I discovered this morning."

"He sent them to you knowing you would protect them."

"His mistake."

"Jack, she's nobility."

So was he, but his men didn't know it. When Sebastian had caught the offered pouch, the clinking of the coins inside had signaled the severing of Tristan's bloodlines. None of his men knew the truth of his origins. Even when he returned to England and helped establish his older brother's place in Society, Tristan had kept his two distinct lives separate. With a foot in both worlds, he wondered if he might be in danger of losing his balance.

"Relax, Peterson. I've never yet incurred a woman's wrath."

"There's always a first time, Captain."

She didn't know why she was nervous. It was after all only dinner. Before she'd gone into mourning, she'd had dinner with all sorts. Royalty even. She'd thought little of it. She could carry her portion of a conversation. She knew how to present herself well.

Dining with a sea captain should be nothing at all. Yet when she was in his company, she couldn't help but wonder when he would demand payment. She did wish he would do it soon. She didn't much like debt hanging over her head.

"Did you wish to change your attire?" Martha asked.

Anne glanced over at the open trunk. She'd brought a gown for dining. She wasn't certain what had prompted her to do so. She'd also packed a lilac gown that had been Walter's favorite, but she wouldn't wear it until she was ready to disembark the ship in Scutari.

She shook her head. "No need for anything formal. I'm sure his invitation was a result of politeness."

"I've not noticed him being particularly polite."

She grinned. "I'm not certain how you can say that when he had one of his men prepare something to settle your stomach."

"I don't like the way he looks at you."

"And how would that be?"

"As though he's contemplating devouring you."

"It's just his way to constantly appear intimidating so he doesn't have a mutiny on his hands."

"Know him that well do you?"

Anne placed her hands on her hips. "Your brother recommended him."

"Yes, and I'm thinking perhaps he's lost his mind."

"Don't be silly. Everyone is polite. No one has done anything untoward."

A quiet knock on the door ended their conversation. Was it time already? Anne's heart fairly jumped into her throat.

But when Martha opened the door, it was to find the lad—Mouse—standing there holding a pail.

"Cap'n was thinkin' ye might want some warm water."

"Yes, thank you." Martha reached for it.

He stepped back. "I kin carry it in."

"Yes, well—"

"We'd appreciate that," Anne said, interrupting what she was certain was going to be Martha's refusal to allow him entrance. Martha gave her a confused look, but Anne was fairly convinced it was the boy's pride speaking up.

He walked in with his uneven gait, and she could see now that his leg was severely bowed.

"Have you been with the captain long?" she asked.

"Ever since he saved me from the shark," he said with no inflection, as though he might be saying that the captain had merely spread jam on his toast. He concentrated on pouring the water into the bowl without splashing a single drop.

She waited until he was finished to inquire, "The shark?"

He faced her. "I was born funny-lookin', no one wanted me, so they used me to bait the sharks."

"I don't understand." Although she feared she did, and the thought horrified her.

"Tossed me in the water. I didn't know how to swim then, but the cap'n taught me later. Anyway, I'd thrash about. They'd pull me out when the shark got close enough so they could spear it."

She heard Martha gasp. As for herself, she thought she might be ill. "And the captain?"

"They were sailin' by. He jumped in, cut me free, and took me aboard his ship." He grinned mischievously. "Then he fired a cannon, blew their boat out of the water. Sharks had a feast that day."

"I see." Her stomach had tightened into a painful knot. To think she was angry because her father wanted her to begin making the social rounds again, to attend balls, soirees, and dinners. She wasn't in danger of being eaten.

"Will ye be needin' anythin' else?" he asked, as though he hadn't just told her the most horrific story she'd ever heard.

"No. Thank you."

He doffed his cap and limped from the room. Once he left, Martha sank into a chair. "You don't suppose all that was true, do you?"

"Why would he lie?"

"Sympathy. Or perhaps he simply enjoys spinning a good yarn."

Anne crossed her arms over her chest. "It's strange, Martha, but I can very well see Captain Crimson Jack jumping into the sea to save someone."

"You're not starting to fancy the fellow are you?"

"What? No." She walked to the windows and gazed out on the choppy water. "I have, however, decided to wear my proper dinner gown."

Martha made a snort of disapproval, but Anne couldn't have cared less. Tonight she would pay her debt. Get that matter over with, so he would leave her alone, because the more she learned of the captain, the more he intrigued her. And that path could only lead to disaster.

Chapter 6

She'd dressed in an exceedingly distracting sleeveless gown with a low décolletage that bared a good deal of her alabaster skin to his discerning eye. The only thing that pleased him more was the appreciation that had lit her face, tipped up the corners of her mouth, when he'd entered, because he, too, had taken the time to dress appropriately for dinner as though he were attending an affair in London.

Jenkins had done a superb job of arranging the dinner: starched white tablecloth, two flickering candles, fine red wine, and four courses that would have done Mary proud. Not that he was particularly hungry, except for feasting on the sight of Anne. He considered revealing his musings out loud but he suspected she would see it as false flattery. If he was learning anything at all about her it was that she seemed unaware of her allure. She was modest in the extreme and that made her so much more captivating.

The only thing that ruined the tableaux was the rapid clicking of knitting needles as her blasted maid sat in a corner keeping watch over her mistress.

"I'm quite impressed with the fare," Anne said after taking a small bite of the glazed chicken. "I'd not expected such fine accommodations."

"I spend a good deal of time away from ports. A first-rate cook was on the top of my must-acquire list when I gained my own ship."

"Your crew is exceedingly polite. I'd feared they might be a bit rough."

"They can be when the situation warrants." He studied her over his wineglass, wondering where she was going with this. "I have the luxury of determining who I hire. I'm quite particular. If I'm going to be in the company of a man for months at a time, I want to at least like him."

"You seem rather educated."

"My father insisted." He swirled his wine, and within the vortex he could almost see what his life might have been if his uncle hadn't killed Tristan's father. "I had a tutor for the longest. Then when I was fourteen I went to sea."

She leaned forward. "Why?"

"Why does any young man go to sea? For adventure." Although in his case, it was to get beyond his uncle's grasp.

"From what I can gather, you certainly found it. The lad, Mouse, told me that you saved him from being eaten by sharks."

Tristan downed his wine and poured himself some more. "You know that boy didn't talk for weeks after we brought him aboard. Now he's a regular magpie."

"So what he said is true?"

Her brow was furrowed, her concern evident. He'd planned to use dinner to charm her into his arms, not discuss the brutal aspects of his life. "We were off the coast of a small island in the Pacific. Because he was born imperfect, he was thought to have no value. We were leaving the island, when we spotted them hunting for sharks. I couldn't very well sail away without doing something."

"You told me that you found him in the hold. I assumed he was a stowaway. You must have known what I thought."

He shrugged. "We did find him in the hold, on numerous occasions. He was afraid, so he'd hide down there."

"He also told me that you blew up the boat that he'd been on. Have you killed many men?"

"None that didn't deserve it."

"You lead a rather brutal life."

"It's not as brutal as it once was."

She released a scoff that might have been a laugh. "The first night I met you I thought you were a blackguard. Now I'm not so sure."

The tempo of the knitting needles was increasing in rhythm. Her maid was obviously not at all pleased with that revelation. Maybe he should see if Peterson or Jenkins had an interest in the woman. It would be nice not to have her constantly hovering. "I explained in the beginning, Princess, that I would never be what you expected."

She set aside her cutlery. "Why do you call me that?"

"Because when you first walked into that smoke-filled haze of a tavern, I thought you looked like a princess from a fairy tale."

This time there was no mistaking her laughter or amusement. "Not difficult to accomplish considering the clientele."

Her cheeks flushed, and he wondered if she might be embarrassed that she was enjoying his company. They spoke of books. She preferred those with a romantic bent to them. When he sneered at the very idea, she challenged him to give Jane Austen a try and had her maid fetch *Pride and Prejudice* from the trunk.

She told him of growing up with four brothers, of being spoiled, of being thought to be the very princess that he mocked her as being. Sheltered, protected.

"Perhaps that's the reason that I was so determined to make this journey on my terms—to simply prove that I could do it."

"I don't imagine they were too pleased with your plans," he said.

"Oh, they know nothing about them. I left my father a brief note with no details, so yes, I suspect they are quite beside themselves at this point. I'm on the cusp of three and twenty. I felt the need to be rebellious. A woman should have a moment in her life when she's rebellious, don't you think?"

"When it places her on my ship? Absolutely."

She laughed then, the unselfconscious tinkling

that reminded him of the clinking of fine crystal. He couldn't imagine her ever being boisterous or loud or crude. She was a lady down to her core and this gent to whom she was betrothed was the younger brother of a lord. A man who didn't shy away from acknowledging his place in Society. Tristan didn't want to think about the lucky bastard who would have her in his bed, while all Tristan would have of her was a kiss.

He finished off his wine. "Take a walk with me about the deck."

"Do you ever ask?"

"I suppose I'm accustomed to giving orders. While it might not have sounded like it, it was an invitation. You can refuse."

"I could use some fresh air."

The clicking of knitting needles came to a stop as Tristan rose. He pulled out Anne's chair and whispered near her ear, "I don't think you really need the chaperone, do you?"

He was aware of a stuttering in her breathing before she said, "Martha, see to tidying up the cabin so that we might retire when I return."

His heart nearly slammed into his ribs with the vision of him and Anne retiring—

Then fantasy collapsed and reality crashed in as he realized she was speaking about her blasted maid retiring with her. He was a fool. From her, he would only ever get the promised kiss. He was an idiot to consider that she might gift him with anything else.

It was cool on deck, with the wind whipping around them. She hadn't considered that, hadn't thought to grab her pelisse before they left the cabin. She was considering returning for it, when he shrugged out of his jacket and placed it on her shoulders. The warmth from his body was lovely as it enveloped her. She drew the jacket closed as they stared out at the inky blackness of the sea.

He stood near enough to provide a partial buffer from the breeze. She would only have to move a hairsbreadth to be nestled up against him. Perhaps she'd had too much wine, because she felt slightly off-balance and was half tempted to lean into him, to let him hold her up.

Instead she gazed up at the twinkling velvety sky. A star arced across it, quickly followed by another. She released a small laugh. "I'm not certain I've ever seen stars so clearly before."

"Because there's nothing between us and them. No dirty air, no gaslights, no fog."

"Do you think it fell into the ocean?"

"I'm certain of it. That's where starfish come from, you know."

She peered over at him. "That's a fanciful thought. You don't strike me as a man who would have them."

His white smile flashed. "I've seen mermaids."

"No."

He tilted his head slightly. "They looked like mermaids. But when they came out of the water they did have two legs instead of a tail."

"I can't imagine all the things you've seen."

"None compare to you."

She laughed. "You are impossible with your flirtation."

"Why do you not believe me?"

The seriousness of his tone informed her that he was baffled by her reaction, was truly curious regarding her reasoning. "I own a mirror, Captain. Several in fact. My features are not particularly appealing."

"Did your fiancé never—"

"He told me I was pretty; pretty is not beautiful. I don't wish to talk of him." Not tonight. Not when she'd enjoyed dinner with a charming man, when that same man brought her senses to life as they'd not been in a good long while.

A deep mournful moan echoed in the distance.

"What's that?" she asked.

"A whale."

"That's a rather lonely sound, isn't it?"

"He's probably searching for his mate."

She found herself looking at him once again, studying him. "Do you ever get lonely out here?"

He didn't answer right away, but his gaze was focused on her as though he were striving to determine how much to reveal, how much to trust her. "Sometimes," he finally said quietly. "But I'm not lonely now."

She wasn't certain when, but he had moved closer and the motion of the ship caused them to brush up against each other from time to time. His stance was steadier than hers, but she no longer fought the rolling toward him. They didn't have much more moon tonight than the night before, but with no fog the stars stretched into eternity. His face seemed to be lost in fewer shadows, although perhaps it was only that she now knew every mountain and valley that comprised his strong, noble features.

How simple it would be to just lift up on her toes and press her mouth to his. Give him the kiss he demanded. She had no doubt that it would be as slow and leisurely as he'd promised. But she also thought it would be incredibly warm and very, very intoxicating.

She heard another whale, the lowing slightly different from the first. Was it the whale's mate? Or just another desolate creature? Until this moment she hadn't realized how terribly lonely she was, how she longed for this emptiness inside her to be filled.

She had no doubt that the man standing near could fill her to overflowing, but then he would leave and she would once again be empty. Was it better to have the fullness for a little while than to never experience it at all? Was it worth the pain that would surely follow?

Her lips tingled, her *breasts* tingled. Her toes curled. She realized that her fingers were clutching his waistcoat and she wondered when she'd released her hold on his jacket and grabbed him instead. They were facing each other, and that, too, she didn't remember making a conscious decision to accomplish. But here they were, so close again that their breaths were mingling, his warming her cheek. "Are you going to kiss me now?"

"No."

"Why?"

"Anticipation will serve only to make the moment that much more unforgettable."

"It might also serve to disappoint, to build up expectations that cannot be met."

"I think that highly unlikely."

"You do realize that you're tormenting me."

He flashed a grin. "Not nearly enough. Not yet. One kiss is all I shall have, Princess. When I claim it, I want you yearning for it so desperately that you hold nothing back."

"I won't hold anything back now."

He lowered his head. She closed her eyes, felt his lips skimming along her cheek.

"Not yet," he said in a low voice near her ear, sending shivers of pleasure gliding through her.

She almost grabbed his hair, yanked on it, and forced his mouth onto hers. But if he could resist, so could she. Inhaling deeply, she opened her eyes. "You're a cruel man, Captain."

To her surprise, chuckling low, he turned her to face the sea, stepped behind her, and wound his arms around her. "So I've been told."

She didn't know why at that moment, protected by the curve of his solid body, she was happier than she'd been in a good long while.

Why the devil was he tormenting himself? He hadn't a bloody clue. He could have had her tonight—a kiss and more. He was almost certain of it. It was the *almost* that had him waiting. Unfortunately, in spite of all his reassurances to her, he wasn't going to be satisfied with only a kiss.

Dammit all! No woman had ever plagued him as she did. When he escorted her from the deck, he'd been so tempted to follow her into his cabin and chase out the silly maid and her clacking knitting needles. Instead, he simply retrieved Jane Austen. Poor substitute.

Since her hovering maid wasn't using the first mate's cabin, Tristan decided to bed down there. It wasn't nearly as comfortable as his own quarters. He'd had all his furniture handcrafted to accommodate for his height and broad shoulders. He'd also paid extra for comfort. Few homes could boast nicer accommodations than what he provided for himself. What was the point in accumulating wealth if one didn't enjoy the fruits of one's labors?

He could hear soft murmurings from the room next door. He was half tempted to hold a glass to the wall and press his ear to it so he could hear the exact words. Instead, he simply lay there with the lamp still burning and listened to the feminine lullaby. Eventually it drifted into silence, and when it did, he opened the book. On the inside of the cover was an inscription:

> *To my darling Anne*
> *With all my love always,*
> *Your Walter*

Tristan wondered what other gifts the pup may have given her. As he valued books, he couldn't fault this present, but he wondered if she possessed jewelry or hair ribbons or gloves that her betrothed had bestowed upon her. Perhaps when he returned to London he would send her a gift for remembrance. Something naughty. Stockings perhaps. Something that would glide over her toes, the arch of her foot, her heel. Something that she would slide up her calf, over her knee, along her thigh.

Why was he allowing his thoughts to travel down such wicked paths that resulted in little more than pure torture? He couldn't remember the last time he had a woman. He'd quickly grown bored with the ones in London two years ago. During his travels since, none had managed to entice him. He would think he'd become a eunuch if he didn't react so strongly to Anne's presence. What was it about her that called to him?

After the brief flirting on the deck, he'd been content to simply hold her in his arms. He wondered if she was aware of the sigh she'd released as she nestled against him. If she hadn't been wearing a gown with so many layers of skirts and petticoats she'd have realized how very difficult it had been for him not to kiss her then. She'd have been aware of his immense desire.

He wouldn't be sleeping tonight. Not unless he took a quick dive into the waters to cool his ardor. Not a wise move at night, but then he was beginning to doubt that he was as smart as he'd always thought he was.

When it came to Lady Anne Hayworth, it seemed he had no sense whatsoever.

Chapter 7

He ignored her. A new strategy, Anne was fairly certain, he'd adopted, designed to torment and lure at the same time. He would discover she was made of sterner stuff. He had, however, gone to the trouble of having some sort of sheeting suspended so a portion of the quarterdeck was in shade. She and Martha could sit there without having to worry about winds whipping away her parasol. In addition, Martha discovered two wide-brimmed gentlemen's hats tied to the outside knob on their door that morning. Squinting against the sunlight reflecting off the water, they wore them now as additional protection against the harsher elements. In the distance she could see dolphins frolicking. She found herself wishing she could be so carefree.

She also felt a tad guilty that she was doing little more than enjoying the day while around her the men worked. Some scrubbed the decks, others wove rope, a few scampered up the sail rigging.

She suspected if she and Martha weren't out on the deck that a good many of them would be running about without shirts. As it was a good many buttons were left undone. From what she could see of their skin, the men were dark from the sun beating down on them. Leathery, tough skinned. But not the captain. His flesh was more bronzed than anything. Perfectly shaded.

"How old do you suppose he is?" she asked.

Martha startled and Anne realized she'd been absorbed in watching Mr. Peterson going about his labors. "Who?"

"The captain."

"Oh, I don't know. Late thirties, early forties, I suppose."

"So old? No, I think he's much younger."

"He has his own ship."

"Still, I can't quite picture him not being captain of a ship. I think he would pull at the traces if someone else were holding the reins. I think gaining his own ship would have been a priority for him when he was very young."

"You seem quite infatuated with him."

"You must admit he's a fascinating specimen. He's nothing at all like the gentlemen I've met in ballrooms." Nothing like Walter, or his brother. Or *her* brothers for that matter.

"He could bring you a great deal trouble, m'lady."

Oh, she didn't half know that. *But only if I let him.* "Please give me some credit, Martha. I'm not completely without experience when it comes to gentlemen."

"But they were gentlemen. He's more scoundrel."

He was temptation. Anne couldn't help but think that if the devil wanted to lure women into sacrificing their souls for pleasure, he'd have used the captain as his lure.

"The lords will be glad to have you back in Society," Martha said.

"Oh, yes, I suppose." She came with a nice dowry, something the captain certainly didn't need. "I don't think ladies should come with a dowry," she mused. "Makes it difficult to know if the gentleman is choosing the lady or security."

"Any gentleman would choose you."

She smiled at her maid's devotion. "Perhaps." She pointed toward the horizon. "What do you suppose is going on out there?"

Martha glanced toward the black clouds that seemed to be touching the water. "Oh, I don't like the look of that."

"Mr. Peterson!" Anne called. When he glanced over, she said, "What do you make of that darkness in the distance?"

"Storm coming in."

"Don't you think someone should make the captain aware of it?"

"He's aware, m'lady. He's busy now trying to determine how best to avoid it."

"Ah, well, then," she said half to herself, half to Martha, "we've nothing to worry about."

A couple of hours after sunset, the storm caught up with them—or they caught up with it. Anne wasn't quite certain of the particulars except for the fact that she was exceedingly disappointed in the captain's navigating skills. When the ship had begun tossing her and Martha about the cabin as though they were ragdolls, they both ran up to the deck and watched in horror as water lashed over the sides.

The captain grabbed her arm in a bruising hold and jerked her about. The fury reflected in his eyes rivaled the storm's. "Get below and stay there!"

"What about you?"

"Now!"

And he shoved her. *Shoved her!* Then the bulk that was Peterson was doing the same with Martha and blocking the doorway. "Into your cabin immediately!"

Now she and Martha were curled on the bed, taking turns hanging over a bucket, even though neither had anything left to bring up. She tried to console herself that the ship had no doubt been through many storms, that the captain no doubt knew what he was doing. But the fierceness with which the boat lurched was terrifying. Her stomach sank and rose with the swells of the sea. She wanted to die, wished she was dead.

The ship groaned and creaked. How could it withstand the bombardment? What if it didn't?

She thought she heard a knock. Was it the ship splitting apart? Then it came again and the door opened. The captain stood there with strands of his drenched hair having worked free of his leather thong. He removed his greatcoat and tossed it to the floor where it landed with a wet slap.

"Are we going to sink?" she asked.

"No, we're through the worst of it."

"It doesn't feel like it." She wanted to tell him that if anything it felt worse, but at that moment her stomach pitched and she grabbed the bucket. Oh, it hurt, it hurt to heave and have nothing come up.

Suddenly he was crouched beside her, rubbing her back. "Easy now," he cooed, before yelling, "Peterson!"

The large man stepped through the doorway. "Aye, Cap'n?"

"Take the maid to your quarters."

"Aye, Cap'n."

He leaned over the bed and lifted a feebly protesting Martha as though she were a feather pillow. "Easy, woman. No one's going to hurt you."

To Anne's surprise, Martha sagged against him and began crying.

"I know, I know, girl. It's frightening, but it's all over now. You'll feel right as rain soon enough."

She was also surprised by the soothing tone of his voice, and she wondered if he'd been watching Martha that afternoon as much as Martha had been watching him. The painful cramps stopped, and she rolled back. "He won't . . . hurt her, will he?"

"No, but with the bed bolted down and one side up against the wall, it's too difficult to try to take care of you both here. He's big, but he'll be as gentle as a lamb."

"And you?"

"Gentle has never been my style. I can't believe you're still in your blasted corset."

"I thought we might have to abandon ship."

"Which is exactly why you should have taken it off."

"I didn't want to wash up onshore improperly attired."

"Sweetheart, we're so far from any reachable land that you would have been drowned. You wouldn't have cared."

She didn't like his scolding her and was going to explain that Martha had loosened it some, but she was distracted by his fingers rapidly unbuttoning her bodice. She slapped at his hands with what little strength she could muster. "Don't."

He'd already completed the task and was working on her corset. She was wearing a chemise beneath it, but still she tried to roll away from him, only he held her in place.

"Don't be so modest," he growled. "I'm not looking."

She relaxed. "Truly?"

"Of course I'm looking. I'm a man, aren't I?"

She laughed, then groaned as her stomach protested the movement. "You're so refreshingly honest. I think I may have done some damage here."

"It's always harder on your body when your stomach is trying to empty itself and there's nothing to bring up."

"Hardly polite conversation."

"But the truth. You'll be sore for a couple of days."

If she survived. At that moment she couldn't quite believe that was a possibility. Her corset loosened, he removed it with an efficiency that she would have protested if it didn't feel so lovely not to be confined. He dragged the gown and petticoats down her legs and whipped a blanket over her before she could complain about the precarious immodesty of her position. Through half-lowered lids she watched him making his way around the room, but couldn't quite find the strength to ask him what he was doing. The ship was still bucking. How did he maintain his balance so easily?

She imagined him moving about a dance floor with the same grace. He would be poetry in motion, and the woman held within his arms would be swept away. How could she not? He returned to the bed, sat on its edge.

"Face the wall," he ordered.

"Why?"

He held up a brush. "So I can do something with your hair before it becomes a tangled rat's nest."

"I can sit up." She was halfway to her goal when the room swirled around her and her stomach roiled. She fell back and rolled to her side, wishing the world would stop spinning.

"Ah, Princess, I bruised you when you came up on deck."

She felt his callused fingers skimming over her upper arm so lightly, as though he was afraid of hurting her again.

"I'm sorry," he said. "I shouldn't have treated you so roughly. Forgive me." He brushed his lips over her discoloring flesh, and in spite of her misery, she felt pleasurable tingles all the way down to her toes.

And disappointment. A kiss. The time of his choosing. She opened her mouth—

"That does not qualify as a kiss," he said in a low purr.

She released a small laugh. "I could argue that, but I won't."

She felt a tug here, a gentle pull there as he began removing the few pins that remained in her hair. It tumbled down and he gathered it up. She thought she heard him mumble, "Glorious." But how could anyone consider anything about her glorious at that moment? She was a miserable, tired, aching wretch.

Then the brush was gliding through her hair and nothing had ever felt so marvelous.

"You've done this before," she murmured.

"Never, actually." He slid a hand between her head and the pillow, carefully lifted, dragging the brush through the strands, pulling them taut, before lowering her.

"You're very good."

"I'm a quick study."

She was being lured into sensations she wasn't quite comfortable feeling. They seemed naughty. She should send him away now. Instead, she didn't want him to ever stop his tender ministrations. She had never expected such care from him. She thought he would be like a tempest: powerful, uncontrollable.

Nothing about this man ever seemed to be as she anticipated.

"Peterson said you were going to go around the storm," she chided, not quite pleased with herself for making the words seem accusatory.

"We didn't have enough room to maneuver. We could have possibly outsailed it but I thought it better to continue forward, skirt it as much as possible. It didn't look too threatening."

"But it was."

"Not really."

She glanced back. "You've been in worse?"

He grinned. "Much worse. Cape Horn is notoriously treacherous. At least in these waters, we don't have to deal with icebergs."

"Does nothing frighten you?"

He grew somber, his gaze gliding over her before he began once again to concentrate on her hair. Knowing that he wasn't going to give her an answer, she turned her attention back to the wall, studying the knotholes in the wood, relishing the feel of his hands gathering up the silken strands, taming them with the brush. She supposed she should be scandalized to be wearing the barest of undergarments beneath the blanket while a man sat on the bed stroking her hair. If she didn't feel so awful she would demand he leave. But she did feel awful, except for where he touched her. Why should she not take comfort in that?

He parted her hair and began to plait it.

"You're really quite nice, aren't you?" she asked of the wall.

"Because I won't take advantage of a woman who might heave her stomach contents over me? You don't have very high standards, Princess."

Oh, dear God, but she wanted to laugh hard, but she knew her sides and belly would protest, so she settled for a wide smile that he probably couldn't see. When he was finished with his task, he draped her braid over her shoulder and she fingered the strip of leather that had been holding his hair in place.

With his large warm hand, he began stroking her back.

"I'm feeling somewhat better," she said. "You don't have to stay."

"I'll stay until you drift off."

It felt so lovely. She couldn't remember the last time someone had given her so much attention. That it was him could not have surprised her more. He was a man of varying facets, complex and interesting.

Her eyes grew heavy. She didn't want to go to sleep, didn't want to give up the press of his fingers along her spine, the circling of his palm over her shoulders. But the lethargy weighted her down and drew her into oblivion.

"**D**oes nothing frighten you?" she'd asked.

She frightened him, terrified him in fact. When he'd seen her first come to the deck during the storm, terror had ripped through him. She could have tumbled, been hit by a broken mast, washed overboard. Anything could have happened and it had rocked him to his core to consider her gone . . .

Before he acquired his payment. That was what was so troubling about the whole blasted situation. The woman seemed to have no care regarding debts owed. He'd follow her into hell to claim what was due him.

Unfortunately, he suspected she was headed for heaven, which was barred to him.

Rubbing her neck, Tristan listened to her soft breathing. Her arm was bared, and his gut again clenched at the sight of the mottled flesh where he'd grabbed her. She'd have a nasty bruise by tomorrow. If he could only touch it and draw it upon himself, he'd gladly do so. He doubted she'd ever been so brutally handled.

He was truly the barbarian that the Londoners considered him.

He was also—in spite of wearing a coat out into the storm—damp and chilled. If she'd not been drowning in her own misery she might have noticed and insisted he change into dry clothes. Not that he would have with her awake. But with her asleep . . .

He eased his hands away from her. She didn't stir. As gingerly as possible he rose from the bed and crept to a chair where he removed his boots. Then he grabbed a linen towel and rubbed it briskly over his wet hair, before finger combing the strands back. He was exhausted. Every muscle ached from fighting the storm.

What he truly wanted was to lie in his own bed,

curl his arm around her, and sleep the sleep of the dead. But he supposed for tonight it was either the floor here or a hammock in the area where his men slept.

Wearily, he forced himself to his feet and wandered over to the chest where he kept his extra clothes. He dragged his shirt over his head and tossed it aside, before lifting the heavy lid.

"Oh, dear God, whatever did they do to your back?"

He froze, fighting against the need to hide the unsightly latticework of scars that marred his back. He forced a casualness into his voice that he was far from feeling as he grabbed a shirt. "I thought you were asleep."

"No, only drifting about. Those are lash marks, aren't they?"

He slammed down the lid and shoved his arms into his shirt, before jerking it down over his head and shoulders, welcoming the knowledge that with the material in place, the ugliness was once again hidden. "They're nothing."

"They must have hurt terribly."

"For a short time, yes," he gritted out.

"But the pain long remembered, I should think."

Shoring himself up to ignore the pity in her eyes, he gazed over at her. She was sitting up, clutching the blanket high at her throat with both hands, as though that could protect her from him. Her eyes were wide damp saucers. Damnation but he never flaunted his scars and he hated that she'd seen them. "I believe that's the point, Princess."

Chapter 8

He was angry at her, furious in fact, judging by the tautness in his features. And so profoundly proud, standing there so magnificently, almost rebelliously, trying to show that the scars didn't matter, that they were nothing. She wished she hadn't seen how terribly he'd been hurt. But she had and she couldn't undo what she'd seen. She felt sicker in her stomach now than she had during the worst part of the storm.

He'd been a lad when he'd gone to sea, seeking adventure, not much younger than Mouse. Had he been as slender, as vulnerable? Had he been near that age when he felt the bite of the whip? Had he screamed? Had he cried? Had he begged them to stop?

"How can men do that to another?" she asked.

"It's standard practice on a ship when someone isn't behaving . . . quite properly," he bit out.

"Do you take the lash to your men?"

"No, but then none were forced aboard my ship

against their wishes. They share in the bounty. They work together because it adds coins to their pockets."

"You said you went to sea for adventure. Were you forced—"

"No," he interrupted before she could finish her question.

A knock sounded, and relief washed over his face as though the disturbance would bring a natural end to this conversation, which he obviously loathed. She watched as he strode across the room, his hair freely grazing over his wide shoulders. She wondered what he would say if she offered to take a brush to it, to sift her fingers through it, to provide comfort to him as he had to her. He opened the door and Mouse scurried in with his rocking gait. On the desk, he set a tray with a teapot and some cups on it.

"Mr. Peterson thought ye be needin' this."

"Good lad."

"She gonna be a'right?"

"Should be. Just a bit of seasickness." He placed his hand on the boy's shoulder. It seemed a tender gesture, even though he was guiding the lad out of the room. Had anyone placed a kind hand on the captain's shoulder or brow after the flesh on his back had been ripped apart?

When they were again alone, he returned to the desk and poured some tea into a cup, then added a splash of amber liquid to it.

She settled back against the pillows, ever conscious of keeping the blanket high.

"This should help settle your stomach a bit," he said as he handed her the cup and saucer. The china seemed incredibly delicate in his large paw.

As for himself, he poured a generous helping of spirits into a glass before pulling over a chair and sitting beside the bed.

She supposed as things were settling down that Martha could rejoin her now, but she didn't suggest it on the off chance that she was sleeping. She didn't want to disturb her. More, she wasn't quite ready for him to leave. She took a sip, recognized the flavor, and smiled. "Brandy."

"Your indulgence of choice, I believe."

"Only because it was the easiest bottle to swipe from my father's liquor cabinet." She studied him more closely. He appeared older now than he had before, and she realized fighting the storm had taken a toll on him. She missed his ready smile and teasing.

His eyes contained a distance, as though he were looking inward rather than outward, and she wondered where his thoughts traveled, if he was thinking about the pain he'd endured when they whipped him or how he battled the sea or . . .

She knew so little about him, knew it was foolish to want to know more. Once they were again in England, she would never see him again. They would take diverging paths, hers leading her to ballrooms and his returning him to the sea.

She wanted to talk, but the brandy was having its way with her, swirling warmth and lethargy through her bones. She supposed she shouldn't have been surprised, considering that nothing remained in her stomach to absorb it, to halt its progress.

After finishing off the tea in one long unladylike swallow, she set aside the cup and saucer on the table beside the bed. Then she snuggled beneath the blankets, slipped her hands between her cheek and pillow, and watched Jack. He didn't quite look like a Jack to her. His lids were half lowered, his glass empty, and she wondered if he was feeling as languid as she. "Why did they whip you?" To her surprise, the words came out slowly, slightly slurred.

"I won't discuss my back, Anne."

The anger was still in his voice and he studied his glass as though it were far more interesting than her. She didn't know why that stung.

"Where did you grow up?" she asked.

Finally, he shifted his gaze over to her. "On the sea."

She smiled, or at least she thought she did. Her mouth definitely moved. "Before that."

"Yorkshire."

"Lovely country."

Leaning forward, he brushed back some wayward strands that he'd failed to secure in the braid. "You should sleep now, Princess."

"So should you." She furrowed her brow. "Where do you sleep . . . since I have your room?"

"In the room next door or in a hammock on the berth deck." He cradled her chin, his thumb stroking her cheek.

"Doesn't sound comfortable."

"It's not."

"You should have taken my two hundred pounds to make it worth your while."

"It's worth my while."

He sounded as though he meant the words. How could a kiss make up for all the discomforts he endured?

"Are you going to kiss me now?"

"Not when you're too weak to return the kiss with enthusiasm."

"You seem to have a rather high opinion of your kissing talents. I might not have any enthusiasm for it at all."

"You will."

Such an arrogant cad, she thought dreamily as she fought to keep her eyes open. "I thought we were going to die tonight," she whispered.

"I would never have allowed that to happen."

He said it with such confidence, as though he commanded the sea. She trusted him, believed in his skills, and had to reluctantly admit that she even liked him. "You had a rough night of it, didn't you?"

"Very rough."

"You must be exhausted."

"Terribly."

He shouldn't have a hammock tonight. He should have his bed. Only she was in it. She certainly didn't want a hammock. "You could sleep here . . . on top of the covers," she hastily added.

His response was a tender smile that caused

her heart to flip. She didn't remember moving, but between one blink and the next, the cabin was in darkness, she was on her side, and he was spooned around her. In the vaguest corners of her mind, she thought she should stiffen, elbow him in the ribs, or shove him away with a reprimand of, "Not so close."

Instead, she snuggled more securely against him, his soft moan wafting around her as she sank into the land of dreams.

With her body pressed against his, she felt better than he'd anticipated. Even with clothing and blankets separating them, he couldn't recall ever being quite so aroused with so little effort. Especially as his body felt as though it had been transformed into an anchor and was dragging him down.

He'd spoken true. He was exhausted. Beyond measure. He wasn't certain that he could have made his way out of his quarters to a hammock below. In all likelihood, he'd have been able to do little more than slide out of the chair and land in an unconscious heap on the floor.

The weariness had slammed into him the moment he'd finished braiding her hair, the moment he'd realized that her bout of sickness had passed. The moment he'd acknowledged to himself that she would survive, that she would recover. Until then, he'd been so focused on seeing to her needs that he'd had no time to consider his own.

He'd never been selfish when it came to women.

He'd always put their pleasures first, but he'd never been quite so consumed with a female to the degree that he was when he was around her. Pain, aches, weariness ceased to exist for him until she was clearly out of harm's way.

It was a strange . . . thing. He didn't quite understand it.

But he did understand that being this near to her was dangerous. Very, very dangerous.

From the moment he'd seen her, he'd wanted her beneath him, his body pounding into hers with a fierceness that would cause the ship to rock on still waters. But with her in his arms now, he feared he'd not be content with having her only once. He would want her again. When they returned to England.

He wished he could work up the energy to skim his fingers along her cheek, down her neck, across her shoulders. When he woke up with her, he might very well be unable to resist the lure of a kiss—but he would have to remain strong, stronger than he'd ever been.

Because he just realized with startling clarity that he couldn't kiss her before they arrived at Scutari. No, he would have to wait until afterward, until they were nearer to England.

Her fiancé would no doubt kiss her when he saw her, kiss her when he said good-bye, and his mouth on hers would wash away anything that remained of the kiss she would share with Tristan. Therefore, it stood to reason that he would have to remain in purgatory a bit longer.

Because when they arrived at England's shores

and she walked away from him, he wanted his kiss to be the last upon her lips.

It was a bittersweet awakening for Anne. The captain was gone, so she was spared the uncomfortable awareness of being in his arms. She ignored the disappointment that struck her because he had taken his leave so quietly, so unobtrusively.

Which left her to deal with the guilt and the immense longing to have such a memory of being held through the night with Walter. He'd wanted it, had asked for it, and she'd denied him. Of course, what he wanted involved more than simply holding her. But she now had an inkling of how lovely it might have been. It was no longer just a wispy imagining. She knew the feel of a man's body pressed against her, the warmth, the scent. She knew the sound of his breathing luring her as though it were a lullaby.

She was beginning to regret that she'd decided to take this sojourn, but it was far too late to turn back.

Stepping onto the deck, a much recovered Martha at her side, Anne shielded her gaze from the brilliant sunlight reflecting off the blue water. After what they endured several hours before, she expected to encounter some remnants of a storm, but instead all appeared as though it had never been. Men were working. The breeze toyed playfully with the sails.

"If I didn't know better, I'd think we imagined the horrors of last night," Martha said.

Only Anne did know better. The leather strip with which the captain had bound her hair was tucked into a hidden pocket on her skirt.

"Oh my God, land." She walked to the edge of the ship and gripped the railing. "We can't be too far from our destination, do you think?"

"Not too far," a deep voice responded.

She spun around, her heart seizing as she gazed at the captain. He, too, looked as though last night had never happened, as though he hadn't held her, as though they hadn't shared a strange sort of intimacy. She wanted to reach out, touch him, curl her fingers around his shirt, and bury her face in his shoulder, inhale deeply of his now familiar fragrance. Instead she balled her hands into achingly tights fists. "How soon?"

"A few more days."

They turned out to be the longest and loneliest of her life. He didn't have dinner with her. If she was on deck, he was below or on the opposite side of the ship. She knew it was just as well that they weren't in each other's company. Each day she recovered a little more from the illness she experienced during the storm, but as they neared their destination a weariness settled over her.

Finally, she saw the spires of the city as they pulled into the harbor. They were here. They had arrived.

But a secret mourning part of her wished they hadn't.

Chapter 9

Standing on the deck in the predawn, Tristan waited for the night to retreat.

They'd arrived in the harbor yesterday afternoon. He'd expected Anne to go flying off the ship to be with her fiancé. Did she even know where he was? Surely, she did.

Instead, she retired to her quarters, maid in tow. Mouse reported that she'd asked for hot water, enough to fill the copper tub. Tristan had forced himself to stay on deck, because he wanted nothing more than to burst through the door and watch as she luxuriated in the bath. At first he'd imagined a soapy cloth skimming over her skin, but then the cloth became his hands. Beginning at her neck he would glide his large hands along her shoulders and circle around until he cupped her breasts. He could almost feel the weight of them against his palms. He thought of going into his quarters and claiming his kiss then. Leaning over the tub, taking her mouth as though he owned it. Claiming it. Claiming her. Making it clear that when she returned to the ship, he would be waiting.

He'd barely slept last night, twisting and turning in the blasted hammock, almost upending himself. A foul mood hung around him when he returned to the deck before the sunrise. He wanted to be there when she left. He would be there when she returned.

It occurred to him, belatedly, that he'd never asked her how long she wanted to be in port. As she'd said that she wanted to travel on her own schedule, she no doubt wanted to remain here for days, possibly weeks. He'd become so obsessed with obtaining the kiss that he'd given little thought to the inconvenience of it all.

He didn't like being here. The war was over, but still the ghosts of it remained. Sebastian had been here, recovering from the wounds he'd suffered during the devastating battle at Balaclava. Tristan had been half a world away, but still he'd sensed when his brother was wounded. Perhaps because they were twins, they shared a connection. Tristan seemed to have the stronger bond, was often troubled when Sebastian suffered. He frequently prayed that Sebastian never knew how much he himself endured during their time apart.

Strange that they were not in each other's company now, but Tristan no longer viewed them as being apart. Simply separated by distance, no longer hiding from their dreaded uncle. Amazing how the blighter's death could restore a sense of rightness. As the sun began easing over the horizon,

Tristan could make out the spires of a large building. He wondered if Sebastian had gazed at them, how much might have changed in the few years since he was here.

"That's the hospital," Anne said softly coming to stand beside him, bringing her lavender and citrus scent with her.

Her hair was pinned up beneath an elegant hat with a broad brim decorated with ribbons and delicate bows. Beneath her pelisse, her lilac dress had prim buttons and a high collar. He didn't like considering that her fiancé might be loosening those buttons shortly after the sun set, if not before.

"Florence said I would recognize it by the spires," she continued.

"Florence Nightingale?" His voice came out terse, angry, but she seemed not to notice. He was regretting that he'd brought her here. He wished the ship had gone down in the storm, that she and he had swum to a deserted island where they could be alone forever.

"Yes. There are other hospitals, but that's the Barrack Hospital where she did most of her good works. She provided me with a map of things so I could find my way. The General Hospital is where I need to go."

She finally lifted her gaze to his. He was surprised by the doubts and uncertainty he saw there.

"I was wondering if you would be kind enough to go with me," she said. "Martha's not quite recovered from her seasickness during the ordeal of the storm."

The words that he recognized to be a lie came out in a rush and he wondered why she would want him at her side when she met with this Walter fellow. She had to know it would be incredibly awkward. "Your fiancé won't be pleased by my presence."

"He won't mind, I assure you. Besides, I suspect I'd be safer walking the streets with you there."

"I could send some of my men with you—"

"No, I don't want . . . people about. It's part of the reason that I didn't purchase passage for other means of getting here. I didn't want to run into someone I know or might have met on the journey. I need this to be private."

Was she going to call things off with him? Why not simply pen him a letter? Why go to all this bother? No, all she needed was for Tristan to accompany her, then things would become private between her and her fiancé. Tristan would be expected to return to the ship. Could he do it? Could he leave her in another man's keeping?

He was half tempted to kiss her now or to ask for an additional kiss for the service of delivering her safely through the streets. If she hadn't been looking at him so beseechingly he would have bargained. As it was he could say little more than, "When do you want to leave?"

"Now."

"Good." Before he had any time to consider the ramifications and to change his mind. Smart lass. He contemplated shaving, making himself a bit more presentable, but what did he care what this bloke thought of him? And if she used the opportunity to compare them, he could undo any damage when they returned to the ship. It was chilly out, he had his coat, and quite honestly, he wanted this done with. "Let's be off then."

After disembarking she handed the map to him. He wished he was familiar with the city. He could navigate the world, certainly understood the lines on a map, but preferred the stars to guide him. But there were none out now, so he studied the scrawled lines and the scribbled words and the occasional arrow. Florence Nightingale was meticulous but things were not drawn to scale.

Anne kept her hand on his arm. From time to time, she'd squeeze and he realized it was her way of coping with nervousness. He supposed after four years that she might be a bit apprehensive about seeing this man. If her fiancé was at the hospital, Tristan wondered if he was recovering from wounds, but that seemed unlikely after this length of time. Perhaps he was a physician who had stayed behind to help the people. Maybe she had come here to persuade him to return to England.

He fought not to growl at the thought of the man on his ship.

It seemed to take forever, but it was only a distorted passage of time brought about by his lack of desire to go where she wished him to lead, and eventually they did reach the General Hospital. At their arrival, the lethargy seemed to leave her and a purpose in her step took hold.

As they came around to the front, she said with confidence, "This way."

A short distance away was a sign: British Cemetery.

He was no longer leading, but following as she passed through the entrance. She strode past several marked graves until she came to an area that housed no headstones, where the land simply stretched down to the glistening blue waters of the Bosporus Strait.

She staggered to a stop, tears welling in her eyes. "More than five thousand are buried here," she rasped. "With no markers. However shall I find him?"

"He's dead?"

Her answer came as she sunk to the ground and sobbed softly, leaving Tristan to feel like an absolute bastard. He'd considered killing the man himself. Now he was irrationally furious at her fiancé for causing her this pain.

He knelt beside her, drew her into his arms, and held her while her shoulders shook with the force of her grief and her tears dampened his neck where she had pressed her face. If he still possessed a gentleman's heart, he thought it would break at her mewling, her trembling.

If he had a heart, he would know how to comfort her. But all he knew to do was to hold her and swear softly in between uttering her name.

Oh, it hurt, it hurt so terribly much. She'd known it would, known that no matter how much she prepared for it, the reality of being here would undo her.

She had also known that the captain would hold her and comfort her, just as he had when she'd been ill during the storm. Martha would have comforted her as well, but with her slight frame it wouldn't have been as reassuring. He was solid, firm, and strong. His large hands caressed her back, her arms. He held her until she had no more tears to weep, and then he walked with her along the water's edge where birds darted about and swooped down to capture fish.

"Even knowing that Walter was laid to rest in an unmarked grave, somehow I thought I would be able to find him, that I would know where he was. That I would sense his presence. But I don't feel him here. I had so much that I needed to say to him."

They walked on in silence. No matter how she had imagined things, she hadn't envisioned it being like this. She thought she would regain something she'd lost. Instead, it remained beyond reach.

"Why didn't you tell me that your fiancé was dead?" he asked over the cries of seagulls.

"I never said the words to anyone. It would make it more real. A letter from his brother alerting me to his death, his condolences, a notice in the paper—they made everything seem so distant. He died of cholera. Such an ignominious ending. I'm not even certain if he ever saw battle."

"Doesn't make him less of a hero. He was willing to fight, to die."

She peered up at him, at his strong features. "Thank you for that."

"I'm not simply muttering words, you know. He was a soldier. That says a lot for his character." He glanced out toward the sea. A muscle in his jaw tautened. "My brother fought in the Crimea. Was terribly wounded. Lost half his face."

"Oh, my God. I'm sorry."

"I didn't reveal that to garner sympathy. Rather I wanted you to know I understand the price your fiancé was willing to pay. I'm certain he would have much preferred staying with you than coming here."

He could have stayed with her, but he had chosen the army because he was weary of living in his brother's shadow.

"He was the second son of a nobleman," she said, shielding her eyes from the sun. "He wanted to make his own way in the world."

"Which makes him even more worthy of you."

She couldn't quite stop the soft smile. Flattering women was simply a natural part of the captain's charms. She suspected most of the time he probably gave no thought to the compliments he tossed out. She turned and glanced back toward the consecrated ground. "It's peaceful here, isn't it?"

"Quite. And he's with his brothers in arms."

Yes, he was. Having come here, having seen where he was laid to rest, she thought she might be able to move forward at last.

Chapter 10

As soon as they returned to the ship, she indicated that she was ready to leave the harbor. Tristan had not expected the short stay, the hasty departure, but he set his men to the task.

In the days that followed it was like having a wraith floating about the ship. She seldom spoke, never smiled, didn't laugh. She dined alone. Spent far too much time in her cabin. When she did finally appear on deck, her eyes had a faraway look to them, her mouth downturned. She spoke in a monosyllabic tone that was as flat as the horizon in the distance. Where was a good storm when he needed one, anything to shake her out of her melancholy?

He wanted to give her a kiss that would melt her bones, sear her flesh. She wasn't betrothed. She wouldn't suffer guilt or betray anyone. She could enjoy the kiss as much as he intended to, but not when she was engaged in this blasted moping about.

Leaning back against the railing he crossed his arms over his chest and contemplated the full moon. The winds were in their favor. They had no cargo weighing them down. They'd passed through the choppy Strait of Gibraltar. His ship was slicing through the water with ease. His time was running out.

"That look never bodes well."

Tristan grinned at Peterson as he came to stand beside him.

"What are you scheming now?" his first mate asked.

He studied what he could see of the masts against the star-filled sky. "Considering our passenger."

"We have two."

"Yes, but I'm only interested in the one. You're interested in the other."

Peterson didn't bother to argue. He simply grumbled, "She's a fine lass, but not too keen on a man who's married to the sea."

"It's a rare woman who is."

"Do you ever think of giving up this life?"

Tristan heard a whale lowing somewhere off in the distance. "When we were in England two years ago, I constantly felt as though I would crawl out of my skin. I've been too long on the water, Peterson, to be content on the land."

He had his swine of an uncle to thank for that. If he hadn't had to run, he'd be a very different man. He would be a man who visited Rafe's gaming establishment and enjoyed the vices he could experience there. He would be welcomed at balls. Mothers would *want* their daughters to catch his fancy rather than shielding them from his sight. He would be proper. He would be tamed.

Having known nothing different, would he be content? The answer mattered little. He was what he was, set in his ways, too old to change. He would never settle into marriage. He would never be embraced by Society.

Once they returned to England, he would never again see Anne.

But they'd struck a bargain. It was past time he collected payment—whether she was ready to give it or not.

Lying in the bed, Anne watched as sunlight filtered in through the mullioned windows. She was sad, remarkably sad. She'd known she'd weep at the cemetery. Had known grief would overcome her, but she'd expected to cry and finally be done with it.

Instead she continued to think about the last time she saw Walter and how awful it had been. The argument, the unkind words, the tempers flaring. Oh, if she could only have that night over—

But she couldn't. And that's what hurt the most. She'd made a dreadful mistake and she had no way to right it.

At Martha's insistence, she finally dragged herself from the bed. Raising her arms, she stretched from one side to the other. "I must have finally become accustomed to being on a ship. I feel as though we're doing little more than bobbing."

"We are only bobbing," Martha said. "When I went to the deck earlier for some fresh air, the sails were down."

Anne lowered her arms. "Why?"

"I don't know. You'll have to take it up with the captain."

"Is there another storm brewing?"

"Not that I saw."

Why was he delaying their return to England? She hired him to make a short trip of it. She didn't want her family worrying about her any longer than necessary.

"Quickly. Help me to dress."

She had just finished buttoning the final button at her throat, when a knock sounded. She and Martha exchanged quick glances before her maid hastened to the door and opened it.

"May I come in?" the captain asked, and yet the authority in his voice indicated it wasn't truly a request.

She'd seen him very little since leaving Scutari. She'd almost forgotten that he was a man accustomed to being obeyed on all matters.

Martha opened the door wider, and he strode in. She was surprised by the newly acquired deep lines on his face, as though he wasn't sleeping any more soundly than she. She didn't want to admit how many nights she had contemplated seeking him out, asking him to simply hold her while she fought for sleep. His gaze traveled over her, and he seemed none too pleased by what stood before him. She straightened her shoulders, angled her chin. She had a right to grieve, but this journey was supposed to allow her to put it all behind her. Why didn't it?

"You're wasting away," he said.

Self-consciously she plucked at her skirt. The dress did seem looser than it was when she wore it to travel through the streets of Scutari. "The sea is not agreeing with me. Why are we stopped?"

"I have a surprise for you." He tossed a bundle of clothes to her. She juggled them before finally securing them in her grasp. "Put those on."

It was a small bundle. She peeled away a pair of trousers and a shirt. "These are britches."

"I'm not in the habit of carrying around items without knowing what they are."

"Ladies do not wear britches."

"Those who wish to look out from the crow's nest do."

She clutched the garments to her chest. Opened her mouth. Closed it. Was he implying what she thought he was? "How do you propose I get there?"

"You'll climb."

He said it with such assurance that she couldn't help but laugh. "And if I fall?"

"You won't. You'll be secured with a rope and I'll be there with you."

She shook her head. "It's far too dangerous."

"You never struck me as cowardly."

"I'm practical," she bit out.

"Scared," he taunted.

"I'm not." He made her feel like a child, but it wasn't the height or the climb that terrified her. It was the thought of falling, not to the deck but into his arms.

"I'll show you a view of the world you may never have an opportunity to see again."

"I can't parade about in trousers in front of your men."

"They're all below deck, except for the three I need to assist in getting you into the crow's nest."

"Will they be climbing with us?"

"No, but we've rigged a winch and pulley. Someone has to man it." He touched her cheek with a featherlike graze. "Trust me, Princess."

Hadn't she from the beginning, when she'd had no true cause to except for another's word? But always something about him, something deep within him had calmed her nerves, quieted her doubts. If she believed in magic, she'd consider that he might be a sorcerer weaving his spells over her. But if nothing else, the state of his back proved he was merely a man.

"I'll need a few moments," she said flatly, quelling any anticipation she might be feeling at the prospect of what she was about to do.

"I'll be waiting." He headed for the door, stopped, glanced back. "No shoes. It'll make it easier. But do wear gloves."

He quickly left. She met Martha's gaze. "Do you suppose I should wear a corset with this attire?"

Martha smiled. "No, m'lady. I suspect for this

adventure, it would be best if you wore as little as possible."

When she was finally in the shirt and trousers, she felt rather very much like a heathen. A rope threaded through loops on the trousers kept them hugging her waist. She had to roll up the hem to prevent herself from stepping on them. Now her ankles were exposed. Scandalous. The shirt was loose, the linen fine, and it felt almost as though she wore nothing at all. Martha had braided her hair, securing it with the leather strip she had yet to return to the captain.

She had no cheval glass in which to peer. Martha removed the captain's shaving mirror from the wall, but it only provided glimpses as though she were pieces of a puzzle and not the whole.

"I'm certain my appearance will suffice," she said succinctly. After all, what did her clothing truly matter when she would never again see these people once she got off the ship?

He was waiting for her on the deck. His feet were also bare, and her toes curled at the intimacy. His feet were long, slender, as bronzed as his face. She'd never looked at a man's feet before—not even her brothers'.

With his bare hand, he took her gloved one, and she had an irrational urge to remove the protection so her skin would touch his. Ludicrous. Where were these strange notions coming from?

He led her to the mast where the crow's nest perched near the top. The sea was calm, yet a slight breeze gently lolled the ship. She craned back her head. "It's so high."

"Imagine the view."

Shifting her eyes to his, she could see within his blue depths that he understood her hesitation. He wasn't mocking or chiding. He was waiting patiently for her to gain her resolve. Taking a deep breath, she angled her chin. "I don't want to imagine it. I want to experience it, to see it."

With a jerk of his head, he signaled Mouse and Jenkins over. They brought with them the lassoed end of a rope. Strips of what she was fairly certain had once been woolen blankets were wrapped around it, offering a bit of padding. She raised her arms and the captain lowered it over her, securing it beneath her arms.

"This is only to stop you if you fall," he said. "They won't be pulling you up. You'll be doing that on your own." He explained the climbing process, showing her notches and handholds.

She did wish that she hadn't been so prim and proper growing up, that she'd followed after her brothers, racing barefoot across fields and climbing trees. But then, if she hadn't been so prim and proper, she probably wouldn't be weighted down with regrets and so she wouldn't be here now. She would have said yes to Walter when he asked of her what he did. She would have scoffed at Society's rules as he'd wanted to. Instead, she'd remained steadfast in her determination to hold to the higher ground.

Yet here she was wearing clothing that outlined

her form to such a degree that she might as well not be wearing anything at all. Nothing prim or proper in that.

But then who was to see except for the four males in view of her now, Martha, and the occasional porpoise that leapt out of the sea?

At the captain's urging she pressed against the mast and used his wrists as her handholds. She didn't know how this would work at all if he wasn't so much taller than she. He wedged his right foot into a notch, then instructed her to place her foot on his. She did—

And froze.

The top of his bare foot was warm and soft beneath her sole. It shot sensations through her. Naughty, wicked sensations. She'd never touched a man so intimately. It was unsettling, yet reassuring at the same time. It was marvelous. It was—

"The other." His silky voice danced around her ear.

"Pardon?"

"Place your other foot on mine. I'm hanging here, Princess. Can't hang forever, you know."

Why not? Why couldn't she stay here where his nearness distracted her from her misgivings?

"Yes, of course. I'm sorry." She rose up, placed her foot on his.

"There we go," he murmured. "Now, just relax and climb with me."

Relax? With him cocooned around her, with her clinging to him as much as she was to this cylinder of wood?

"If you're afraid of heights, I'd advise you not to look down," he added.

She didn't think she was afraid of heights, but then she'd always looked out through a window. This, she realized as they slowly made their way upward, was a very different kettle of fish.

His foot slipped, she screeched. He snaked an arm around her waist, held her tightly against him, as his other arm wrapped around the mast. She was breathing heavily while he seemed not to be breathing at all.

"I won't let you fall," he said quietly.

She nodded jerkily. "Yes, all right."

"Calm your breathing."

"How can you not be rattled?"

"Because I've done this a thousand times."

"Taken a woman up to the crow's nest?"

He had the audacity to laugh. "No, you're the first. But I've climbed often enough that I'm intimate with every knothole. I know the rough grain, where to place my hands and feet for the best purchase. I've never fallen, Princess. I'm not about to today. Besides we're almost there."

She glanced up at the basket high above her. "I'm not certain you have a clear understanding of the term 'almost.'"

He chuckled low. "Come on, up we go."

He guided her with gentle murmured words, his hands, and his feet. Before long, she was scrambling over the side of the basket and into the crow's nest. What surprised her was how small it was, how inconsequential it seemed. Especially when he joined her. She thought that she should have felt as though he were crowding her. Instead, she found that she simply wanted to lean into him.

She also discovered that she wasn't terribly afraid of heights, especially when such an incredible vista swept out before her. The deep blue water melting into the light blue, billowy white cloud-filled sky.

"Oh," she said as her breath escaped. "It's stunning. What is that shadow over there in the distance?"

"England."

Her stomach nearly dropped to the deck. "We're almost home."

"Tomorrow evening, most like."

"Tomorrow." Holed up in her cabin, mourning, filled with sadness, battling regrets, she'd lost track of the time. One day had rolled into the next and she'd not been counting. The purpose of this journey was to prepare her for reentering Society. She would be expected to attend balls, to embrace gentlemen's advances, to encourage their interest in her. To engage in flirtatious banter. To place herself back on the marriage block. "I don't know if I'm quite ready."

"Say the word, Princess, and we'll sail right on by."

She tilted back her head to study him. It was a lovely thought, but she couldn't do that to her family. Become a vagabond, a gypsy. To turn her back on what was good and proper. Regretfully, she shook her head. "No, that would accomplish little except to confirm that I'm a coward."

"A coward would not have hired me to take her to a place with a past tainted by horror in order that she might say good-bye to someone she cared for."

"Someone I loved," she felt a need to point out. But not enough. If she'd loved him enough, she would not now have so many regrets. "I thought it would heal this terrible hole in my heart, and yet at times I still feel as though I'm drowning in the sorrow." Tears stung her eyes. "I wish I could have brought him home. I hate that he's there."

Gently, he touched her cheek. "What do you see when you look out?"

"So much water."

"All the way to the horizon and beyond. When a man dies on a ship, he's given to the sea. Over the years, Anne, I've learned that it matters not where a man is buried. It matters only where he is remembered."

She thought she'd cried her fill in Scutari, but it seemed she had more tears to spill. They rolled over onto her cheeks and he gathered them with his thumbs.

"I would take your pain if I could," he said in a low rough voice.

When she thought her heart could ache no more, he bent his head and tenderly brushed his lips over hers, before gathering her into his arms and holding her near.

Nothing he might have said or done could have devastated her more. He understood loss, he understood pain, he understood walking away when one dearly wanted to stay.

For the first time in so long, the fractured remnants of her heart felt as though they might finally heal.

Chapter 11

Damnation! Through the long nights and days since he met her, when he envisioned claiming his kiss, he certainly had never envisioned it being so uneventful. It was never supposed to offer comfort; it was never supposed to be little more than a brief touch, a quick taste.

Blast it all! It was supposed to be designed to have her gasping and clinging to him. It was supposed to have her begging him to take it further. It was supposed to end with a tumble on his bed.

As he jerked free his unruly cravat to once more begin to properly tie it, he wasn't certain he'd ever been more disgusted with himself. He couldn't very well deliver the sort of kiss he'd dreamed of when she was moping about. Hence the journey to the crow's nest.

But she'd seemed so vulnerable, the pain still in her eyes. Whatever had possessed him to utter such poetic nonsense about where people were buried?

If that was not embarrassing enough, he'd dipped his head and grazed his lips over hers as though his body were not in a constant hardened state by the mere thought of her.

Now they were going to have dinner together—their last dinner together—after which he would not be at liberty to claim her mouth as though he owned it, because—dammit all—he'd already claimed the promised kiss!

Not only that. He hadn't bothered to give her a kiss that any woman in her right mind would want to experience again. There had been no heat, no passion, no swirling of tongues.

Good God, it might as well have not happened.

But it had happened, and she would hold him to it. Debt paid and all that rubbish.

If he wanted another kiss, then he was going to have to well and truly seduce her. Tonight. Because the sails had captured the wind and they were nearer to England's coast.

Whatever had he been thinking this afternoon? He hadn't been thinking at all. The woman had the ability to send his thoughts scattering. It was unsettling, this strange influence that she had over him.

His cravat finally to his liking, he grabbed his jacket and slipped it on. He'd bathed and shaved. He hadn't bothered to cut his hair because he didn't want to appear totally civilized. He didn't want her thinking of him as anything other than the sea captain that he was.

He wondered if he sailed by England without

delivering her to its shores, if he would rot in hell. Having spent a considerable number of years in that horrendous pit, he supposed he shouldn't be giving it any thought, and yet he couldn't quite quell the niggling temptation to keep her with him for a time at least, until he grew tired of her. He always grew tired of women. Never had there been one that he wanted to keep for any length of time. He just hadn't had his fill of her yet.

Hadn't even had a proper kiss.

He cursed himself once more, then headed out of Peterson's cabin and into his own.

If Anne's experience with Walter had taught her anything at all it was that she was far more likely to regret things she *hadn't* done than those she *had*.

So as she sat there dining on exquisite fare and drinking fine wine, both of which rivaled anything served at her father's table, she contemplated the regrets that might haunt her where Captain Crimson Jack was concerned. When they arrived at the docks on the morrow, she would disembark from his ship and never see him again—except in her dreams. She was fairly certain he would frequent her there. Much to her chagrin.

She'd not expected to like him, to be drawn to him, to be fascinated by him. She'd not expected to be able to peer beneath his rough exterior and discover a kernel of goodness within him that rivaled that of the most generous lords she'd ever known.

"Where will you go?" she asked. "When next you leave England?"

His plate now empty, he leaned back and swirled the wine in his glass, but his gaze was riveted on her. She was no longer uncomfortable by the intensity of it. Rather she found it oddly soothing, indeed flattering, that he would give so much attention to her as though she were all that mattered in his world. "The Far East most likely. Would you care to come with me?"

Her heart stammered at the improper suggestion, even as a small corner of her mind considered it. What would it be like to be free of all societal constraints? She suspected in time that she'd miss them terribly. It was what she knew, what she understood. "I wasn't made for this vagabond of a life you lead. Does it not become mundane, traveling about, with no permanence in your life?"

"I have permanence, Princess. The men who serve with me, the sea always around me, and the knowledge that I'll discover something new on every journey."

"Even this one?"

His eyes never leaving her, he took a slow sip of wine before saying, "Especially this one."

She was incredibly tempted to ask him exactly what he'd discovered. But that was only her vanity nudging her. They'd formed an odd bond of intimacy that she couldn't deny. It was something else that she'd not expected to happen.

"A bit scandalous not to have your maid in here watching over you, isn't it?" he asked.

"Her clacking needles were about to get on my last nerve," she said. A partial truth. Dare she voice the real reason she was alone with him?

He chuckled low. "Especially when they speed up in disapproval."

"Yes." She felt the heat suffuse her face. Martha would most certainly disapprove of the journey her thoughts were now taking because they led to the captain not leaving these quarters until the sun rose. "I've—" She cleared her throat. "I've instructed her to stay in your first mate's empty cabin for the night."

"Have you now?"

She nodded, her throat threatening to knot up. "I think she rather likes him. Your first mate. Mr. Peterson."

"He's quite smitten with her."

"Is he?" She couldn't stop herself from smiling. "How lovely for her. I suppose. It would be a rather lonely life, though, wouldn't it? With him at sea?"

Before he could answer, a knock at the door had her nearly leaping out of her skin. She didn't know why she was so skittish. Perhaps because her not having Martha in attendance had little to do with her irritating knitting needles and more to do with the fact that she was seriously contemplating giving him far more than a kiss.

She wanted to announce that she trusted him, but all she trusted him to do was misbehave. She was counting on it, in fact. It was as though she had changed on this journey, had become as liberated as his ship. It had the power to carry them anywhere, to reveal sights never before seen. It tempted her—*he* tempted her—to do her own exploring. What would she discover of him . . . and herself? Did she want to know? Or did she wish to remain forever naive?

They said that ignorance was bliss, but she was learning that it was little more than irritating. Better to know than to forever wonder.

With the lithe movements to which she'd grown accustomed, he got up from the table and opened the door. Mouse and Jenkins skittered in and cleared away the dishes. When the door closed on their retreating forms, she found herself standing, not certain what she should do next.

He was leaning against the wall, studying her, his arms crossed over his chest. Had she really considered that he could pass for a gentleman? His attire was well tailored, fit him to perfection. She suspected he'd paid a pretty penny for it. But still, beneath it hovered an untamed element, like the tempest that rose up unexpectedly. His life was coarse and harsh, had shaped him into the fascinating creature that he was. But just as his ship didn't stay at port long, she suspected he wasn't one to stay in her life for more than a short period.

They would never have more than this time together. And it was quickly drawing to a close.

"Can I interest you in a bit of after-dinner brandy?" he asked.

She nodded, grateful for something to do with

her hands as the silly things wanted to reach out and touch him, skim over his chest, his shoulders, his back. "Yes, please, thank you."

He prowled to the corner cabinet where he kept his spirits. She watched as he poured liberal amounts of brandy into two snifters before bringing them over to where she stood like a blasted mast. Whatever was wrong with her?

She took the glass he offered and he *clinked* his against hers. "To the end of a successful voyage."

"Is it something to celebrate?"

"We survived."

"Was there any chance we wouldn't?"

"There's always a chance, Princess. We can't control the seas."

Or our own destinies, for that matter, it seems.

She took a healthy sip, savoring the flavor, felt the familiar burn as the liquid went down but the vapors wafted through her nostrils, stinging. She smiled.

"What's so amusing?" he asked.

"I was recalling the first time I sipped brandy, after pilfering it from my father's cabinet. I went into a wretched coughing fit. My worst fear was that he would hear me, come to investigate, and discover what I was about." Not daring to look at him, she tapped her finger against the glass. "I always strive to be so damned proper."

"You say that as though you're not quite pleased with that aspect of your character."

She lifted her gaze to his. Why was it that he seemed to know her so well? She swallowed hard.

"I believe there are times when one shouldn't be quite so proper."

"Like when climbing a mast for example?" he asked with a twinkle in his eyes.

"I was quite daring, wasn't I? And the reward—the view from atop the ship—was so very worth it." She took a deep breath. "You claimed your kiss there."

He released a long suffering sigh. "Yes, I did, didn't I?" He then proceeded to finish off his brandy.

She followed suit, and this time, it felt as though the vapors invaded her brain. She felt lightheaded and bold. "It wasn't as you promised."

He arched a brow. "Oh?"

"You said it would be slow, leisurely, and long. It was none of those things. Quite honestly, Captain, I'm not certain you've been fully paid for your troubles."

"I did say *a* kiss, the moment of my choosing."

"But I think it was a kiss brought on by pity."

"Never. I don't pity you, Princess. It was simply that I could no longer resist and we did have an audience."

"We don't have one now."

"No, we don't."

He was watching her intently, and she realized that he would never force her, would never take what she was unwilling to give. She'd instinctively understood that of course. She'd have not boarded his ship otherwise, but now she fully comprehended that all the power was hers. "This long, slow, leisurely kiss of which you spoke . . . where does it lead?"

"Wherever you want it to."

She felt the weight of responsibility, but more she sensed the depth of yearning for something she'd been denied. "I believe I would like to . . . explore the possibilities."

"And where exactly do you want it to lead?"

"I don't want to say. In case I get frightened and change my mind. But we've shared so much on this journey. I would like a little more."

He touched her cheek. "At any time, all you have to say is 'stop.' "

"And you'll stop?"

"Even if it kills me."

"You'll get angry."

"I won't."

Walter had. He'd called her a tease, because she'd dared to allow him to kiss her until they were both breathless. She didn't want to think about that now. She only knew that she was drawn to this man who stood before her, and she didn't want to look back on these moments with regret. She knew only that if she heard of his death, she didn't want to have to journey to the other side of the world to beg his forgiveness. She knew that the kiss he'd given her in the crow's nest was not the one he'd envisioned that long-ago night when he'd stood in her bedchamber and made a bargain with her.

During the days and nights since, she'd come to anticipate what he'd promised. She didn't want to leave the ship without acquiring it—and perhaps a bit more.

"Well, then, Captain, I don't see that the kiss you bestowed upon me this afternoon—as lovely as it was—really fulfills my obligation to you at all."

A corner of his mouth hitched up. "I certainly wouldn't want you to disembark tomorrow feeling as though you've failed to live up to your part of the bargain."

Never taking his eyes off hers, he wrapped his long fingers around her snifter and set it on his desk. He was progressing so remarkably slowly that she wanted to shout at him to get a move on. Did he not want to truly kiss her? Did he not find her desirable? Perhaps that was the true reason that he'd been willing to be content with a light brushing of lips.

But when he turned back to her, she saw desire smoldering in his eyes, and she saw with alarm how very good he'd been at holding his true feelings at bay. She almost backed up, almost changed her mind, but before she could fully acknowledge that she was suddenly terrified by the intensity of what she saw, he snaked an arm around her waist, brought her up flush against him, cradled her face with one rough callused hand, and lowered his mouth to hers.

No light brushing of the lips, this. No sweetness, no gentleness.

It was as though he were a starving man, devouring his first meal after years of deprivation.

His mouth pressed firmly against hers as his tongue enticed her lips to part. He explored as she'd discovered he did everything: boldly and without hesitation. His tongue thrust and parried, gentled and waltzed. Of their own accord, her arms wound around his neck, bringing her closer to him. His hand skimmed along her throat, halted. She could feel her pulse thrumming against his fingers as his mouth continued its leisurely plunder. He tasted of rich brandy, fine wine, tart oranges. He tasted of desire. His mouth was hot, wet, and so very, very talented.

Lethargy seeped into her bones, heat swirled through her, pooled between her thighs. Her toes curled, her fingers dug into his scalp, keeping him near. Not that she expected him to leave.

She didn't think it possible, but the kiss deepened, became more, became everything until nothing existed except for him and the incredible sensations he was stirring to life. She had been dead for so long. She hadn't realized exactly how dead she'd been, but now she was being brought back to life—her body, her soul, her heart.

They were all beginning to regain a sense of awareness. They could *feel* again. They *wanted* to feel again. She thought she should be terrified by this immense awakening that she was experiencing, but all she knew was a gratitude that threatened to overwhelm her, to make her weep for what she'd denied herself for so long.

His mouth continued to work its magic, never leaving hers, never ceasing its explorations. She was beginning to wonder if she'd ever truly been kissed, because this was like nothing that she'd before experienced. It affected her entire body, made her want to crawl over him, made her want to sink into him until they were one. The cabin had grown so very warm that she wanted to rip off her clothes. Or maybe it was her, heated from the inside out, from the outside in. She barely knew any longer. Had little rational thought save for *pleasure, pleasure, pleasure.*

Long. Slow. Leisurely. It was all there, and yet in spite of that, the kiss was wild, untamed, unyielding. It commanded, it tempted, it seduced. Thoroughly, irrevocably. She understood better now his restraint, because what he was unleashing had the power to conquer her, to have her writhing in his arms with no care for the consequences that would follow. She wanted what he was offering, wanted it all. Wanted nothing to go unexplored.

His hand slid lower and cupped her breast. She moaned with the intimacy of it, the pleasure that tripped through her when he skimmed his thumb over her pearled nipple.

She broke off the kiss, pressing her mouth to his chin, his jaw, his neck. She damned the cravat and the blasted buttons that kept her from going where she wished, from tasting him fully. Why tonight of all nights had he decided to prove that he did indeed understand the purpose of buttons and buttonholes?

He cradled her face between his strong hands, forced her to meet his smoldering gaze.

"I was wrong, Anne. I won't be able to stop. So tell me now: do I take you to my bed or do I jump into the sea to cool off?"

She wanted to laugh, but all she seemed capable of doing was pleading, "Don't go."

Thank God, Tristan thought. Thank God.

He'd known she'd be exquisite but none of his imaginings had prepared him for the reality of her responsiveness, her flavor, her heat. His burgeoning desire astounded him. He wanted her more than he'd ever wanted anything in his life. Even his past hunger for revenge was dwarfed by the need clawing through him to possess her completely and fully.

He wanted to exhibit the slowness with which he'd taunted her but he wanted her too badly. And she was wearing so damned many clothes. In between kisses he released buttons, untied ribbons, dragged off petticoats—

In between kisses she unknotted his cravat, gave his buttons their freedom, tugged at his clothes—

Between caresses he removed her slippers, rolled down her stockings—

Between caresses she pulled off his boots, drew his shirt over his head—

It seemed hours but he knew it was only mere minutes before they were breathing harshly, taking each other in.

"You're so beautiful," he rasped. Her breasts were high and firm, her nipples a pale pink that he

longed to taste. Her belly was flat, her hips narrow.
He watched as her gaze traveled over him, and he
couldn't mistake the appreciation in her eyes. It
was without arrogance that he knew he had much
to offer, but he also knew that for a virgin it could
be frightening to see the clear evidence of his desire
for her. He should have doused the blasted lamps.
He should have—

She placed her warm hand on his shoulder, met
his gaze. "I want you."

She devastated him with so little. Lifting her
into his arms, he carried her to his bed, set her on
the sheets with care, then followed her down.

Anne welcomed the weight and length of him as
he covered her body with his and once again took
her mouth. She wanted to touch all of him, every
inch. He was magnificent. Long legged, strong,
powerful. She'd seen his muscles bunching with
his movements as he made his way about the ship.
In her innocent imaginings, she'd never envisioned
that a man could look so beautiful. A handsome
face, yes, but a beautiful body that promised something that went beyond pleasure. It was a fanciful
thought, but it had raced through her mind when
she'd finally managed to unveil him. She thought
perhaps she should be frightened by what was to
come, but she seemed to be capable only of anticipating it.

She skimmed her fingers over his chest, his shoulders, his back. She felt the raised welts that marred

that incredible expanse of muscles and sinew and
wanted to weep, knowing that he had once suffered such damaging punishment. She wrapped her
arms around him, squeezed him tightly, wishing
she could take the painful memories from him.

But she supposed they were partially responsible for shaping him into the man he'd become, the
man who fascinated her, the man she now yearned
for more than her next breath.

His mouth left hers to trail along her throat,
and while she almost cried out at the loss, she welcomed the new sensations that arose with his explorations. He seemed to be intent on not leaving
an inch of her unknown to his questing tongue.
He lightly nipped her collarbone before easing
down. He skimmed his lips over the swells of her
breasts. He was wedged between her thighs. She
rubbed her soles over his calves, arched her hips
upward—

"Not yet, Princess."

"Is this too to be long, slow, and leisurely?" she
asked on a sigh.

"Long, slow, but hardly leisurely, once we're
into the thick of things."

She wanted to laugh. Instead she moaned as
he closed his mouth over her nipple and suckled
gently. Conflicting sensations poured through her.
Tension and lethargy battled. She wanted to relax
beneath him, tighten herself around him.

He journeyed to her other breast and bestowed
upon it the same attentions. She'd never imagined
such dedication, had never realized the full extent

of caressing, tasting, touching that making love would entail. She had always thought it would be over quickly. Instead she was discovering that it might last forever.

He ran his tongue up and down the valley between her breasts, turning his head one way to kiss an inside swell, then the other. She scraped her nails along his scalp, welcoming the long strands of his hair curling around her fingers. Easing lower, he dipped his tongue into her navel and her body tightened in response.

She raised her shoulders from the bed, clutched his, tried to pull him toward her. "I want another kiss."

His eyes were heavy-lidded, held a hint of wickedness in them as he met her gaze. "I intend to give you one. Only on another set of lips."

"Whatever—"

"Relax, Princess. I've thought of this too long to deny myself the pleasure of it."

"The pleasure—"

His breath stirred the curls between her thighs and whatever words she might have been on the verge of saying scattered from her mind. She thought a proper lady would object, but tonight she was anything except a proper lady.

And as his tongue swirled over her, he made her glad for that fact. Never had she experienced anything so decadently wonderful. Sinking back on the bed, she drew up her knees, welcomed the intense sensual sensations cascading powerfully through her. She dug her fingers into his shoulders, needing purchase because she was in danger of being cast upon the winds of a storm and carried away.

Long. Slow. Leisurely. She wondered distractedly if this was the kiss he'd been referring to when he'd made his original bargain. Was this where he'd always intended to take her? Had the other been a ruse?

It didn't matter. She'd always suspected that the bargain wasn't as innocent as he'd made it seem, but she couldn't be angry, not when her nerve endings were dancing wildly and a tempest of pleasure churned around her.

Then the tempest grew, threatened to drown her. "Oh my God!"

"Let go, Princess," he murmured against her sensitive flesh. "Just let go."

When his tongue returned to its task, she did. She fell into the storm and found herself being hurled through a vortex of intense pleasure. She cried out, certain she would die from it, but when it passed, she was still breathing—though harshly—and she opened her eyes to find him staring down on her, a satisfied smile on his handsome face. Had he felt it, too? How could he look so pleased if he hadn't?

He lowered his mouth to hers, kissed her deeply, and she tasted the salt of her skin on his lips. Decadent.

She felt him nudging between her thighs and lifted her hips to receive him. She'd heard that it would hurt. Then, she couldn't deny that she experienced discomfort, but more she felt the joy of having the length and weight of him filling her.

Sliding a hand beneath her bottom, he raised her slightly and she was aware of him sinking even further into her, welcomed the fullness of him.

"God, you're incredibly hot," he breathed near her ear. "Wet. Tight."

Squeezing her eyes shut, squeezing him, she relished the intimacy, the closeness. That he could say such things to her, that she could hear them without igniting.

Then he began rocking against her, and her body responded in kind. Sensations began to build again. Planting her feet on the bed, she met his driving need. She clamped her hands against his backside, felt his muscles bunching with his powerful thrusts as he drove himself into her, over and over. It was madness. She was lost in the storm again, only this time he was lost in it with her. She knew from his grunts, his tautening body, his increased rhythm. When the storm reached its apex and she cried out, she heard his guttural groan, opened her eyes to see his head thrown back, his jaw clenched. His body jerked, a final deep thrust, and he growled through gritted teeth.

Opening his eyes, he stared down on her as though he couldn't quite remember who she was. Tears suddenly stung her eyes, because in spite of everything, she very much hated herself at that moment.

Chapter 12

Bloody damned hell. Tristan rolled off Anne and stared at the beams of the ceiling, waiting for his heart to calm, his breathing to settle. She was unlike any woman he'd ever known. She gave so much of herself, gave so willingly. He'd never felt so shattered, so vulnerable, so . . . lost.

He wanted to take her again, but it was more than her body that he wanted to possess. That strange yearning made little sense. He'd never experienced it before. He enjoyed women, enjoyed the pleasures that could be shared. But he'd never gone beyond that. Had never wanted to. Had never been tempted to.

Perhaps it was because she'd been a virgin. He'd never taken a virgin before. He felt a sort of responsibility toward her, a need to protect—

She sat up, the sheet gathered at her waist, her legs drawn up, her arms wrapped about them, her glorious hair cascading down her back and pooling at her hips. He skimmed his finger along her arm, but she neither acknowledged the touch nor looked at him.

"Regrets already, Princess?" he asked, shoring himself up for the brutal blow of the truth, wondering why he should care if she had misgivings. He'd gotten what he wanted from her, what he'd wanted from the moment he'd seen her walk through the door of the tavern on that rainy night.

With her knuckle, she swiped at her cheek. He didn't want to acknowledge the clutch at his heart because his actions had brought on her tears. It was all he could do not to sit up and begin kissing them away, but he knew once he was wrapped around her that it would be hell not to continue on to another sated adventure.

"I lied," she rasped.

His gut clenched and a fissure of unease went through him. He narrowed his eyes. "About what precisely?"

"Walter. I didn't see him off at the railway station. I assume he was in uniform and that he looked as handsome as always. I don't know if he said anything about being home in time for pheasant hunting. I heard the Duke of Ainsley's brother did. I stole it for my memory, because I had none. The night before we had an awful row and so I didn't go to say a final good-bye. Our last words to each other were spoken in anger. He wanted this from me and I said no."

"This?" He sounded like a bloody echo, but he didn't want her dead fiancé here now, between the sheets with them. By God, the man's ghost had been with them on the entire journey. Couldn't Tristan at least have tonight without the man haunting them?

She waved her hand over the bed. "This." She sniffed, scrubbed at her eyes. "We were walking in the garden. He wanted me to slip out of the house later, meet him in the mews. He said he'd take me to a room at a hotel, that no one would ever know. But I said no."

She twisted around, clutching the sheet with one hand to her breast, doing an incredibly lousy job of covering herself because one nipple was playing peek-a-boo and distracting him.

"A proper lady says no," she continued. "I wanted this"—she jerked her hand back and forth between him and her—"to mean nothing. But it's so intimate, so personal. I wanted proof that what I had denied him was of no consequence. But it wasn't. It's important. It's larger, more than I expected it to be. He must have died hating me for denying him this."

"No." He cradled her cheek, urged her down until her head was nestled in the nook of his shoulder. "I can assure you that he did not hate you."

"How can you be so sure?"

"Because you are the sort of woman a man could never hate."

He had expected her to be stiff in his arms, but as always she melted into him. He wasn't accustomed to talking afterward. Generally he would simply go to sleep, but something was to be said for lying here in the lethargy of lovemaking—even if the conversation revolved around another man, one he was coming to loathe.

"You should know, Anne, that a man will always strive to get a woman into his bed. It's our nature. Even when he expects the lady to say no, he will still try to convince her otherwise. He may be disappointed if the lady turns him down, his pride may sting, but he won't hate her. If anything, it was his pride talking that night. Not his heart."

She tightened her arms around him, and he felt warm tears trickle onto his chest. "Yet, here I am with you, someone I don't love. Being intimate."

"It's easier if you don't love the person. If you make a mess of it you can just walk away. Besides, we're not in Society. Out here there are few rules. Who is to care what we do?"

"And you're safe, I suppose," she said quietly. "I'll never see you again. I can pretend this didn't happen."

Could she? Could he mean so little to her? And why did he care if he meant nothing at all to her? What did it matter if he was simply an itch that she had a need to scratch? How many women had he left in ports throughout the world and never given another thought to them?

Why was he certain that he would not so easily forget her? The one woman he *should* forget.

He became aware of her soft, even breathing. Gently he slid out from beneath her and covered her with the blankets. He'd never had a woman sprawled in the bed on his ship. Now he would always see her there.

After drawing on his trousers and a shirt, he slipped silently out of his quarters. The ship creaked and rocked, and he found comfort in the familiar sounds as he made his way to the quarterdeck. Gripping the railing, he stared out at the vast expanse of black sea and star-blanketed sky. He remembered the first time he'd done so. How small and insignificant it had made him feel. How frightened. He hadn't known then what awaited him. He'd never felt so alone or betrayed. All he'd thought about was making his uncle pay for sending him into hell.

In time he'd conquered his terror, mastered the hell to such an extent that he couldn't envision leaving it. He was a ship's captain. Traveling the world was what he knew. In spite of what he and his brothers had accomplished two years ago, he couldn't imagine giving up his roving life, his ship, his unencumbered existence.

He didn't know why his thoughts were trudging along this path.

Perhaps because she had not wanted him per se; she had simply wanted the sensations. He thought of all the women he'd taken to his bed over the years—for pleasure's sake. Had they left his bed feeling as . . . used, as dissatisfied? Were they as he was now: wanting more?

Why? Why did what he shared with Anne suddenly seem as though it wasn't enough?

"Jack?"

"Tristan," he said quietly, so quietly he wasn't certain she heard. She stepped nearer until he could feel the warmth emanating from her body, could smell the lavender and citrus scent that was such a part of her, but layered now within it was the fragrance of their lovemaking.

"Pardon?" she asked softly.

"My name is Tristan. Jack is simply . . . a name I use on the sea."

Out of the corner of his eye, he saw her wrap her hands around the railing. After all they'd shared, he should place his arm around her, but that somehow seemed far too intimate, more so than what had transpired in his cabin. He was floundering here, like a fish tossed onto the sandy shore. He didn't like it, wasn't certain how to regain his footing, because everything seemed to be shifting beneath him.

"Why? Why do you use a different name?"

"I lied," he forced out, repeating the simple words that she'd used earlier, "when I said I went to sea for adventure. I went to sea because someone was desperate to kill me."

"Dear God, why?"

"It doesn't matter. That part of my life—" He tightened his own hold on the railing. How could it not matter when it had shaped him into the man he was? He didn't want it to matter; he didn't want to consider that in some perverted way his uncle had won. "—is unimportant."

Her delicate hand crept slowly across until it was resting on his. He wanted to fling it away. He didn't want comfort. He hadn't had comfort in years, fourteen to be exact. Half his life he'd lived without tenderness or care. It unmanned him. His eyes burned. Damned salty air. Or maybe it was the breeze causing his eyes to water. But it wasn't her. He wouldn't allow it to be her.

If not for his uncle, he might have grown into a man who would be worthy of Anne. He'd have been embraced by Society, instead of perceived as a pariah. He might have met her at a ball before she'd come to love her fiancé. He might have been the young lord she'd denied, although for the life of him he couldn't imagine that he'd not have enticed her into his bed. From the moment he'd spied her, he'd wanted her too desperately.

"Why Crimson Jack?" she asked.

He swallowed hard. He didn't want to tell her and yet he seemed incapable of holding in the words. "The captain named me Jack. He knew I was running from someone. At first I was angry, wanted to smash something. Got into a fight with one of the mates. Roughed him up good. Captain said I had to apologize. I wouldn't. They took the lash to me. Still wouldn't apologize. I was a bloody mess when I finally lost consciousness."

He heard her tiny cry of dismay, knew if he looked he'd see tears in her eyes. So he didn't look. It was easier not to feel anything.

"Crimson."

"Yeah. After that I was known as Crimson Jack and no one wanted to risk upsetting me."

She squeezed his hand. "I hate that they hurt you so badly."

He didn't want her sympathy. It made him feel weak, not quite the man he knew himself to be.

"It all worked out satisfactorily in the end." He turned to face her. Her hair was loose, flying in the wind. The moon was full, and her features were limned by its pale glow. Touching her cheek, he felt the dampness of her cooling tears. "But what am I to do about you?"

She smiled sweetly. "Remember me, perhaps." Her inflection was that of a question, doubt, insecurity.

"That I most certainly will do."

He captured her mouth, relishing the taste and feel of her. That she scared the bloody hell out of him was something to be dealt with another day, another night. For now, he was greedy for whatever more she would give him. He would leave her in port. He would watch her march away, disappear into the fog-enshrouded shadows—

He would be left behind, but this time it was what he wanted. He wanted to sail the seas. He wanted to command his ship, his men. He wanted only memories of her.

She would waltz in ballrooms, walk through parks, and flirt with gentlemen. She would be sought-after, desired. She would have a husband and children. She would possess everything that he had no aspirations to own.

So it was with a measure of regret for what he could not give her that he swept her into his arms and returned to his bed for what he could bestow on her.

Tristan, Tristan, Tristan.

She murmured his name as she nibbled on his neck and ear while he carried her to his cabin as though she weighed little more than a cloud hovering on the distant horizon. How strange that she had never thought he looked like a Jack to her, had never called to him by what she thought his name was until after they'd made love.

And only then to discover that his true name was Tristan. It suited him. Jack was too common. But Tristan belonged with the dashing sea captain.

He shouldered his way into his quarters and kicked the door closed without releasing his hold on her. He set her on her feet near the bed. She quickly undid the buttons on her gown and let it slide down her body. It was all she'd bothered to put on before seeking him out on deck.

She saw his eyes darken with appreciation just before he dragged his shirt over his head. He unfastened his trousers and dropped them. Would she ever tire of the sight of him straining with desire for her?

When he made a move to come in for another kiss, she stayed him with a hand on his chest. "Not yet."

She knew once he claimed her mouth again, she would be lost to the sensations and would allow him to steer the pleasure. "I want a moment at the helm."

He flashed a purely masculine predatory grin. "By all means."

Out of the corner of her eye, she saw it dim when she eased behind him.

"Anne—"

"Shh, Tristan." She studied the crisscross of lines marring his back. "How many? How many lashes?"

"The first time or the second?"

His voice held no emotion. He might as well have been asking if she preferred marmalade or jam. "It happened more than once?"

"I had a lot of anger in me."

She trailed her finger over the longest, thickest welt. Crimson Jack. Covered in blood. "How old were you?"

"Princess, this is hardly conversation that will lead to seduction."

"How old?"

She felt him tense beneath her touch, heard him swallow.

"Fourteen."

She slammed her eyes closed. She hoped she'd been wrong. That he'd been a man better able to withstand the pain and humiliation of it. She pressed her lips to the center of his back, for the boy he'd been, the man he was.

"Is he still alive . . . the man who did this to you?"

"Yes. A captain called Marlow. Our paths cross from time to time."

"I hope you beat him."

"I never blamed him. He needed order on his ship

and I was of a mind to create havoc. The one I blame is the man who wanted me gone. He's now dead."

"I'm glad."

"No more than I."

He twisted around, cradled her face with his palms, and gathered her tears with his thumbs. Only then did she realize that she was crying. "Don't weep, sweetheart. As I've told you before: it was a long time ago. I never think of it."

How could he not? It had shaped him, was part of his life. She supposed it was a testament to his character that he had moved on, that he thrived in spite of knowing that the world could be unkind. He didn't wallow in self-pity or bemoan the un- fairness that had been bestowed upon him.

She wanted to be as strong as he, to remember the wonderful moments she'd spent with Walter, to release the regrets. The regrets no longer served a purpose. She saw that now. She had said good-bye. She must move on.

Like Tristan. She had to turn her attention toward the horizon where better things awaited. While she knew he would not be waiting for her there, he was here with her now.

She couldn't waste these moments with sorrow or remorse. She needed to relish the joy that being with him brought.

Peering up at him beneath half-lowered lashes, she gave him an impish smile. "I see your interest in me has dimmed. Pity."

He gave her a cocky grin. "I can be at full sail before you hit the bed."

With a laugh he grabbed her and tumbled her onto the rumpled sheets. The fragrance of their previous lovemaking wafted around her. As he nestled himself between her thighs, she wasn't surprised to discover that he was true to his claims. He was ready for her.

"Are you tender?" he asked.

"Yes, some, but we have only tonight."

She saw an emotion pass over his eyes that she couldn't quite decipher. He nibbled on her ear.

"Tell me if you experience discomfort. I know other ways to enjoy each other."

She'd learned that quickly enough. She supposed there was a comparable way to pleasure him, but then his mouth was again ravishing hers and she wasn't supposing anything at all.

Chapter 13

"Just because we're in dock doesn't mean we have to leave the ship."

Deciding her hat was as straight as it could get, Anne turned away from her reflection in the mirror to the man leaning against the door. He wore black trousers that hugged his thighs, boots, and the familiar loose white shirt with its rebellious buttons. Only an hour before, he'd been sprawled in glorious nudity over the bed. She suspected in spite of all the time it had taken for her to dress with his assistance that he could have her naked and beneath him before she took her next breath if she but encouraged him.

"My family is no doubt desperate for word from me. If I don't leave now, we would only be delaying the inevitable."

"If it can be delayed, perhaps it's not inevitable. Pen them a missive. Tell them you've decided to see the world. I can have us back at sea by dawn."

Oh, she wasn't half tempted. "I have responsibilities here." A Season to endure, a husband to find, a father to please.

She crossed over to him, placed her hand on his chest, right where his heart beat out a steady rhythm. "We're from different worlds, you and I. As lovely as it's been, I can't stay in your world. Not for the long haul."

"Then for a short haul. A year. Eighteen months."

"I would return a ruined woman with no hope for marriage prospects or children." She shook her head. She wanted him to say that he'd marry her, but if he offered it would be foolish to say yes. She couldn't go gallivanting around the world. What sort of life would that be for their children? Nor could she stand the thought of months on end, waiting at home for his return. But she also suspected that he wasn't a man willing to take a wife. He'd lived his entire life unencumbered. "You know that *we* can't be."

In answer, whether acknowledgment or denial, he captured her mouth with his, shoved the fingers of one hand into her hair, and used the other to press her flat against him. She thought she would never tire of his kisses, the heat and passion of them, the way they encompassed all of her. Rising up on her toes, she wound her arms around his neck.

This would be their last kiss. She would be strong; she would walk away once his mouth was finished ravishing hers. But she was so tempted to stay, even knowing the disaster it would beget. She had known all along that their association would come to an end. Between them was unbridled passion, but no love. She wouldn't even contemplate that she could possibly love him, because how would any man ever measure up to her courageous, strong, and unyielding captain?

She would have to forget him, cast memories of him to the locked corners of her heart, only to be visited on the very rarest of occasions.

His tongue swirled with hers, a familiar waltz now, and yet desperation clung to her as she swept hers through his mouth, searching for anything she'd not yet explored. She didn't want to look back and wish that she taken one more swipe, nibbled a little longer, tasted more deeply. With him, she wanted no regrets. He'd given her a night that would sustain her for the remainder of her life. But it was time now to say good-bye.

Drawing back, he pressed his forehead to hers. "You should know that I'll never forget you."

She squeezed her eyes shut because she couldn't give him the same promise, even if it was true. It wouldn't be fair to the man she would eventually marry. She must forget him. She must condemn him to a faint wisp of memory.

Reaching behind him, he opened the door. She walked into the passageway and felt the heat suffuse her face at the sight of Martha standing there with Mr. Peterson. She wondered if they had heard her moans, sighs, and cries through the night. Then she decided what they might have heard was of no consequence, and it was far too late to worry over.

The captain led her up to the deck. She'd known it was night, of course, but somehow it seemed the right time for her parting. Although she was so tempted to stay with him until dawn. But her family had waited for her return long enough.

She heard him issue orders for someone to get her trunk. Then he escorted her down the gangway and along the docks. His arm remained inappropriately around her, nestling her against his side. She couldn't bring herself to step away.

When they reached the area where hackneys waited, he hired two and she watched as her trunk was loaded into one.

"I should go with you," he said.

"No. I want to say good-bye here, to remember you here." Turning into him, to face him fully, she touched her gloved hand to his jaw. "May the winds always deliver you safely to your destination."

"Anne—"

Rising up, she brushed a quick kiss over his lips before scrambling into the hackney. Martha settled in beside her and the wheels were soon clattering, carrying them away.

"We will never speak of this, Martha," she said tersely, shoring up her resolve not to weep.

"Yes, m'lady."

"We must move forward. See to our duties."

"Yes, miss."

No matter how much it pained them to do so.

Tristan watched the hackney roll away into the night, the emptiness engulfing him similar to one he'd experienced fourteen years earlier on the Yorkshire docks. It didn't bear thinking about.

"What now, Cap'n?" Peterson asked.

"I intend to get bloody well drunk. Care to join me?"

"What in God's name were you thinking?"

Anne stood within her father's study. Knowing that she would be brought to task for her actions did not make the actual *bringing* any easier. Her father and brothers had not yet left for their clubs when she arrived home. It was the one night of the week that her father insisted they enjoy a meal together. She'd arrived too late to partake in dinner, but early enough to receive a scolding.

Her brothers had taken up various positions around the room, arms crossed, stances erect, obviously fully in support of the tongue-lashing she was on the cusp of enduring.

"As I discussed with you previously and reiterated in my letter, I needed to say good-bye to Walter so that I could move on with my life, fully embrace the upcoming Season, present an engaging front, and entice a lord into finding me worthy of becoming his wife. That is my duty, is it not?"

"Your duty is to obey your father and I had forbidden you to go."

"Yes, well, I'm home now so it seems rather

pointless to harp on what I've done. I achieved my goal and am ready to reenter Society."

She'd never seen her father appear so flummoxed. He blinked, opened his mouth, shut it.

"Upon what ship did you book passage?" Jameson asked. As her father grew older, so her brother was beginning to assert himself, to prepare for the day when he would step seamlessly into their father's shoes. "I made inquiries but had little success in determining—"

"I hired a ship."

"What do you mean you hired a ship?"

"Honestly, Jameson, did you lose your comprehension of the English language while I was away?"

"You'll answer your brother," her father snapped, obviously regaining his faculties.

"I hired a captain willing to sail on my schedule."

"Who is the captain? What ship?" Jameson barked.

"I don't see that it's relevant. The matter is done."

"Do you have any idea what could have happened?"

"He came highly recommended."

"By whom?"

"These pointless questions are becoming quite tedious."

"Your reputation—"

"Did you tell people what I'd done?" she snapped.

"Absolutely not. We said you had determined you were not yet ready to step out of mourning, required additional seclusion, and returned to the country."

"Then my reputation remains untarnished. And I'm quite weary from my travels so if you'll excuse me, I wish to retire."

She turned to go.

"I'm not finished with you yet," her father shouted.

She sank into a chair, folded her hands on her lap, and met his gaze. "By all means, then, proceed."

"I don't believe you fully comprehend the seriousness of what you did."

"And I'm not certain you fully comprehend that the matter is done. It's unlikely that I'll ever have another need to leave England's shores. Hopefully it shall be many years before I lose someone else whom I love. And even then, he shall in all likelihood die here. I shall have no further adventures."

More's the pity, a little corner of her mind squeaked.

"It is only that we love you and were worried," her father reiterated.

"I know." She gave him a warm smile. "I believe your clubs await."

"Indeed they do."

Grateful that the matter was being put to rest, she rose.

"The Greystone ball is next week," Jameson informed her. "I assume you will attend."

"Most assuredly. And I shall put my best foot forward."

She strolled from the room, thinking how odd it was that the house didn't pitch at all. It seemed she'd finally gotten her sea legs when it was a bit too late.

In her bedchamber she found Martha putting away the last items from the trunk. Her maid looked up as though guilty. "Did all go well?"

"As well as it could." She began tugging off her gloves.

"I found something in the trunk. I'm not sure what it is. I put it on your vanity."

Anne walked to the vanity and discovered a small paper-wrapped parcel. The paper was more suited to serving as stationery but it had been crumpled and folded, secured with string around an object. Slowly she untied the string and pulled back the paper to reveal a starfish.

On the paper was written: *For making a wish when there are no stars to be seen.*

Tears stung her eyes. So many things to wish for, but only one mattered: *Be safe, Captain. Please always be safe on your travels.*

Carefully she flattened the paper, then folded it and placed it, along with the starfish, in her jewelry box.

"I'm tired, Martha. Help me prepare for bed."

When she was dressed and Martha had left, Anne sat in a chair by the window and gazed out as the fog rolled in. The gaslights offered a meager attempt to hold it at bay, but they lit a path to the residence. She wished now that she hadn't left the ship so soon. Perhaps Tristan wished the same. He could climb the tree. He could come to her. She wouldn't turn him away. Just one more night.

But morning found her asleep in the chair, alone.

Chapter 14

"**I**'m so glad you're finally back in London. I've missed you dreadfully."

Reaching across the small round table in the garden, Anne smiled and squeezed the hand of her dearest friend, Lady Sarah Weston. "I've missed you as well."

"I can serve as your chaperone this Season."

Anne laughed lightly. It had been three years since Sarah had married the Earl of Fayrehaven. Anne had attended her at the wedding, served as her maid of honor. She had always planned for Sarah to assist her when the time came to exchange vows with Walter. They had decided to toss aside the societal rules that said a married lady could not stand beside a bride. They were going to allow it to happen. It was silly now to wonder if the possibility of flaunting convention had been responsible for fate's nasty turn.

"You will find someone else, you know," Sarah continued.

Anne wanted to confess that she *had* found someone else. But that had been a temporary holding. She'd been home all of three days now and she'd almost gone to the docks during each one of them to see if the *Revenge* was still in port. But going to the docks was not something that ladies did—although it had not stopped her before.

She wondered if he spent his evenings in the same tavern where she'd first seen him. Did he wait for other ladies to approach him? Would he compare them to her? Would he find them lacking? God help her, she wanted him to find them lacking.

"I have heard . . ." Sarah began, leaning forward as though the blooming flowers had the ability to gossip, "that Chetwyn has set his cap for you."

"He has said nothing to me."

"Well, you've hardly been in London long enough, have you? I called on you a month ago, when I first arrived in town and was told that you weren't in residence. I was so disappointed. I'm remarkably glad you sent a note round letting me know that you were indeed in the city. Did you need a bit more time in the country?"

Anne nibbled on her lip. "No, actually. If I tell you, you must hold it a secret."

"Of course."

Now Anne was lowering her voice, which was ridiculous because no one was about. "I went to Scutari, to say good-bye to Walter. It was a remarkable trip, liberating."

Sarah furrowed her brow. "Did your brothers take you?"

"No, I went by myself. Well, with my maid. I wore trousers. I climbed a mast. I stood in a crow's nest and looked out on the world. I felt small, yet significant. It was a strange dichotomy."

She realized she was throwing out everything in a nonsensical manner, but she'd been unable to share it with anyone and it was just there, bubbling to the surface.

"Not to mention scandalous," Sarah said with a measure of disapproval that Anne fought to ignore.

"Yes, I know. Which is why you mustn't tell anyone. I haven't told my father or my brothers everything that I did. Only that I went to Scutari. They wouldn't understand."

"I'm not quite certain that I do either."

"Do you ever consider that we behave a certain way because it's expected of us, but no one ever truly explains why we must behave as we do?"

"We behave as we do because it's the way one behaves."

She had once thought the same, but now she questioned the staidness of her life. But how could Sarah understand when she'd never ventured from it?

Anne heard a servant approaching and glanced up to see one of the younger maids carrying a tray. Earlier she had brought them tea. Now she set on the table some scones and a bowl of orange segments. Anne couldn't help but think of that first morning on the ship when she had bitten into one. "Those look tempting."

"They're very good, m'lady," the girl said. "Cook had us taste them to make sure there was nothing amiss. A crate of them just showed up on the steps."

"From the shops? Cook purchased them?"

"No, miss. We don't know who sent them."

Tristan. She was as certain of that as she was of her name. She wondered if it had been a final good-bye gift, knowing that she would never again eat an orange and not think of him. She wondered if he would think of her when he tasted one. She'd not anticipated that so many things would remind her of him.

"Are you in love?" Sarah asked.

Anne snapped her gaze over to her friend. "Pardon?"

"You're staring at the bowl rather oddly, as though you care deeply about oranges. If you want one, simply take it."

Anne did. It was as succulent and sweet as she expected.

"So continue with your story," Sarah commanded. "What was it like to wear trousers? And why would you? Were you a stowaway or something equally atrocious?"

Anne smiled. "I paid for my passage, but after going to Scutari I became melancholy. The captain thought it would brighten my outlook to gaze out on the world. But I couldn't very well shimmy up a pole in skirts."

"You actually climbed a mast?"

She released a short burst of laughter. "Yes."

And I climbed a ship captain. But that memory was for her and her alone.

"Better keep it to yourself. Gentlemen prefer their ladies less adventuresome."

"Oh, I fully intend to tell no one. But I wanted to share it with you, although I realize now that I haven't the words to paint a true portrait of the experience." She popped another orange segment into her mouth. "Sarah, are you happy being the wife of a lord?"

"Absolutely. Fayrehaven treats me very nicely. I'm fortunate in that regard. I daresay that by the end of the Season you'll be on your way to becoming a wife as well."

"Perhaps."

"You can't dally, Anne. Your prospects next year will be fewer than they are now. A new batch of eligible ladies will be stepping onto the marriage block."

"You make it all sound so frightfully appealing."

"It's marvelous. Truly. With a husband comes children." Sarah had given birth to a son fifteen months after her wedding. "It's a tragedy that you've been denied so much for so long, which is the reason that I'm ecstatic to have you in London this Season. We shall find you a husband with all due haste. If not Chetwyn then someone else who appeals."

An image of Tristan flittered briefly across her mind. She was giving herself leave to think of him until she attended her first ball. Then she would have to pack up the remembrances, store them in a corner of her heart, and never visit them again. Except perhaps when she was old and withered and looking back on the life she'd led. She would write her memoirs, and include the scandalous journey and the dashing sea captain with whom she'd felt the first stirrings of happiness after being dead inside for so long.

"Have you ever known any lady who didn't marry into the nobility?" she asked Sarah.

"The former Duchess of Lovingdon. She married that Dodger fellow, but then he's obscenely wealthy so sins are easily forgiven."

She was fairly certain that Tristan was wealthy, yet she couldn't imagine him remaining patient with Society's rules. He'd always be chomping at the bit to return to the sea.

"What if Walter hadn't asked for your hand in marriage?" Sarah asked. "Who would you have wanted to marry then?"

"I never gave it any thought. From the moment I met Walter . . . we were so alike with so many common interests." She and Tristan didn't meld nearly as well. Well, except when they were physically melded together. They fit perfectly then.

"Are you blushing?" Sarah asked.

Anne touched her cheeks. Was she? The man had the ability to warm her from the inside out even when he was nowhere in the vicinity. "No, it's just an unseasonably warm day."

"I think you're not being quite honest, that there is someone other than Walter who caught your fancy. Whisper his name and if he's still unmarried—"

"There's no one," Anne said sharply, trying not to remember how many times she'd whispered Tristan's name during the throes of passion.

"There will be. Have no worries. As soon as you attend the first ball of the Season, I shall do all in my power to assist you."

Anne thought she'd prepared herself for the whirlwind that awaited her. She'd anticipated her first Season with an air of giddiness and anticipation. Now she merely wanted this Season to all be over.

It had been ages since Anne had been to a ball and her arrival was causing quite the stir. She did wish that she hadn't waited so long to return to Society. An awkwardness hovered about as people approached her. Should they mention Walter? Should they not? Should they offer condolences? Should they carry on as though nothing were amiss?

Gentlemen didn't seem to know if they should ask her for a dance. How did one treat a lady who had the baggage of a widow, but wasn't a widow?

The only one who seemed at all comfortable with her was Chetwyn, as he expertly glided her over the dance floor.

"My brother would be pleased to see you smiling again," he said.

It was strange, but she saw little of Walter in him. His blond hair seemed more easily tamed. Not a single freckle dared to mar his skin, where Walter had always been cursed with an abundance that had only served to make him more endearing.

Chetwyn's smile was more stately and sedate. Walter's had always been filled with fun and mischief. But what really surprised her was that she could think of Walter now without hurting, or feeling guilty, or longing for what could never be. She had been correct that she needed her sojourn. She was ready now to face whatever the future held.

"I'm frightfully behind on the gossip I fear," she said, smiling warmly, striving to carry the conversation away from the past and their shared loss.

Chetwyn rolled his eyes. "With your brothers—the worst gossips in all of England—about? I rather doubt that."

She laughed. It felt good to laugh beneath flickering chandeliers while an orchestra wooed the dancers with gentle strains of harmony.

"I should like to see Jameson married this Season," she said.

"He should like to see the same of you."

She couldn't miss the speculation and interest in Chetwyn's eyes. It wasn't that he was an awful fellow, but he didn't make her heart speed up or her body yearn for nearness. But then she suspected few men would have that influence over her.

"I was going to ask if you knew of any prospects with whom I might entice my brother into walking down the aisle," she said, hoping to direct them off a path she wasn't ready to travel. Her own possibility of marriage was far from her thoughts. Tonight she simply had to survive her reentry into Society.

"Perhaps I could come to call later this week and provide a list at that time," he suggested.

Oh, she'd been too long out of the flirtation game, felt as though she'd maneuvered herself into a trap. "Do you not worry that your brother would always be between us?"

"No. He and I were very different. I daresay, my mother often quipped that if she wasn't present at the birthing, she'd have not believed we were brothers."

She felt the heat suffuse her face. Not exactly a proper topic, and she wondered briefly if he was slightly nervous about being in her company. It couldn't be easy to be with a woman who had a past with his brother. "Well, then, I suppose a call later this week would be lovely."

The music wafted into silence and without another word he escorted her to her aunt, her father's sister, who was serving as her chaperone this evening. In spite of Sarah's offer to take on that role, her father thought she needed a more seasoned lady. Especially as he wasn't here, but had elected to spend the evening at his club.

"He is such a handsome devil," her aunt Penelope said after the marquess had wandered away.

"Yes, he is."

"I've heard he's set his cap on you."

"So I've been told."

"You could do far worse, my girl."

"That is a ringing endorsement."

All the wrinkles in her aunt's face shifted around until she looked rather like a dried prune. "Whatever do you mean by that?"

"It just seems that one should set one's standards a bit higher than simply not going with the worst."

"You're close to being on the shelf. You can't be particularly picky. You had your love, which is more than most women have. Now you must settle in and do your duty."

"Is one allowed love only once?"

"I daresay, if at all, once is all that one can hope for."

"That's a rather sad state of affairs for women, isn't it?"

"It is the way of it, m'dear. I'm a bit parched. Perhaps you'd like to come with me to the refreshment room."

So she could continue to be bombarded with such demoralizing commentary? "No, thank you. I believe I shall watch the dancers."

After her aunt left, Anne moved farther back into the fronds. It wasn't that she didn't like being here. She loved the gaiety and the music and the lovely gowns. She enjoyed watching the gentlemen flirt, but she couldn't quite relish them flirting with her. She caught speculative glances from time to time, knew they were sizing her up. She'd forgotten how calculating everything was. Perhaps she should simply drop every eligible bachelor's name into a hat and draw one out. It seemed as good a solution as any if her aunt was correct in her assumption that love wouldn't be part of the bargain. It would certainly save her time, humilia—

"I never took you to be a wallflower."

Her breath hitched at the familiar silken voice

that rasped near her ear. The tang of orange wafted around her. Fighting for composure, she slowly turned. Her heart pounded at the sight of Tristan, so devilishly handsome in his black swallowtailed coat. His face was bare of whiskers. His hair, while still long, had been trimmed. His light blue eyes were filled with devilment. "You," she croaked.

He grinned, a grin that spoke of secrets shared. "Me."

"Whatever are you doing here?"

"Speaking with you obviously."

"But—" She was fighting not to panic. He shouldn't be here. He *couldn't* be here. "However did you get in?"

"Through a door."

Oh, God, the infuriating man! "Invitations were required."

"And I managed to gain one."

"How?"

"I had hoped you'd be a bit more pleased to see me, rather than seeking answers to such trivial matters."

"But this isn't your world."

"Unfortunately it is." Some emotion that she couldn't identify flickered in his eyes. Loss, grief, sorrow. "I don't believe we've been formally introduced. Allow me." He tipped his head slightly. "Lord Tristan Easton."

Lord? Impossible. He was untethered, did as he pleased. He grew up on the sea, he—

Then the name he'd spoken registered at the back of her mind.

"Easton?" The word came out on a choked breath. "Your brother is—"

"The Duke of Keswick."

She fought to remember everything her brothers had told her, what she'd heard over the years. She'd been a child when they went missing, yet she could remember the nightmares that had visited her, the fear that she, too, would suddenly disappear. "One of the lost lords. Why didn't you tell me?"

"I'm a lord by birth and blood, but not by life. I don't fit comfortably here as you can well imagine, since you know something of my life beyond London. To be honest, I had no particular interest in claiming my place in Society until I realized that it would provide me with much easier access to you."

"But you're a ship captain."

"Must a man be only one thing?"

She had shared her body, her soul, perhaps even a portion of her heart with this man, and yet she knew so little about him. It made her feel tainted in some way, less than she should be. "It was your uncle you were running away from, the one who wished you harm."

The glimmer of teasing dimmed. "Yes."

"Was he really going to kill you?"

"We had evidence to indicate so. But that was long ago. I'm much more interested in claiming a dance than talking of the past."

How like him to avoid revealing the mysteries behind the myriad of stories that surrounded him.

"A dance?" she squeaked, irritated that she could not appear as composed as he.

"Yes, it's an activity where one—"

"I know what a dance is. I'm simply having a difficult time comprehending your being here. I thought never to see you again."

Which had made it so much easier to be with him on the ship. What they had shared would sail away with him. But he hadn't sailed away. He was here. And if he told—

"Anne?"

She jerked around to find Jameson studying her while managing to glare at Tristan at the same time. "Jameson, allow me to introduce Lord Tristan—"

"Easton. Yes, I know. Unfortunately, I saw him arrive with his brother."

The duke was here? That must have set tongues to wagging. How had she managed to miss it? Was she so wrapped up in her own worries that she wasn't paying attention to everything else happening around her?

"Lord Tristan, my brother. Viscount Jameson."

"M'lord," Tristan said with a slight bow. "A pleasure. I was about to ask your sister for a dance."

"I fear you'll find her dance card filled."

Shock at his rudeness rippled through her, and she couldn't help but blurt, "Pardon?"

"I believe the next dance is mine," Jameson said, wrapping his hand possessively around her upper arm. He never danced with her, and she certainly didn't appreciate his interference now.

"On the contrary. It belongs to Lord Tristan."

"Anne."

The warning in his voice was unmistakable but

she had to speak with Tristan, and on a crowded dance floor was the perfect place because if she sought a tryst in the garden, he would no doubt use the darkness to advantage and she would find her back up against a rose-covered trellis with his mouth devouring hers. She'd be so absorbed by the kiss that she'd not notice the prickle of thorns.

"Release her," Tristan snarled, his voice low, but his threat evident.

"Or what?" Jameson challenged.

Tristan grinned, but there was nothing pleasant in it. Rather it reminded her of a predatory cat anticipating its next meal. "You'll discover that I am the barbarian you and your brothers whisper me to be."

"Jameson, please. It's only a dance. If you don't release me I shall be forced to kick you. And such unladylike behavior will no doubt make it much more difficult for me to secure a husband. Don't make a scene and ruin my entrance back into Society."

He released his hold, but not before saying, "One dance and then you leave her be."

The very worst words he could have said. Tristan wouldn't stand down. She knew him well enough to know that.

"Oh my word. Lord Tristan, I thought it was you."

As Anne turned to the newest intruder, out of the corner of her eye she saw some emotion she couldn't quite identify wash over her brother's face. Longing, followed by stoicism? She couldn't be sure. Then she was staring at a gorgeous lady with blond hair. The largest green eyes that Anne had ever seen were fastened on Tristan as though he were her favorite sweet.

He bowed slightly. "Lady Hermione."

"Why ever did you not let me know you'd returned to London?"

"Yes, my lord," her brother stated succinctly, "pray tell, why ever did you not inform the lovely lady of your return?"

"I've had other serious matters that required my attention."

Anne felt herself floundering. What did this young woman mean to Tristan?

"It truly doesn't matter," Lady Hermione said. "You're here now. I daresay that I'm free for the dance that's just starting."

"I've already promised to partner with Lady Anne," Tristan said, a gentleness in his voice that reminded Anne of lying beneath him and hearing murmurings in the same tender tone. Had he bedded this girl? She certainly seemed to have cause to believe she meant something to him.

"Oh." Lady Hermione looked at Anne. "Lady Anne, my apologies. I didn't notice you standing there. You're out of mourning, I see. Such a tragedy. To lose your love at such a young age. I daresay, the man can never be replaced. It is so kind of Lord Tristan to take pity and dance with you."

Before Anne could respond to her assumption that it was pity he bestowed on her, the girl turned to Tristan. "But I must claim the next dance, my lord. Please."

"It will be my pleasure. Perhaps Lord Jameson will partner with you for this dance."

"I don't take another man's leavings," Jameson said before turning on his heel and striding away.

Anne gasped at her brother's callousness but Lady Hermione didn't seem at all bothered. Anne was fairly certain the girl heard nothing that was not uttered by Lord Tristan.

"If you'll excuse us?" Tristan said to Lady Hermione, while offering Anne his arm.

She wasn't certain she should take it. She felt as though she'd stepped into the middle of some sort of drama.

"Yes, of course," Lady Hermione answered brightly. "I shall wait here with bated breath for your return."

He arched a brow at Anne, and in spite of her reservations, suddenly well aware that they were capturing the attention of others standing nearby, she placed her hand on his arm.

"What is she to you?" she heard herself ask as he escorted her toward the dance floor.

"An annoyance."

"She seemed incredibly smitten."

He stopped. "I promise you, Anne, I never gave her reason to believe she was anything more than a dance partner—twice. Two years ago."

He took her in his arms and swept her over the floor, and God help her—if he had danced with such skill two years ago, if he had gazed on the girl with the intensity that he now gazed at Anne, she could well understand how Lady Hermione might have fallen under his spell. He was so very masculine, so very earthy. She had succumbed to his charms easily enough. Why shouldn't every other lady in the room?

"You should have told me who you were," she said, her words clipped because she had to shore her resolve that things between them were over.

"Why?"

"Because you made a fool of me."

"That was never my intention. Nor did I ever intend to return to this madness. Your brother is not the only one here tonight who has expressed dissatisfaction over my presence."

"Then why are you here?"

His jaw tightened. "I can't stop thinking about you. I wanted to make sure that you were all right. That your family didn't ship you off to a convent or something."

She laughed lightly. "Why ever would they do that?"

He shrugged his broad shoulders without missing a step. "I've heard of it being done."

"I was given a scolding but nothing worse than that. But they wouldn't send me away when they are quite desperate for me to marry."

"The chap you were dancing with earlier . . . is he whom they wish you to marry?"

She almost stumbled with the realization that he hadn't just arrived at this affair. He'd been here for a while. He'd been watching her.

"The Marquess of Chetwyn. Walter's brother. And yes, he has apparently expressed interest. But

I haven't settled on him." She didn't know why she felt compelled to say the last. Perhaps because she feared he might get into a row with Chetwyn. Seek to stake his claim. A claim he didn't truly have.

As her hand rested in his, as his other hand cupped her waist, she tried not to think about how marvelous it had been to have those hands roaming over her flesh. To have him rising above her. To have him bring her pleasure. She was fairly certain, though, that her cheeks were flaming red, because she saw satisfaction in his gaze and feared he knew what paths her thoughts traveled.

"I found your gift. The starfish. Thank you. Where did you find it?"

"I've seen them along many a shore, but that particular one I found in Yorkshire."

Her laugh, though light, sounded as though it was on the edge of hysteria. "I imagined it came from the Far East or somewhere equally exotic."

His gaze darkened, and she saw secrets hidden there.

"No, it came from my youth. The morning I left England."

"Why give it to me?"

"I don't know. Perhaps because of your fanciful tale of stars falling into the sea. Just something to remember me by."

As if she could ever forget him.

"The oranges. You sent those."

"Yes. I can't eat one without thinking of you.

I hoped the same could be said of you regarding me."

As much as she wished it wasn't so, she did very little that didn't remind her of him.

"Don't you have journeys that await you? Obligations that must be met? You transport goods, do you not?"

"The advantage of owning my own ship is that no one commands me."

Even if he didn't own his own ship, she suspected no one would command him.

"But you must earn a living, you must . . ." She felt as though she had so much to learn about him.

"All I must do, Anne, is dance with you."

Each time he called her Anne, it spoke of intimacies. She wished he'd revert to calling her Princess. It kept her hackles up, made it easier to deal with him, to keep her distance. He was a lord and it gave a new meaning to everything they'd shared.

"The duke, your brother, I've never seen him. Is he about?"

"He's dancing with his wife, Mary. To your left."

As unobtrusively as possible, she glanced over her shoulder and nearly lost her footing. The left side of his face was heavily scarred and he wore an eye patch.

"He's my twin," Tristan said quietly.

"I can see a bit of resemblance." The dark hair, the jawline—

"Most people don't look beyond the scars."

She studied the duchess. She had vibrant red hair and was smiling up at her husband as though she adored him, as though he had no hideous countenance to look upon.

"She doesn't seem bothered by them."

"But then she loves him."

That much was obvious. She returned her attention to Tristan. "Do all of you bear scars?"

"None we can't live with."

Why could others not see what these brothers had endured to reclaim what they'd lost? Why were they not welcomed? Because they'd not grown up within the familiar confines, because they stood out as different.

She realized the music had drifted into silence as their movements came to a halt.

"Will you keep your promise to Lady Hermione?" she asked.

"If would be cruel of me not to, don't you think? But I want another dance with you."

"That would be most unwise."

She hated the words even as she spoke them. He didn't argue. He simply began to lead her from the dance floor. Tense and bristling, Jameson was standing at its edge. She was surprised he didn't charge into the fray and snatch her away.

Just before they reached her brother, Tristan said, "The last dance of the evening is mine."

Before she could object to his possessive tone—or admit how it thrilled her—he released her and strode away.

For the first time that night she was truly looking forward to something, and that filled her with a certain amount of dread. Nothing could exist between them beyond what they'd already shared. In spite of his being a lord, his life was the sea. Hers was here.

Chapter 15

"The ladies are all atwitter," Sarah said as she cornered Anne in the ladies retiring room.

"Ladies are always atwitter," Anne responded coolly. She'd needed a moment alone to regain her composure. Lie, lie, lie. She'd needed to be away from the dance floor so she wasn't watching Tristan waltzing about with Lady Hermione. He smiled at her; he spoke with her; he was holding her in his arms only moments after doing the same with Anne. She wasn't jealous. That would be ridiculous. But she didn't much like seeing him with another lady. Especially as he seemed to be enjoying himself so much.

"You danced with Lord Tristan," Sarah said.

"I'm well aware with whom I danced. He wasn't in disguise, for goodness' sake."

"He's dangerous, Anne."

I'm well aware of that, and in ways you can't even imagine. "It was merely a dance."

"You weren't here when he and his brothers returned two years ago. They were savages."

"Because they reclaimed what was stolen from them?"

"It was the manner in which they did it. They burst in, uninvited, to Lord David's ball and ordered him to leave the residence."

"It was their residence, was it not? It was Easton House, wasn't it, which belonged to their father and thus his son, the next duke?"

"Well, yes, I suppose if one were to be literal about—"

"I don't see how one could be anything else."

Sarah glared at her. "The residence aside, they made quite the spectacle of themselves. Why the eldest brother almost choked his uncle to death."

Anne wasn't certain she could blame him for such an action.

"And poor Lady Lucretia has been in seclusion ever since," Sarah continued.

Their uncle's wife. "She's a widow now, isn't she?"

"Quite. After her husband's mysterious death. Slipped from a tower, in the rain. Supposedly."

"What do you think happened?"

"I think they killed him."

She didn't want to admit that she could quite easily see Tristan killing someone. But not without very good reason.

Tristan stood in a darkened corner of the terrace and smoked on a cheroot. Dancing with Lady Hermione had been an exercise in frustration. The silly chit talked incessantly. She invited him to ride with her in the park, to have dinner with her family, to dance with her again. He'd made up one excuse after another. Perhaps it would have been kinder in the long run not to have danced with her, not to give her any hope at all that more could be between them.

Two years ago, he had wanted nothing more from her than a bit of innocent flirtation. He'd certainly never considered wooing her into his bed. She was a child. She didn't have Anne's allure.

Now, Anne . . . damnation, but he was obsessed with thoughts of her. She invaded his waking hours as much as she did his sleeping ones. He would be studying charts or discussing with merchants the possibility of carrying their cargo—and there she would appear. He thought he should be envisioning her hair draped over her nude body or her slender form writhing beneath him. And he did visit those images from time to time. But more often than not, he thought of her smile or her laughter or the way it had felt to have her standing near him on the deck, listening to the whales. Or sharing meals with her. Verbally sparring with her, the challenging glint in her eyes when she gave no quarter.

He should be back at sea, yet here he was in a place that he loathed. He thought one more sighting of her would have satisfied him, but he'd seen her and wanted more. To speak with her.

He'd spoken with her, and it wasn't enough. He wanted a dance.

He'd had his dance, and now he wanted one more.

He wondered if he could lure her into the garden for a kiss. Just one more—

"Lord Tristan."

At the sound of Lord Jameson's commanding voice, Tristan took a last drag on his cheroot, dropped it to the ground as he exhaled, and snuffed out the sparks with his boot. He turned to find four fair-haired gents blocking his way. "Ah, Lord Blackwood's sons, I take it."

"You are never to go near our sister again," Jameson said.

"Your sister strikes me as a lady with a mind of her own. If the words come from her, I'll heed them. From you, no, m'lord."

"How do you know our sister?" one of the others asked. He appeared to be the youngest. A year, maybe two older than Anne.

"How does any gentleman know any lady?"

"The problem there, Lord Tristan, is that none of us consider you a gentleman," Jameson snapped. "We watched as you cut your swath through London's ladies two years ago. Our sister will not succumb to your charms."

She already has, m'lord, hung at the edge of his tongue like some poor blighter forced to walk the plank in shark-infested waters. Those words would earn him a sound beating from the gents who stood before him. But more, they would anger

Anne and he wasn't quite done with her yet. Of course, neither was he done taunting Lord Jameson. He had decided that he didn't much like the fellow. He could hardly signify that this man was Anne's brother.

"Lady Hermione didn't succumb, my lord. We never shared more than a dance."

Even though they were in shadows, enough light filtered in from the garden path for Tristan to see the fury ignite Jameson's eyes. He'd noticed the way the man looked at Lady Hermione, and Tristan was fairly satisfied to see that he'd guessed correctly at some of what might lie beneath the man's animosity toward him. *You're welcome to her, old man.*

"Why the devil would I care about that?" Jameson asked.

"Because you fancy her, my lord."

"You know nothing. Stay clear of our sister or you'll know the weight of our fists." The man charged toward the doors leading back into the ballroom.

His brothers weren't so quick to leave. They each took a moment to glare at Tristan, issuing their silent challenges, before sauntering away.

He glanced up at the hazy sky. Damn but he hated London, Society, the rules. He needed the wind around him and the sea beneath him. He'd been residing at Sebastian's residence, but tonight, he decided, he'd sleep on his ship, just to have the rocking motion that had so often lulled him.

"Tell me that barbarian is not the sea captain you hired."

Anne was grateful for the dark confines of the carriage because she was relatively certain based on the heat searing her face that she was now scarlet. Jameson had just delivered their aunt to her residence and was now escorting Anne home. Her other brothers had departed from the ball at various times to head to their clubs. It seemed Jameson, however, was taking his role of oldest brother to the extreme.

"Good God, he is, isn't he?" he asked.

"I knew him only as Captain Crimson Jack," she admitted rather reluctantly, but she couldn't see lying about it. She didn't need him making inquiries along the docks. Sooner or later he was bound to uncover the truth anyway. Better to control the discovery and subsequent consequences.

"What a colorful moniker."

"He came highly recommended and he was a perfect gentleman on the ship."

"He is not a gentleman. He gave Lady Hermione cause to believe he would ask for her hand and he did not. He left with nary a word and she has been pining for him ever since. Now he is back and he didn't even bother to call on her."

Now Anne wished for some light so she could study her brother's face in the shadows. His voice held such distaste that she was surprised he wasn't spitting. "You seem more concerned with his treatment of her than my acquaintance with him."

"I'm only telling you of his behavior so you understand he is a blackguard of the lowest order. Not to be trusted. I forbid you to speak with him again."

Forbid her? She almost snapped that it wasn't his place to forbid her anything. Instead she stared out the window. Tristan had claimed her for the final dance of the evening. She wasn't certain where he'd been all night. After his dance with Lady Hermione he had disappeared. She'd feared that he'd left. A silly thing to worry over but she had wanted another dance with him.

But then he'd appeared, as though out of thin air. Perhaps he'd been playing cards. It didn't matter. She was back in his arms, and while she knew it was a very dangerous place to be, she couldn't help but feel glad to be there. They didn't speak this time. Not a single word. Yet there had been so much communication. She'd recognized the appreciation in his light blue gaze, and the longing that mirrored hers. She'd fallen into the welcoming depths of his eyes and found herself yearning for dark forbidden corners where their bodies could share secrets.

It was all so wrong. Yet the knowledge did little to curb her desire.

She didn't want to contemplate that he might have taken advantage of Lady Hermione, that he might be the sort who left broken hearts in his wake. Surely he understood how vulnerable hers was. Although she had no intention of giving it to him. What they shared was the physical only. She couldn't allow it to be more. She couldn't risk being hurt again. Love led to unparalleled pain that couldn't be assuaged so easily. Always there would be a final separation.

Much better to live one's life with a man whom she could like, but in whom she would not invest her heart and soul. Chetwyn came to mind. He would be such a man. No passion. No risk to her heart. No worries.

Proper. It would all be very proper. She suspected even his lovemaking would be proper. No sweating bodies, cries of pleasure. No torrid breathless moments.

The carriage came to a halt and she realized that they'd arrived home, her wayward thoughts careening into oblivion.

"Do we have an understanding?" Jameson asked. "Regarding Lord Tristan."

"Yes, Brother. I understand perfectly what you said." *Doesn't mean I'll heed your orders.* But she did understand them.

She retired to her bedchamber, rang for Martha, and an hour later was prepared for bed, though her emotions were in such a swirl that she knew she'd be unable to sleep. She considered going to the library to fetch a book, but she doubted she'd be able to concentrate.

"Will there be anything else, m'lady?"

From her bench in front of the vanity, she peered over at Martha. "No. Thank you. Sleep well."

When the door had clicked shut behind her maid, she turned her attention back to her reflection in the mirror. Her first ball after so many years away had not gone so terribly badly. She supposed she would survive the Season.

Leaning toward the mirror, she watched as a boot-clad foot and tight britches appeared through the window. Coming to her feet, she spun around and stared as Tristan made his way ever so calmly into her room.

He grinned. "I thought she'd never leave."

Chapter 16

"**W**hat are you doing here?"

She didn't seem alarmed, so much as curious.

"I came to see you of course."

"My brothers are—"

"At their clubs. As is your father."

"Still, this is my father's home and for me to allow you to stay . . ."

Her voice trailed off, and he strove not to let show his joy at her considering allowing him to stay. Damnation but the past week had been hellacious. He suspected, and tonight it had been confirmed, that his calling on her would not be welcomed by her family. Before tonight he had no opening, no way to explain how he knew her. Now an introduction at a ball opened doors . . . and windows.

He strode over to her, cupped her face in his hands, and tilted up her chin so he could gaze squarely into her silver eyes. "Tell me to leave and I will."

"God forgive me for my weakness," she whispered, rising up to meet him as he lowered his questing mouth to hers.

It felt marvelous to once again have the taste of her, the scent of her, the feel of her. Why did she call to him so? Why could he not leave? He'd readied the ship for departure. He wanted to be back on the seas. He wanted to hear the wind slapping the sails. He wanted to look out and see nothing that hindered him. He'd stood on the deck prepared to give the order to set sail and the words that had come out of his mouth surprised him as much as his men. "We're staying in port."

He'd gone to Sebastian's, knowing that Mary would have an inkling as to which ball held the promise of attracting most of the nobility. He hadn't confessed his interest in Anne to her, although she'd certainly given him a speculative look. Once he returned to his brother's residence, she'd no doubt pepper him with questions regarding what she may have witnessed this evening. Small sacrifice for what he had now gained.

Anne was as greedy as he was, her mouth matching his eagerness, her tongue darting and exploring as though she'd only just discovered a treasure map and needed to memorize the paths that would lead to gold. Bold, so very bold. Her hands skimmed over his shoulders, his back, up into his hair. He couldn't get enough of her touching him, but he wanted it to be flesh meeting flesh with no clothes between them.

Breaking away, she staggered back, her hands pressed to her mouth, her eyes dimmed with misgivings. "Not in my father's house."

"Get dressed. I'll meet you in the back and we'll find a room in a hotel where we can be alone."

"As though I'm some common doxy?"

"As though I shall go mad if I don't possess you."

A bubble of laughter burst from her mouth, lighting her eyes, even as she shook her head. "It's too tawdry. A room somewhere in which other people have slept."

"You didn't seem to mind my climbing into bed with you when we were on my ship."

"It was another world. Far away. Not . . . here."

God help him, he wanted to push her, but he'd seen how she'd suffered with the refusal she'd given her fiancé. He wanted to do nothing that brought back memories of the man who had once—and possibly still—held her heart.

"Seems you could at least be hospitable and offer me a drink. Still hoarding your father's brandy?"

He saw the gratitude wash over her features because he was squelching his desires. *Only for now, sweetheart.* Misjudging an adversary on the sea could cost a man his ship and possibly his life. Tristan was not in the habit of misjudging. He was very skilled at biding his time until the moment was right.

With a nod she turned and headed toward her wardrobe. He wandered over to the sitting area and stared into the empty hearth. He couldn't help but imagine what it might be like to be with her in winter, snuggled beneath a layer of blankets, seeking warmth.

"Here you are."

He took the snifter she offered, glad to see that she had one of her own. Brandy would serve much better for seduction than a fire.

He wondered if she read his mind, because a wariness touched her voice when she asked, "Would you care to sit?"

"Delighted."

She sat on one end of the small sofa, drawing her feet beneath her, while he sat on the other, stretching out his legs. She looked young and innocent, cupping the snifter with both hands, watching him over the rim. "My brother informs me that you gave Lady Hermione cause for hope that your interest in her went beyond the ballroom."

Damnation! It could be Lady Hermione more than this being her father's residence that had Anne hesitant to welcome him into her bed. "I didn't."

"But you are in the habit of leaving women . . ." Her voice trailed off into an unasked question.

At every port. "Yes."

"So this between us is—"

"I don't know what it is."

"Or how long it will last?"

"Does it matter?"

"I'm not sure." She sipped on the brandy.

"Your brother warned you away from me."

"Yes. He believes you to be barbaric. I told him

he was wrong, that you were a perfect gentleman on the ship."

Tristan couldn't hide his surprise. "You told him you were on my ship?"

She nodded. "He guessed. He wasn't happy, and I shall no doubt be brought to task by my father in the morning."

"What exactly did you tell your brother?"

"Only that you were the captain of the ship. Certainly nothing about the intimacy that we shared." She gave him a shy smile. "I'm not certain if he would have killed you or dragged you to the altar."

"I suppose it goes without saying that neither option appeals."

"And yet you said it." Her voice had an acerbic edge to it. She furrowed her brow. "Have you no plans to ever take a wife?"

He wished a fire on the grate was producing writhing flames into which he could stare contemplatively rather than into her eyes. But she deserved him holding her gaze. "Surely you weren't foolish enough to see me as the marrying sort?"

"No." She sipped her brandy, then licked lips that he wanted to once again kiss. She studied the contents of her snifter as though she could read the answer there. "It was one of the things that made you safe for a night's indiscretions. You would never demand or desire anything more of me than a quick romp."

"It was hardly quick." He set aside his snifter and slid across the cushions until her eyes widened with alarm. He skimmed his fingers along her throat, felt the fluttering of her pulse against his skin. "And I'm still safe. I'm a blackguard to the core. I've never claimed otherwise. All I want from you is passion and pleasure. To give. To receive. You don't want me for a husband any more than I want you for a wife. But you can't deny there is an attraction between us, like the moon to the tides."

"And which am I?" she asked on a breathy sigh. Before he could respond, she answered, "The moon, of course. I stay put in London Society while you come and go where the sea takes you."

"Yet here I am, with you pulling me toward you. Let me come nearer, Anne."

It was a bad idea. An awfully bad idea. Anne could think of a thousand reasons to say no, but she didn't object when he took her snifter, finished off its contents, and set it aside. She didn't snatch free her braid when he took hold of it and slowly unraveled the strands. She didn't move back, only swayed forward when he cradled her face with one hand, her nape with the other, and covered her mouth with his. Lovely, so lovely. Molten heat flowed through her as his thumb stroked the underside of her chin and his mouth worked its magic. She could taste the brandy on his tongue, more intoxicating there than in the glass.

She maneuvered herself around until she was in his lap, straining to get as close to him as she could. She shoved his jacket off his shoulders, worked it free of his arms, never breaking the kiss. The familiarity astounded her. It was as though she had been with him forever, as though the days separating them had never occurred. She dispensed with his cravat next, then began working on the buttons of his waistcoat while he nimbly freed those on her nightdress. She felt the air cool her flesh, then he was warming it again, trailing his mouth along her throat before dipping into the valley between her breasts. She dropped back her head, relishing the rasp of his rough tongue as it circled a nipple.

"Yes," she breathed, then he was drawing it into his mouth, tugging and suckling. The pleasure coursed through her, pooling between her thighs. She was acutely aware of the straining bulge against his trousers.

Suddenly he was standing, she was in his arms, and he was carrying her to the bed. "You'll be the death of me," he growled.

She stifled her laughter. It seemed wrong, here in her father's house, to take joy in such wicked pleasures, but she couldn't have sent Tristan away now if her life depended on it. He laid her on the bed and whipped off her nightdress. She felt no need to cover herself from his heated gaze. The appreciation that lit his eyes only served to warm her further. She watched as he hastily removed his own clothes. In this larger bedchamber, he shouldn't have looked as powerful as he had on the ship, he shouldn't have caused the room to seem dwarfed. But he did.

He dominated everything. He crawled onto her bed, near her feet, and skimmed his fingers up her legs, along her hips, her sides, easing up until he was looking down on her.

"What sort of spell have you cast over me?" he whispered before lowering his mouth to hers.

It was marvelous, having him so near, having the weight of his body resting on hers. The scent of brandy and oranges wafted around her. Wrapping her legs around him, she raked her fingers up his strong broad back, feeling the uneven flesh. Her husband wouldn't be marred like this. He would have lived a leisurely existence fraught with few dangers. Would he stir her to life like this? Would he have her writhing and panting beneath him?

Or was this wild abandonment limited to the wicked?

"You're beautiful, so beautiful," he rasped, worshipping her body with his mouth, hands, and words.

How quickly she'd grown accustomed to the manner in which they waltzed in bed. Holding her gaze, he rose above her. "Be sure, Anne."

"I am."

He plunged into her. She cried out with the pleasure of it, the rightness of it. It felt so good to have him pounding into her, as though each thrust was a return home. She met his movements with a determination and fierceness that astounded her. She wanted to claim him, possess him, own him. She'd never felt this way. She hadn't liked watching him dance with Lady Hermione. She'd wanted to tell the girl that she couldn't have Tristan because he belonged to Anne. Only he didn't.

He belonged to the sea.

And she knew that she would have to give him back to his demanding mistress. Anne was only for now. Tonight. Maybe one more. Already she was contemplating one more.

But each night would only add to the weight of sorrow when he finally parted from England's shores. She knew he would leave. The sea would call to him and he would answer.

Yet at this moment, it was her cries that he responded to. It was his answering grunts that echoed around her. His eyes held hers. He measured her pleasure, increased it with deeper, more forceful thrusts. She dug her fingers into his buttocks, anchored herself to him as a deluge of sensations rocketed through her.

As she cried out, he covered her mouth, swallowing her screams, giving her his grunts just before he arched back and shuddered above her in a magnificent display of pure masculinity. As replete as she was, she still managed to find the strength to trail her fingers over his glistening chest.

He cursed soundly before rolling off her onto his back and drawing her up against his side. Staring at the canopy, in between harsh breaths, he muttered, "I didn't think to protect you. Damnation."

After the first time they'd made love, he'd begun withdrawing, spilling his seed on the sheets rather than in her. She understood the precautions that were needed, but it always left her wanting. While she didn't want to find herself with child, a distant part of her thrilled with the possibility. But it would be such a disaster. She should remind him to leave her, but when he was inside her, her only thought was that she wanted him to stay.

She cradled his taut jaw. "It doesn't always happen immediately. It took my friend Sarah six months to get with child."

He chuckled low. "I gave no thought to anything except the wonder of being inside you again."

She felt the heat suffusing her entire body at the crudity of his words. One didn't talk so pointedly about such things.

He shifted his gaze to her and a corner of his mouth quirked up. "After what we've shared how can you still be embarrassed?"

"The words are so . . . raw."

"Shall I tell you how scaldingly hot you are inside?"

She furrowed her brow. "Does it burn you?"

"No, it feels bloody marvelous. Hence my inability to remain focused on what I should do as a gentleman. Rather, I become lost in being a scoundrel."

"Are you complimenting me?"

Turning onto his side he tangled together their legs and threaded his fingers into her hair. "Never doubt for a moment that any woman can compare to you."

"As you unravel the mystery of me, perhaps you'll become quite un-enthralled."

"Impossible. I suspect there is always a new mystery to discover."

"I'm not comprised of as many secrets as you.

Tell me of your boyhood, of why you ran away. What did your uncle do that made you believe he would kill you?"

The teasing left his eyes as he sighed. "It was long—"

"Yes, I know, long ago," she said impatiently. "But it made you the man you are. You can't deny that. It was one thing when I thought you were a ship captain, but now that I know you're a lord . . . Tristan, I don't know what to make of you."

"I'm the same man that I was on the ship."

She flattened her hand against his chest. "But there are so many layers to you. Please reveal this one so that I might understand why you didn't tell me who you were sooner."

He studied her for a moment before releasing a gust of air. "Pembrook. The family estate. More castle than manor. Built before the days of Henry VIII, but used as a stronghold and a prison for that king. It had a dungeon for tormenting those who did not support Henry and a tower for housing prisoners. For adventuresome boys, it was a wonderful place steeped in history. Sebastian and I used to go down to the dungeon and try to scare the other by saying that we heard ghosts. I loved it there. I think he did, too. It was home."

He said the word with a longing that tore at her heart. She understood the history, the traditions, the legacy attached to an ancestral home. She had grown up being taught to appreciate those who had come before her, those who had paved the way for her family.

"I was a child when tragedy struck you," she said quietly. "I barely remember anything that I might have been told. What happened to your father?"

"He died when his horse unseated him, but none of us ever believed it was an accident. His skull was crushed. Uncle said he fell on a rock. We always believed Uncle David bashed his head in. Then after Father's funeral, when all the guests had departed, Uncle locked us in the tower."

"Your mother—"

"Died in childbirth."

"You must have been so afraid being all alone."

"It was winter. Bitingly cold. We had no light, no blankets. No moon filled the heavens that night."

She realized he didn't acknowledge her statement. Rather, he focused on everything that had been going on around him instead of what was happening within him. "How old were you?"

"Fourteen."

"Perhaps another reason prompted him to put you in the tower." She couldn't imagine anyone setting out to murder young boys.

"Mary heard him plotting our deaths. She lived on an adjoining estate. She'd come to see Sebastian. They were close."

She thought of the lovely woman she'd seen dancing with Keswick. She couldn't have been much younger than they. "She helped you escape?"

"Yes."

"I remember vaguely hearing that something

had happened to the lords of Pembrook. I suppose I was about nine at the time."

"What tale did you hear? That we were eaten by wolves, died of the pox, or were stolen by gypsies?"

She skimmed her fingers through his hair, hating the thought of anyone hurting him, and knowing that so many had. "Wolves. My brothers relished telling me the gory details. I remember having nightmares about it. So you went to the sea."

"Sebastian thought we should all separate. Rafe was only ten so we left him at a workhouse. I went to the sea. Sebastian went to the army. We were supposed to return ten years later to reclaim our heritage, but war kept him away. The sea did the same for me. But eventually we met up and the Lords of Pembrook returned to Society—much to Society's chagrin."

Again, he made it sound as though he'd endured little more than a sniveling nose. She cradled his firm jaw, realizing that he must have shaved between the time he left the ball and the moment he stepped through her window. She couldn't imagine her brothers climbing trees and scrambling through windows. "Only because you're quite different from everyone else. They're not quite certain what to make of you."

"You give them far too much credit. They despise us."

"Not you so much as perhaps the adventurous lives you've lived."

"I, for one, could have done without the adventures, thank you very much."

She was familiar enough with his back to know how awful some of them might have been.

"Now enough of this maudlin talk," he said as he eased over her, nudging her opening with his hard shaft. "I want you once more before I leave."

She couldn't deny him any more than she could deny herself. She lifted her hips to receive his offering and as he sank into her, she wondered if a time would come when she would ever not yearn for this joining with him.

Chapter 17

After he made love to her, lethargy settled in and Tristan fell asleep still nestled inside her with one of her legs draped over his hip. He didn't think he'd moved for the remainder of the night, because she was still within the circle of his arms when he awakened. It bothered him to realize how comforting it felt. He wasn't a man accustomed to comfort. Comforts, yes. A good bed, a sturdy ship, well-tailored clothes. But comfort, bestowed by another, was foreign. Yet he couldn't deny the joy it brought him to find her near enough that with only a slight adjustment of his body he could be buried deeply within her once again. A lovely way to greet the day.

"Tristan?" She nudged him. "Tristan, I hear the lark. You must go."

Forcing his eyes open, he greeted her concerned expression with a grin. "Twenty more minutes."

"No. The sun will be up at any moment. I can hear carts jangling about in the street."

"If we were to stay here all day—"

"No!" She shoved on him. "Please, hurry. I shouldn't have let you stay. We can't do this again."

"But it was so worth it." He planted a quick kiss on her mouth before rolling out of bed. He gathered up his trousers and put them on before grabbing his shirt and drawing it over his head. He peered over at her, sitting up in bed, clutching the sheets to her chest, her hair a tangled mess that fell around her. She looked decidedly improper this morning. He sat in a chair and began tugging on a boot.

"Come with me."

Her eyes widened. "What?"

"Come with me. To the ship. We'll set sail by noon and travel the world. I'll show you water so clear that you can see the fish swimming along the bottom. I'll show you islands that have not been touched by modernization and life slows to a crawl. I'll take you to hidden coves where you can bask naked in the sunlight."

She drew up her knees and pressed her chin to them. "How long will this idyllic journey take?"

"A year. Two."

"And then? Upon my return, what shall I do with a tattered reputation?"

He sighed. There was the rub.

"No man will have me," she continued. "My family will no doubt disown me. What will my future be?" She shook her head. "I want a proper life, Tristan. With a husband I see every day and children and a home on land."

"Being proper brought you unhappiness. Being improper . . . Princess, I've seen the way you smile afterward."

"Being improper in bed is one thing. Being improper with my life is something else entirely."

He shoved his foot into the other boot. He would never be happy here, in London, living within Society, with all its blasted rules. He'd always known the sea wasn't a life for everyone. He couldn't blame her for not wanting it. But damnation, it didn't stop him from wanting her.

He snatched up his remaining clothes, bundled them up, and walked to the window. He should say good-bye to her, never see her again. Instead he heard himself ask, "What are you doing today?"

"Making some morning calls. Going to Hyde Park this afternoon."

"Carriage, horse, or stroll?"

"Horse, I should think."

He grinned. "I've never seen you ride a horse."

She returned his smile. "Do you know how to ride one?"

"I'm a lord. Of course, I do."

With that, he slipped out the window. He'd thought one more night and he'd have his fill of her. It was disconcerting to realize that before his feet landed firmly on the ground, he already wanted her again.

"**B**y God, but I'm famished," Tristan said as he strolled into his brother's breakfast dining room and headed for the sideboard where an abundance of delicacies awaited his appreciation. He'd experienced far too many occasions when food was scarce on a ship. All the planning in the world couldn't guarantee good winds and the absence of delay in reaching a port.

"You're not properly attired," Sebastian chided from his place at the head of the small table.

Tristan had dropped his waistcoat and jacket on a chair in the foyer on the way in. He gathered up ham, eggs, bread, and a bit of everything else. "Do you know that I've eaten meals with no shirt on at all?" he asked as he took his seat.

Sitting beside her husband, rather than at the foot of the table, Mary blushed. Tristan had noticed that the two of them always stayed within easy reach of each other. He didn't want to acknowledge the tug of longing that realization brought. How boring life would be to wake up to the same woman every morning. Eventually he suspected he'd just as soon *not* wake up.

"I imagine you did quite a bit on a ship that you do not do in a residence," Sebastian chided. "You're not setting a good example for my son."

"I don't see him about." The little bugger was barely a year old. He wasn't likely to notice anyway. "Perhaps you'd rather I not be here either."

"Of course we want you here," Mary quickly said. "Never doubt that."

"It is simply that you are in Society now,"

Sebastian added, "and certain behaviors are expected."

Tristan relented. A blasted waistcoat, jacket, and cravat weren't worth fighting over and creating a chasm between him and his brother. They'd had too many years apart as it was. "I shall come properly attired in the future."

"Might help if you didn't stay out all night."

Tristan barked out his laughter. "Are you going to deny me all my pleasures?"

"Was it pleasures or creating trouble that kept you out?"

"A little of both, truth be told." He winked at Mary, and her blush returned deeper than before, almost scarlet. She had spent a good many years in a convent, protected from the likes of him. She was fun to tease now, but she could hold her own. She'd proven that with Sebastian. Dammit, she'd proven it when she was twelve years old and helped them escape from the tower at Pembrook. "You should have some oranges, by the way. Prevents scurvy. I'll see that some are delivered."

"We are not likely to get scurvy here."

"It's not a pleasant thing, so humor me."

"Did you ever suffer from it?" Mary asked.

"No, but I've seen plenty who have. I fear I became rather obsessed with oranges. Other fruits work, but oranges are my preference."

He cut into the ham, like a gentleman. Marlow had insisted that his men not eat like savages. Marlow was a contradiction. A man who could order, without compunction, that the flesh be flayed off a man's back one minute and the next offer solace, holding a seaman's hand while he waited for death to claim him. Tristan had experienced both his kindness and his brutality.

"Lady Hermione seemed quite thrilled to see you returned," Mary said, snapping Tristan from his musings.

"She doesn't seem to have matured any during the time I've been away."

"She's simply an excitable girl. I would caution you to take care with her."

"Trust me, Mary, I intend to avoid her like the plague."

"That may prove a challenge at the balls. And elsewhere. She appears to be in pursuit of you."

"I'm quite skilled at avoiding capture."

"On the sea, perhaps," Sebastian said. "It's not always so easy in Society. If her father does little more than *think* you've compromised her, you may find yourself at the altar."

"As I've already said, I have no plans to go anywhere near her."

"And what of Lady Anne Hayworth?"

Tristan's fingers tightened around his knife as he sliced off another bit of ham. His temper was straining its tether. "What of her, Brother?"

"We noticed you dancing with her last night," Mary said softly enough to quiet his anger.

"She's a beautiful woman. I happen to enjoy beautiful women."

"She might be vulnerable. As I understand it,

she's only just coming out of mourning after having lost her fiancé in the war."

"I know exactly what she's coming out of. What have you done? Become the patron saint of unmarried women?"

"Don't speak to my wife in that tone," Sebastian said, his voice seething.

"I'm trying to understand what's behind the bloody inquisition. I'm a grown man free to do as I damn well please."

"Not if others may be hurt by it. This isn't the sea, Tristan. You don't rule here."

Tristan shoved back his chair and stood. "Please give me some credit. I held the woman while she wept over her damned fiancé's bones. The very last thing I would ever do is hurt her."

At their stunned expressions, he spun on his heel and headed for the door, not so much to escape them, but because he feared the words that still echoed around the room and in his head were a lie. He had the potential to hurt her and he damned well knew it. But even knowing it wasn't enough incentive to keep him away from her.

Anne had only just finished her breakfast and was considering a stroll in the garden when she was summoned to her father's study. It did not bode well that Jameson was there or that both men were on their feet before she entered. They were going to discover that their strategy to intimidate held little sway over her these days. After all, she had climbed to the top of a mast. She doubted either of them could claim the same achievement. Although she planned to keep it to herself since she'd been wearing britches at the time. That revelation would no doubt give her father an apoplectic fit.

"Jameson tells me that you traveled with this Pembrook lord."

"I traveled on *his* ship. Hardly the same thing."

"Semantics," Jameson barked.

"Quite. And in this instance crucial to the understanding of what actually transpired."

"Which was?" her father snapped.

"A journey from England's shores to Scutari. I visited the British cemetery. I said my good-byes to Walter. We began the journey home. I weathered a storm. I watched porpoises play. I heard whales moan. And I released the last of my sorrow at Walter's passing. It was a journey of healing. Now I am ready for the Season."

"Yet this man approached you last night," her father said.

"Yes. As did Chetwyn. And the Duke of Ainsley. Lords Malvern, Summerly, and Churchaven. I'm not certain why you're so bothered that Lord Tristan would do the same."

"He does not treat women well," her brother said succinctly.

"Women? Or Lady Hermione?"

Jameson glared so fiercely that she was surprised she didn't ignite into a ball of fire. "Did you have a fondness for her?" she asked softly.

"It is you with whom I am concerned. Your reputation. The possibility for a secure future with a husband and children. You're in a precarious position, Anne."

"Yes, because I'm so old. I must stop leaving my walking stick in my bedchamber lest I discover I'm unable to traipse about without falling on my backside." She was fairly certain Tristan would have smiled at that. Her brother only glowered.

"Chetwyn will be coming by this afternoon to take you on a ride through the park," her father announced.

She jerked her head around to stare at him. "Pardon?"

"He mentioned it at the club last night. I expect you to behave as a woman who could one day be a marchioness."

"I had plans for this afternoon."

He arched a brow. "What were those?"

"A solitary ride through the park," she said, knowing it was a weak excuse that would hold no influence.

"So now you'll have a gentleman to accompany you, with our blessing."

And to be present when Tristan approached her. What could possibly go wrong there?

Chapter 18

Anne desperately wanted to be on a horse but Chetwyn had brought his barouche. The driver had set the chestnut mare from a lovely trot into a leisurely walk once they arrived at the park. The carriage's hood was folded back, allowing the sunshine to wash over them. Anne knew she should relax and enjoy it, but she was anticipating the arrival of a storm.

Chetwyn sat beside her. They had spoken of the weather and the flowers. She didn't know why she was having such a difficult time with ordinary conversation. She certainly had never found herself lacking for words where Tristan was concerned. Their discourse ran the gamut from teasing to serious to sensual to angry to sad to profound. She thought she could talk with him forever and never find herself scrambling for topics. But with Chetwyn—

"What sort of sister by marriage would you like?" he asked.

She looked at him. He had such kind brown eyes. Walter's eyes. "Pardon?"

"I promised to provide you with a list of potential ladies for Jameson. I wondered what your criterion was when it came to a sister by marriage."

"Only that she makes Jameson happy. I shan't be living with her."

"But you shall see her from time to time."

"I can tolerate anything unpleasant for a short period of time."

"Even a husband?"

She smiled. "No, I would like him to be pleasant all the time, although I suspect there will be moments when he'll be difficult."

"I can't imagine that any man who gained your favor would ever abuse such grand fortune. He would want you to always be happy."

She wondered if he was talking of himself. She didn't want to journey into a discussion regarding the sort of man she wished for a husband. She feared her desired qualifications might have taken a nasty turn toward the adventuresome. "You and Jameson have been friends for a good while. Do you know if he ever had any tender feelings for Lady Hermione?"

Clearing his throat, Chetwyn looked out over the green. "He might have found himself fascinated with her."

"Two years ago? Before the lords of Pembrook returned?"

Chetwyn nodded, then shifted his glance over to her. "It seems you have captured the attention of at least one of those lords."

"It was only a dance."

"Two actually."

"Two is proper."

"But he isn't."

She wanted to deny it, but proper gentlemen didn't climb in through windows bent on seduction.

"Does he fascinate you as he fascinates all the ladies?" Chetwyn asked.

"He's not a threat to you or any of the other lords. He has no intention of staying here. He has a ship. He travels the world. Marriage to him would be a lonely affair."

"So you've considered it?"

"No!" She felt herself blushing. She had not wanted the conversation to go here. "I only meant to reassure you that he engages in harmless flirtation."

"Then I need not consider him competition for your attentions?"

Her face, her entire body, grew warmer. She had to tread lightly here. Did she wish to encourage him? She knew him. He was kind and well mannered. She suspected he would not stray from his vows. He would not leave her weeping or angry or shattered. She wanted to reassure him, but instead she heard herself spouting a lie. "He means nothing to me."

Chetwyn nodded. "I still miss him, you know?"

The words made no sense and left her doing

little more than batting her eyes, because she was fairly certain he wasn't referring to Tristan.

"Walter," he added, as though she needed the clarification, and shame on her because for a moment she'd forgotten all about him.

"As do I."

"War is a terrible thing."

"But sometimes necessary." She could not—would not—believe Walter had died in vain.

"It takes a toll on a man," Chetwyn said. "On his family, on those who love him. And on a country actually. A lot of men returned with missing limbs, unable to work."

"I suspect they could work if people would only give them a chance."

He gave her a small smile. "Quite right. But until they are given that chance, some are living in the gutters. I want to change that, Anne. In Walter's memory. I want to arrange a home for soldiers where they can stay until they get back on their feet."

"Oh, Chetwyn." Without thinking, she placed her hand over his where it rested on his thigh and squeezed. "What a lovely idea."

He turned his hand over, threaded his fingers through hers. "I'm arranging a ball, with help from Mother, of course. Only a select few shall be invited as we'll solicit monetary contributions. A crass endeavor in one way, but I feel I must do something."

"I think it's an exceedingly generous undertaking."

He held her gaze. "May I feel free to seek your advice on certain matters?"

"By all means. I would love to be involved."

"I feared it might make things more difficult for you. I know you're striving to move on."

"Moving on doesn't include forgetting."

"My brother was exceedingly fortunate to have you in his life. I don't believe I received a single letter from him that didn't mention you. Although I have to confess that even without his assurances, I knew you were extraordinary."

She wondered if she was blushing as deeply as he was. "You're too kind."

"Hardly."

She tried to imagine what it would be like to gaze across a room every evening and see his face, to hold the majority of her conversations with him, to have him kiss her. She was fairly certain it would all be comforting enough. Pleasant even. She would have no surprises, no—

Her eyes widened as she caught sight of Tristan sitting astride a beautiful ebony horse, trotting toward her. He looked as magnificent as she'd imagined. Did any setting exist in which his mere presence didn't dominate? It was as though the lovely park suddenly became smaller, insignificant. As though—

"Anne?"

She looked at Chetwyn, his furrowed brow, his concern. "I'm sorry. I became distracted."

Then as though her attention had become metal shavings and Tristan were a magnet, she was again gazing past Chetwyn.

"I see," he muttered and ordered his driver to draw the carriage to a halt.

She wasn't certain if that was good or bad. It would certainly make it easier to speak with Tristan, but it would also make it easier for *him* to speak and she dreaded what he might say, how he might insinuate an intimacy between them.

He brought his horse to a halt on her side of the carriage, even though it meant going around the contraption and confirming that his interest was in her. He swept his beaver hat from his head and bowed slightly, his ice blue eyes glittering with a possessiveness that she wanted to deny. "Lady Anne."

She wished they were in the country so they could go galloping over the rolling hills together. She wished she hadn't felt a need to be polite and accept Chetwyn's offer to accompany her. She wished she understood this excitement that thrummed through her simply because Tristan was near enough to breathe the same air as she. "Lord Tristan, what a pleasant surprise."

What in the world was wrong with her voice? She sounded like a pesky little dormouse.

"Surprise indicates that you weren't expecting me. Did I not make clear that I would join you at the park?"

She stopped breathing, waiting in horror for him to reveal exactly when they had the conversation, but apparently even he realized that would be a step too far and would neatly slice her reputation to ribbons. With her worry dissipating, her anger sparked. She'd not have him playing games with her in public that would serve only to start tongues wagging. "During our dance I recall mentioning, offhandedly, that I would be riding this afternoon. I expected to be alone. Instead Lord Chetwyn was kind enough to give me the pleasure of his company." Ignoring the tightening of Tristan's jaw, she turned to her traveling companion. "Lord Chetwyn, allow me to introduce—"

"I've had the privilege." He spoke the last word as though it left a bitter taste in his mouth.

She'd never heard him speak so succinctly, and realized he was no happier than Tristan. "Oh, I see. Of course."

Tristan's gaze dropped to her lap. No, not hers. Chetwyn's. Her hand was still entangled with his. She wanted to snatch hers free, but he closed his fingers so tightly around them that they were beginning to go numb. To separate them now would do little more than cause a scene.

"A lovely day isn't it?" she offered.

"A storm's coming," Tristan answered, and she suspected he wasn't talking about the weather.

"Do you find the park to your liking?"

The right side of his mouth hitched up into a grin with which she'd become far too familiar. It was a portent of teasing. *Don't*, she wanted to beg, *don't say anything that will give Chetwyn cause to believe we are more than acquaintances.*

"I prefer the sea."

"When will you be returning to it, my lord?" Chetwyn asked.

"When my business here is completed."

His gaze settled on her. To her shame, she was keenly aware of pleasure spiraling through her. She was his business. But for how long and to what purpose? A few more nights between the sheets? He'd certainly given no indication that he desired more from her. Even his suggestion that they sail the sea together gave way to the promise of an end. A year or two at the most. Then she would be returned to shore a shattered woman, because she feared during that length of time she would give him her heart.

"Am I correct, my lord, in understanding that you own a ship?" Chetwyn asked.

"You are indeed, sir."

"By what name does it go?"

"What's your interest?"

"Why the secrecy?"

"I simply wouldn't want to go to the docks one night and discover it ablaze."

Anne didn't understand this verbal sparring, but she did know for certain one thing. "Chetwyn would never destroy your ship. Where is the harm in revealing its name?"

Tristan studied her for a moment before saying, "*Revenge.*"

"An homage to your uncle?" Chetwyn asked.

"To my lost youth."

"You may not give credence to my words, my lord, but I, for one, never faulted you or your brothers for the manner in which you treated your uncle. Quite honestly, I found him to be a pompous prig."

Tristan flashed a grin. "My lord, my respect for you has increased tenfold."

He shifted his gaze to Anne and she couldn't help but think that his respect for Chetwyn hadn't increased at all. She wanted each man to appreciate the other, but she felt instead that they were sizing each other up, searching for flaws and weaknesses, analyzing strengths. She very much felt caught in the middle.

"I suppose we should be off," Chetwyn suddenly announced.

"Yes, by all means," she said. Although she didn't really want to go, but she was acutely aware of the storm Tristan had mentioned brewing.

"My lord! My Lord Tristan!"

She thought if he were a man prone to rolling his eyes, he'd have done so at that moment. Instead, he forced a smile that was filled with none of the subtle nuances and emotions that usually accompanied it.

Ladies Hermione and Victoria brought their horses to a halt near Tristan's.

"My Lord Tristan, I was so dearly hoping that I should cross paths with you here today," Lady Hermione said breathlessly, leaving Anne to wonder what Jameson might have seen in such a flighty girl. "I trust you remember my dearest friend, Lady Victoria. She is now married to the Earl of Whitby's second son. She is serving as my chaperone. We were so hoping that you would join us in a turn about the park."

"It would be my pleasure to accompany two such lovely ladies."

Anne didn't know why his words stung. She was here with another man. Why shouldn't Tristan prance about with another lady or two?

He tipped his hat at Anne. "I look forward to our meeting again."

Dear God, help her. She knew exactly when that meeting was going to take place and where. Tonight. Her bedchamber. She was not so much scandalized by the notion of it as she was by her anticipation of it.

As the carriage bolted away, Tristan wondered if Anne knew how grateful she should be for Lady Hermione's appearance. He'd been close to leaning down and snagging her out of that contraption, settling her on the saddle between his thighs, and whisking her away to someplace private so he could claim her. She was holding the blasted marquess's hand with fingers that had stroked him in the early hours of the morning. Tristan's only consolation was that she was wearing gloves.

He didn't know what to make of this fury that was rampaging through him. He'd never been a possessive sort, perhaps because he'd never had to be. When he was with a woman, she was his sole focus and he was hers. There was none of this flitting about from man to man nonsense. When he wearied of a woman, she moved on and he thought nothing of it. The trouble here was that he had yet to lose interest. Far from it, truth be told.

Well, he thought sarcastically, one should specify. He was not bored with Anne. He was bored silly with Lady Hermione.

"—made her look like a ripe strawberry. Honestly, she shouldn't wear that shade of red."

He had no idea which lady she was referring to or why he should care one whit that she had the appearance of fruit. Lady Victoria was trailing along at a discreet distance. It seemed Hermione wanted to follow in her friend's footsteps and marry the second son of a lord. He wondered how she would take the news that she could marry the first son. Anne's brother would no doubt still take her if she were to make herself presentable to him, instead of latching onto Tristan as though she were a trailing vine.

"You don't fancy her, do you?" Lady Hermione asked.

"Women who favor fruit have never appealed to me."

She tsked. "I was referring to Lady Anne Hayworth. It seems whenever my path crosses with yours that you are speaking with her."

"Mere coincidence."

"I'm glad to hear that."

With a sigh, he brought his horse to a halt, and she quickly followed suit. She had such large expressive green eyes. One never had to wonder what she was thinking. Tristan preferred a woman with a bit of mystery to her. Anne had that in abundance.

"Hermione . . ."

"Yes, m'lord?"

He hated the anticipation shimmering off her.

He didn't want to hurt her, but neither could he abide with her following him around like a faithful pup. "You're a beautiful woman. But not for me."

Her face had started to beam with his first sentence, before it fell flat with the second.

"I don't understand," she said quietly.

"I enjoy dancing with you, but you will never have more than an occasional waltz with me."

"Are you tossing me over? It's Lady Anne, isn't it? You do feel something for her. But she is not worthy of you. She loved someone else. It was a grand love. Everyone spoke of it. It was legendary. You cannot compete with that. While I have always loved only you."

He barked out his laughter, then bit off the harsh sound at her crestfallen expression. "Hermione, you can't love me."

"But I do and it wounds my heart terribly—"

"You don't know me and if you did you wouldn't love me at all. I daresay, you'd probably not even like me very much." Did those same words apply to Anne? She certainly gave the impression that she liked him.

"You can't sway my feelings toward you. I know all I need to know."

He wanted to tell her to play a bit harder at getting caught. Every man enjoyed a challenge. Tristan also wanted to confess that he had killed, stolen, beaten, seduced. He was not one to settle down. He went where the winds blew him. At the moment they were blowing him toward Anne.

"—dinner tonight?"

Inwardly he groaned. Lady Hermione was prattling on again. He glanced over at her. She sat a horse well. She was beautiful. She would fall easily into his bed. Yet he had no interest in her whatsoever.

"My family would be so pleased if you would join us." She looked so hopeful. He didn't want to crush her spirit, but she was such a child that he couldn't in all good conscience lead her on. Taking advantage of the innocent had never been one of his sins.

"I already have plans for the evening, sweetheart."

"Tomorrow evening then."

"Have you considered that it will upset your father's digestion to share his table with me?"

"But I want you there and my father never denies me what I want."

Which explained some of her dogged determination. He wanted to be impressed by it. Instead, he was merely annoyed. "Lord Jameson would be a better choice."

"Lord Jameson? He is so terribly droll."

"But titled. More impressive than a second son."

With eyes twinkling, she laughed. "No one is more impressive than you, my lord."

He couldn't help but return her smile. Two years ago she had been a frustrating delight and, to his shame, he'd not minded using a bit of harmless flirtation to irritate the nobles who looked down on him and his brothers. It seemed that the devil that had sat on his shoulder then wanted his due.

Chapter 19

The only thing worse than watching a ticking clock was watching a window.

Sitting in a chair near said window, Anne knew it was ridiculous to waste her time wondering if Tristan would show. She hadn't liked watching him trot off with Lady Hermione—especially as he would have been trotting with her if her family hadn't approved Chetwyn escorting her to the park. For all she knew, perhaps he would be slipping into Lady Hermione's bedchamber tonight. She didn't want to acknowledge the queasiness that thought caused, but there it was—taunting her.

She wanted to shout out that he was hers, but he wasn't of course. She was little more than a passing fancy. Convenient on the ship. Convenient now with the dratted tree growing outside her window. She should have had the gardener chop it down when she returned home late this afternoon. That would certainly send a message to Tristan that his attentions weren't wanted.

But when she heard a faint scraping and saw a booted foot appearing over the window ledge, her gladness mocked her. Blast it! Why did she have to be so thrilled that he'd come to her?

He grinned right before he pulled her from the chair and covered her mouth with his, plowing his hands into her hair. She was vaguely aware of pins pinging as they hit the floor. Mostly she was lost in the sensations that his kiss invoked. Why did he have to be so skilled at causing her body to hum with so little effort?

But she wanted more than the physical. She wanted to mean something special to him. He was beginning to touch her heart and that terrified her. She broke free of the kiss and stepped away from him. "I suppose you'll be climbing into Lady Hermione's window next."

"Doubtful. She doesn't have a tree growing outside her window."

With a fury she'd not expected ripping through her, she pounded her balled fist into his shoulder. He snatched her wrist and jerked her to him, holding her near, their bodies pressed together. "Jealous, Princess?"

"Absolutely not."

Tenderness touched his eyes and he skimmed his fingers along her cheek. "She could have stairs leading to her window, and I'd still not go through it."

She despised the relief that swamped her. There

was no hope for her to have anything with him beyond this—a few nights of secreted lovemaking. He was not a man to be tied to shore. And she was not a woman who could go long unanchored.

She'd learned that lesson well enough after Walter's passing. She'd been too lost with no mooring.

Suddenly Tristan was kissing her once again, scattering her thoughts before they refocused on the sensations he elicited with such ease. She could almost imagine that she would have this for the remainder of her life. He dragged his heated mouth along her throat.

"I hated seeing you with him."

She knew of whom he spoke: Chetwyn. She dropped back her head, giving him easier access to the tender flesh. "He arranged the outing with Father. I couldn't very well say no."

"Say no next time," he demanded.

She heard herself murmuring her agreement to do just that. She thought he could have asked for her soul, and at that precise moment she'd have not argued before handing it over. When he was nibbling at the sensitive spot below her ear, he robbed her of strength, of will, of purpose. She felt buttons loosening, air cooling her dampened skin, and somehow it was enough to bring her round. Wrenching free of his hold, she stepped away.

"We can't do this. My father is still in residence, in his bedchamber, just down the hall. He wasn't feeling well this evening."

Mischief in his eyes, he took a step toward her. "We can be very quiet."

Oh, he was alluring. Temptation in human form. She forced herself to skitter over to the sofa. "No, I can't. I could never relax. I could never stop thinking that he might burst through the door at any moment. That somehow he would know." She shook her head briskly and crossed her arms over her chest. "You should probably go."

He glanced around, before bringing his gaze back to her. "I was disappointed this afternoon. I was very much looking forward to enjoying the park with you."

She sank on the arm of a chair. "I was disappointed as well. Since we've met nothing we've done seems to lean toward the normal. I suppose you could stay and we could visit for a bit, as long as we didn't laugh or speak in loud tones."

"We can kiss quietly."

She released a bitter laugh. "But that will lead to other things, you know it will. I am beginning to feel very much like a trollop."

Stepping nearer, he skimmed his rough knuckles over her cheek. "I don't treat you as I would a trollop. You must know that."

"But neither do you treat me as someone you were courting."

He swung away, toward the window, and it took every bit of pride she could muster not to call him back. She knew the words would strike at the heart of the differences between them. He wanted only now. She wanted forever.

He came to an abrupt halt. "I don't want to go, dammit. All day, I've thought of nothing save being here with you tonight. Even when Hermione was rhapsodizing on about bows on a bonnet"—he faced her—"all my thoughts were on you. I'm not ready to leave."

It was obvious he hated admitting that. She wondered if it was so terribly wrong of her to be so glad. "I noticed you had chess pieces in your quarters, so I assume you play. It's a rather quiet game that wouldn't get us noticed."

"Chess?"

"With a slight change to the rules."

"That I allow you to win? Play with only half my pieces?"

"I have enough confidence in my skill not to require that of you, but I thought it might prove interesting if when we capture a piece we are granted the privilege of asking something of the other, and then the other would be obliged to comply with the request."

He narrowed his eyes. "Such as?"

"Well, I might ask you to describe your favorite island."

"Seems innocent enough."

"Yes, quite, it will be. It'll provide an opportunity for us to get to know each other better."

His gaze leisurely traveled the length of her. "I know you quite well, Princess."

"My favorite color? My dearest friend?"

"Lilac. Lady Fayrehaven."

She stared at him open-mouthed. "How—"

"I'm quite observant."

She desperately wanted to be able to ask questions of him, which meant she needed to entice him into wanting to play by her rules. "Who gave me my first kiss?"

He grinned. "I accept your rule, but I'll add one of my own—whoever wins may demand a boon of the other."

The wicked glint in his eyes might have given her pause if she had ever lost to her brothers. She suspected he was going to be quite surprised to discover that she knew her way very well around a chessboard.

"I accept your rule. Wait here. I shall fetch my father's board and pieces." She hurried to the door, stopped, and looked back over her shoulder. "I'm so very glad you're staying."

"We'll see if you feel the same once I've beaten you"—his gaze slid to her bed—"and claimed my boon, with or without your father down the hall."

After two seconds of misgivings, she almost tossed a taunt back at him, but decided it would be much more fun to have him learn the hard way that beating her would not come easy, if it came at all.

She set up the chessboard on the carpet in front of the fireplace. While she'd been gone, Tristan had started a small fire to create a cozier atmosphere. Now the flames danced and crackled. She'd doused all the lamps. He suspected their game of chess might turn into a game of seduction, especially if he had his way. He thought she knew him, but if she did she'd have not asked him to stay. He wanted her again; he intended to have her before dawn.

They were three moves in before she took his pawn and rolled it saucily between her fingers. "How did you acquire your ship?"

Not at all what he was expecting. It was a fairly innocent question, and yet he hesitated. He never spoke of his life on the sea, had already revealed far more of it to her than he ever had to anyone else. He studied her for a moment before answering, "I stole it from pirates."

"Truly?" Her eyes were wide, and for a moment innocent. He wished he'd known her before her life had been touched by sadness. He wished he could play with the earnestness that she desired, but he had little patience for it—perhaps because much of his life had been simply a game. Hide where no one can find you. Be someone that no one will recognize. Bury everything deep, reveal nothing. Be as a phantom.

Through the years, he had created tales about himself. Not that he ever spread them, but he thought if anyone should ever ask . . . and here she was asking. But he couldn't give her the fictional world of Captain Crimson Jack. So he told her the truth.

"No. I won it playing cards."

"A man would actually bet his ship on the chance of a random draw being in his favor?"

He shrugged. "He wanted the money that was sitting in the center of the table."

"Did you cheat?"

"You'll have to take another piece before I'll answer that." He watched the way she scrutinized him, saw the disappointment flicker in her eyes, and knew it had nothing to do with his not answering, but with her accurately deducing the truth. He had cheated, dammit. But then so had the men with whom he'd been playing. The encounter hadn't been so much about the cards but about how well a man could manipulate them without being caught. As with all things, he was very skilled with manipulation. Hadn't he gotten her aboard his ship when she had decided she didn't want to be there?

"You renamed it *Revenge*."

She hadn't asked it as a question, and he was feeling magnanimous so he replied, "Yes."

Two moves later he captured one of her pawns. "Remove your bodice."

She narrowed those lovely eyes, pursed those succulent lips that he was aching to kiss. "The rules are that you ask a question—"

"Those are not the terms you laid out. You said I could ask of you what I would and you would comply."

She scoffed. "Yes, but—" Then huffed. "Anyone of any intelligence would know what I meant."

"I have no interest in playing a game of questions."

"Have you no interest in me beyond my body?"

He merely arched a brow and quirked up a corner of his mouth in answer.

"I know. You're a man. Of course, you're interested in only my body."

She was upset with him, but she held up to her end of the bargain, even if she nearly ripped off a button doing it. He did want to know the particulars about her but that was so dangerous, more dangerous than having her in his bed. It would create a bond, a deeper intimacy—

Who in the bloody hell did he think he was fooling? The intimacy had been forged in tears when he'd knelt beside her at the British cemetery, and what remained of his heart had nearly shattered alongside hers.

She made her move, garnered no captives, and while it was not very wise strategically, he snatched up another one of her pawns.

"I suppose a corset," she said sharply.

He'd been considering a shoe, saving the best for last. Instead he heard himself ask, "What became of your mother?"

She might have looked less surprised if he'd said, "By the by, I normally wear women's clothing when I prance about the ship."

"She passed," she finally said. "Three years ago. Influenza. Father had a fondness for her. I don't know if he loved her. He barely adjusted his stride."

Tristan didn't like the thought that popped into his head: if he discovered tomorrow that she had died, he'd have no stride to adjust because the devastation of learning she was no longer in the world would drop him to his knees. These were odd feelings, only for now, only while he was in her presence. Once he was back on the sea, they would leave him. He needed them to leave him. How could he concentrate on his charts, the stars, the storms if he was constantly thinking of her?

"I believe that's the reason he lost patience with my mourning," she continued. "It must have been completely incomprehensible to him that I could have been sad and melancholy for so long over someone to whom I was never married."

"Are you still sad and melancholy?" He didn't think so, but then he held a tight leash on his emotions.

She gave him an impish smile. "You'll need to take another piece if you want me to answer that question."

As she positioned her knight, he considered that perhaps she had answered it. Would her eyes be sparkling with such mischievousness if she were still sad over her betrothed's passing? Would she be entertaining Tristan now, matching each of his moves with skill and cunning?

And she was entertaining him, but then she always did. From the moment she'd walked into the tavern from the rain, she kept him on his toes, challenged him, intrigued him, made him resent the moment when she would walk away. Everything about her fascinated him. She could be doing little more than sitting there breathing and he was content to watch her.

She grabbed his rook, let her gaze travel over him, and his muscles tensed as he wondered what item of clothing she'd have him remove. Now the game was definitely going to begin to get interesting.

"When you were a boy," she began, "before you left Pembrook, when you thought of your future, what did you see yourself becoming as a man?"

Another damned question? He'd been halfway toward his buttons. "I'm the second son of a nobleman; I didn't give it a good deal of thought. My options were few."

"But they were still there," she insisted. "Were you going to be a gentleman of leisure? A clergyman—"

"One must believe in God to serve his parishioners."

Her brow furrowed deeply, until he wanted to reach across and smooth it out. "How can you not? With the wonders you've seen—"

"Changing your question, Princess?"

She snapped her mouth closed in a mulish expression. "No."

It had been a long time, a very long time since he'd thought about his youth. As a rule he never let his thoughts drift farther back than the night they ran away. He stretched out on his side and rose up on an elbow to give himself time to arrange his memories. What had he planned? By fourteen, surely he had some inkling as to what he would do.

"You've chastised me before for discussing finances, but our estate provides a very nice income. Part of the reason Uncle no doubt wanted it. I would have had an allowance. I suppose I would have been a good deal like your brothers: drinking, gambling, seeking out the ladies." He shrugged. "Much as I do now. Only now I have my own coins to toss about. And I would probably dismiss anyone who was not like me."

Would he look at Mouse and see a cripple, instead of the potential for what he might be? Would he look at Peterson and see a lumbering hulk instead of a man who would protect his back at any cost? Would he see only Jenkin's surliness and not a man who was hiding secrets, much as he once had?

"My brothers do have a rather narrow view of the world, don't they?" She arched a brow. "That wasn't a question, it was merely rhetorical. But I can't see you being like them."

Neither could he. He knocked over her bishop. "Take off your left shoe."

He didn't like where the questions were going. He didn't want her to pry into his soul, his past, his regrets. He didn't want to consider what he might have missed out on, what he might have gained.

Doing as he bid, she tossed the shoe at him. He caught it easily, studied it, concentrated on what he knew from holding her feet in the palms of his hands. He wanted them there now instead of the distance of this board between them. "You have such small feet. However do you walk on them?"

"You took only one piece, Captain."

"Is that who I am tonight?" he asked. "The captain?"

She scrutinized him. "Aren't the captain and Lord Tristan one in the same?"

No, he was comfortable as the captain. Knew his place, his role, his destinations. He had goals, dreams for what he would accomplish. Lord Tristan—it was as though he no longer existed.

He'd attended a ball for the sole purpose of dancing with one lady. Did gentlemen go because they wanted to be there? She made a move, he took a pawn. "Do your brothers enjoy attending balls?"

"I'm not certain they enjoy them so much as tolerate them." As though understanding what he was truly asking, she added, "Chetwyn seems to enjoy them but then he's hunting for a wife."

"Will he make a good husband?"

She hesitated, and he knew she was trying to decide whether to stick to their rules of one question per piece, but then she said, "Yes, I believe he will."

She boldly moved out her queen. He ignored it for a pawn. That was the piece's purpose after all. To provide fodder, distraction, sacrifice. "Why?"

Anne wasn't certain what she'd expected to accomplish when she suggested this game. She knew she wasn't ready for him to leave. Perhaps she'd hoped to learn more about the mysterious particulars that surrounded him. But his latest question flummoxed her. To compare Chetwyn to Tristan was to compare an unfolding blossom to a raging storm. In both there was beauty, power, something to be appreciated. But they were hardly the same. She had tasted a storm. Could she be content with a rose?

She cleared her throat. "He's kind."

Reaching across, he trailed his finger over her hand where it rested in her lap. "Many men are kind."

"He's generous." Then she realized—

"I'm comfortable with him. I never have to measure my words."

"Or your actions."

"A lady must always measure her actions." She balled her hand into a fist, moved it beyond his touch because she was growing warm. "I don't always measure them with you."

"Do you regret that?"

She hated the stupid game, the questions it was eliciting. She wished she'd never suggested it. She shook her head. "No, I would not take back a single moment but neither would I boast about it. I should hope that you wouldn't either."

"Your secrets are safe with me."

"As yours are with me." She moved her queen. "Have you a secret you wish to share?"

"I didn't notice you capturing a piece."

"Tristan, you don't have to take the rules of the game so literally."

"Well, then there is something I want to share, but you must never tell."

"I won't. I've already promised. You can trust me."

Leaning across the board, he cupped her face with one hand and steadied himself with the other. He stroked her chin, circled his thumb around her mouth. "No one knows this, not even my brothers."

Gazing into his eyes, she could see the seriousness there. "Tell me."

He pressed his cheek to hers. She heard him
breathing in her scent. His lips toyed with her
lobe, before he whispered, "I am very, very skilled
at chess. Checkmate."

"What? No!" Shoving him back, she stared at
the board. He'd somehow managed to move his
bishop into position while leaning toward her. He
had her.

"My boon," he said. "Meet me in the mews tomorrow at midnight. We're going to the ship."

"I'm not sailing—"

"It'll stay moored. You, however, shall journey
into the land of pleasure."

She contemplated not living up to her end of the
bargain. He'd obviously cheated, because she
didn't lose at chess, ever, but she couldn't determine how he'd managed to do it. By distracting
her, she supposed.

Wearing her pelisse with the hood raised over
her head, she slipped out into the night. It was far
easier than she'd anticipated, but she'd taken no
more than a half-dozen steps when Tristan was
beside her.

"I thought we were going to meet in the mews,"
she whispered.

"I couldn't wait to be near you again."

Oh, he was such a flirtatious devil, and yet he
sounded incredibly sincere. Her weak heart chose

to believe in the sincerity. Before she knew it they were in an enclosed carriage traveling through the streets. He sat beside her, his hand wrapped around hers. The intimacy of it astounded her. Chetwyn had done the same and yet this, somehow, seemed more profound, not nearly as casual. Perhaps because she knew what awaited her on his ship.

She was rather surprised that he wasn't devouring her within the quiet confines of the carriage, yet neither could she deny the mounting anticipation.

"Will you attend other balls this Season?" she asked.

"Only if you're there."

"You're so flirtatious."

"I've never said anything to you that I didn't mean."

She looked over at him, lost in the shadows. They'd not lit the lantern inside the carriage, which made their clandestine meeting seem even more forbidding. "I suppose, being with you now that I can no longer deny we're lovers. Have you had many?"

She sensed a stillness in him. If possible, he'd gone even quieter. Finally, he said, "I believe you're my first."

"Lover?" she scoffed. "Now I know you lie."

With the hand not holding hers, he cradled her face and she was immensely grateful for the shadows now. She didn't want him to see how his words sliced.

"I've been with women, Anne. I've never denied that. But the trysts with each of them were few, and there was never this undeniable yearning that no other woman would do. If you had decided not to come with me tonight, I'd have not sought solace with another because I've no doubt the encounter would have been lacking simply because she wasn't you. The words sound trite when spoken. And false. But for whatever reason, you are the only one who appeals to me at this moment."

At this moment. But what of the next? she wanted to ask. How many moments would she intrigue him? How many before he'd had his fill and would look for greener pastures—or in his case, she supposed, bluer water? Yet even as the doubts assailed her, she couldn't deny the truth of what she was feeling. "I know I should be ashamed of my behavior and yet I can't seem to regret it."

"For which I'm incredibly grateful."

She saw him flash a smile in the darkness. Or perhaps she only imagined seeing it. Still she knew it was there. In spite of all he'd suffered, he'd not lost the ability to smile, and that was part of his appeal. He didn't mope about wishing that his life had taken different turns. Instead, he forged ahead on the path that had been set before him.

She wondered if that was part of the reason that her brothers and the other lords didn't like him. They couldn't force him to fit into their world, and they feared they'd find themselves lacking if faced with the challenges that had confronted him. He'd been a boy, younger than Mouse, metaphorically thrown to the sharks.

When they stepped out of the carriage she tried

to imagine what it might have been like those many years ago. With her arm wrapped securely around his, as they walked among crates littering the dock, she asked, "Were you frightened?"

"Pardon?"

"When you were put on your first ship. Were you frightened?"

Occasional lanterns fought to hold the darkness at bay, and she could see the harsh lines of his face. How different they might have been with a less adventuresome life.

"Terrified," he finally said in a clipped voice.

"And yet you went."

"Because it was more frightening to stay."

"You must have been so lonely."

"It was long ago, Anne. Nothing is to be gained by revisiting it."

"But I want to understand you."

"I am as you see me."

But he had been shaped by the past. She suspected it influenced him still.

"Still, I would like very much—"

Suddenly he shoved her away from him. She staggered back, her unceremonious landing softened by a pile of coiled rope. She stared up in horror as four men descended on Tristan like ravenous dogs. Screaming for help crossed her mind, but she feared she'd only distract him from his purpose and draw attention to herself. She glanced around for a weapon, but she saw nothing that she could use. All she had were her fists, her teeth, her feet. She could punch, claw, bite, kick but would she be more hindrance than help if she leapt into the fray?

Still she readied herself for the opportunity when she could strike.

Grunts, the sound of flesh slapping against flesh, harsh curses filled the air. She'd expected Tristan to go down, to be beaten. Instead, he remained standing, tossing a man one way, pounding a fist into another's jaw, sending him spiraling back. A kick into the stomach. A duck. A swing. A hit. Dancing away. Charging.

Dear Lord, even when fighting, he was poetry in motion.

One man ran away. Another limped into the darkness. The other two lay sprawled on the dock.

Breathing harshly, Tristan knelt beside her and tenderly touched her cheek. "Are you all right?" he asked, as though she'd been the one caught in the fracas.

In the dim light, she could see a dark oozing along the side of his beloved face. "You're bleeding."

"It's nothing. Are you hurt? Can you stand?"

"I'm perfectly fine." Not so fine she realized as he slipped a hand beneath her elbow and helped her to her feet. Her knees were weak and she was trembling. She forced herself to remain standing when she dearly wanted to sit.

With his arm at her back, his hand clamped on her waist, he guided her along the creaking dock.

"Who were they?" she managed to ask.

"Troublemakers."

"That much was obvious. But what did they want?"

"They mistook me for a gentleman and thought to rob us."

"But why?"

"Sorry, Princess. I didn't think to invite them to tea in order to determine their motives."

The words stung but she knew his impatience had nothing to do with her. She wondered if she'd not been there if he might have finished them all off.

They reached his ship. Once aboard, they were met by a surprised Jenkins.

"Cap'n, wasn't expectin' you tonight."

"Double the watch, then fetch us some warm water. We ran into some ruffians up to some mischief." He leaned in and said something she couldn't hear.

The sailor nodded perfunctorily. "Aye, Cap'n."

Tristan led her down the stairs to his quarters. Once the door was closed behind them, she rounded on him. "What if they had killed you?"

He grinned. "That wasn't likely to happen."

"You're not invincible."

"No, but I'm quite good in a fight." He strode over to the corner table where he housed his spirits and poured two generous glasses. He offered her one. "This'll take the edge off."

She downed a huge gulp, grateful for the burning in her eyes that covered the tears threatening to spill. "How can you be so calm?"

"I've been in my share of brawls, Anne. I can hold my own."

She rolled her eyes at his arrogance. Did he not comprehend—

"You did quite well," he added.

She glared at him. "I sat there like a ninny and offered no help whatsoever—"

"Most women would have been screaming, crying, distracting me from my purpose." He tucked some stray strands of hair behind her ear. "But not you. You were stoic and brave."

"I was useless."

"Never." He stared into her eyes with admiration and she wondered how he could make her feel courageous when she'd been anything but.

The light rap on the door had them separating. He opened it and retrieved a large bowl from Jenkins before dismissing him. He set the bowl on the table and picked up a towel.

"Sit down," she ordered. "I'll see to your wound."

She expected him to object. Instead, he sat. She angled a chair nearer to him and eased into it. After dipping the cloth into the warm water, she gently lifted the hair from his brow and began dabbing at the gash. He barely flinched.

"It doesn't look deep, but there's so much blood," she said.

"There always is with a wound to the face."

"Have you had many?"

He shrugged.

She pressed the cloth to the wound, hoping to staunch the flow of blood. "Do you often brawl?"

"Not as often as I did in my youth. I don't start the fights any longer, but I don't back down from them either."

"You live a very dangerous life."

He said nothing, and that was answer enough. Walter had as well. Before Tristan left England's shores, she would have to end things permanently with him. It would be lonely enough waiting for his return, but it would be unbearable wondering if he would *ever* return. He could be dead for years before word reached her.

"Why would you choose it? This life you lead?"

"Because it makes me feel alive. I never know what adventures await over the horizon."

"But your brother has reclaimed his title. You don't have to keep wandering."

"I enjoy wandering, Princess."

Moving her hand aside, he came to his feet and drew her up until her hips were pressed against his. "What we encountered tonight was rare. I don't know why they were skulking about the docks, although I've sent Jenkins out to have a word with the two who are sprawled on the ground—if they're still there. If my uncle were alive I'd suspect him of sending them to do me harm. But he's long gone. I suspect you and I just happened to be in the wrong place at the wrong time. But let's not let it dissuade us from our purpose in coming here. If anything, let it make us appreciate that we *are* here."

His mouth blanketed hers. Images and thoughts of lurking rapscallions, blood, danger, fear all melted away as his eager hands and hungry lips quickly carried her away on a tide of pleasure. She could hardly credit her wantonness. It seemed to take so little effort on his part to have her desperate for what they could share.

With unbridled haste, their clothes were in a discarded pool on the floor and they were on the bed in a feverish tangle. She thought she would never tire of the velvety warmth of skin against skin. It seemed, since she now knew his body so well, that all should be familiar and yet she always discovered something new: a small mole on his left hip, toes that weren't quite straight, a tiny scar just above his elbow, bronzed flesh above his hips, ivory below.

His body hinted at tales that she suspected he would never tell. He might say that the past didn't matter, but if he truly believed it, why not talk about it? He revealed bits of himself like the flowing tides. He would give her an inkling of what his life had been like and then he would retreat.

But here, in his bed, when they made love, he held nothing back. He touched her with reverence, worshipped her, taunted her, mollified her. Each time they came together, she became bolder—exploring every inch of him, marveling at the various textures. She ran her hands over him with abandon while relishing his doing the same to her.

He flipped her onto her stomach, grabbed her wrists, and carried her arms above her head. Provocatively, he moved her hair aside.

"Tristan."

"Shh." He kissed his way along her spine while she emitted languid sighs. He nipped her backside. "You have dimples you know."

"When I smile? I think not."

He laughed. "No, here." Releasing his hold on

her wrists, he planted a kiss just below the small of her back, first on one side, then the other. "I like them."

"Is there anything about the female form that you don't like?"

"There's nothing about *you* that I don't like." He flopped onto his back before gathering her close and easing her over him until she was straddling him, her hair forming a curtain that enclosed them until all they could see was each other. Plowing his hands through the thick strands, he brought her mouth down to his and kissed her thoroughly. Oranges and brandy. She could taste neither without thinking of him. Tart and rich. Seductive.

But then everything about him was.

He bracketed her hips, lifted her up, adjusted his position, and brought her down, stretching her, filling her. She scraped her nails over his chest, watched his eyes smolder, before leaning down and running her tongue around a nipple. She nipped at it.

He groaned, low and long. "You are a witch."

One with power that she'd never considered she might possess. She began rocking, and now she was the one to moan as the center of their joining reawakened to pleasure. So good. So good. The reality of it was always so much better than the memory. Each coming together never seemed to be quite the same. The intensity caused her entire body to curl in on itself, to strain outward, to cavort inwardly. She always wondered how she would survive the sensations, and yet she did.

From her position above him, she had a clear view of the tension radiating through him. It served to spur her to greater heights. Cupping her breasts, he kneaded the pliant flesh, scraping his thumbs over the sensitive pearls that had hardened with his touch.

Snaking his arm around her, holding her in place, he sat up and captured her mouth, hungrily exploring as though he'd never kissed her before. She scraped her fingers into his hair, careful of his fresh wound. His chest brushed against her breasts, titillating, increasing her pleasure. The musky fragrance of their lovemaking rose up around them.

Then they were both crying out, arching back, clinging to each other as sensations tore through them. Spots of color danced behind her eyelids. When she opened her eyes, it was to see his taut jaw, his fiery gaze. She kissed his forehead, his chin. He sank back onto the pillows and she collapsed on top of him.

She thought it likely that she would never move a muscle again.

Stretched out, one arm behind his head, Tristan watched as Anne wandered his quarters, picking up items, setting them back down, moving on. After nearly destroying him with their lovemaking, she'd donned his shirt. He enjoyed the way it left so much of her legs bared, legs that had squeezed his hips and thighs as she'd carried him to new heights. "Didn't you have enough of examining my things when you were here before?"

With slumberous eyes that caused his body to tighten, she glanced over at him. "I looked but I didn't touch."

He arched a brow in disbelief. "You didn't touch anything?"

"It felt as though it would be invading your privacy."

"And it doesn't seem so now?"

"Now I don't care. Now I want to know everything about you."

"Didn't you get enough with your infernal questions last night?"

"I suspect a lifetime of questioning you wouldn't be enough," she said distractedly, lifting the lopsided globe from his shelf and examining it.

A lifetime. He could imagine all the questions he'd ask her. He still didn't know who had given her that first kiss. He hadn't asked because if it wasn't her betrothed he might have to kill the fellow.

"Did you make this?" she asked. "Was it to commemorate your travels?"

"Yes. No."

She jerked her head toward him. "Pardon?"

"You asked two questions. I answered them."

"You're being difficult."

"Come back to bed."

"Not until you tell me about the globe, why you're not more forthcoming with information about it."

He sighed. Had he ever met a more stubborn

woman? "I made it for my brother. He seems to collect them for some reason."

"Keswick?"

"No, Rafe. My younger brother."

"Was he at the ball?"

"No, he prefers . . . the darker corners of London."

"Why?"

He couldn't stop the regret from seeping into his voice. "I don't know."

Carefully, she set the globe back on the shelf before gliding quickly but quietly over to him and settling on the edge of the bed. She combed her fingers through his hair. "I can't imagine how awful it was to be separated from your brothers. Mine often irritate the devil out of me, but I know they mean well and that they are always within easy reach if I need something. Even when I was in mourning and wouldn't come to London, I had only to send a missive and they were quickly at my side."

"I don't want to talk about the past. Or the future for that matter. I just want now." He planted his hand behind her head and pulled her down for a kiss. When he was with her, the past barely mattered. He could forget about how awful it had been to be separated from his brothers, his family, from everything familiar. From the moment he'd galloped away from Pembrook, he'd sworn that he would never complain, whine, or cry about the unfairness of life. He'd buried deeply anything that could hurt him, because it had very nearly de-

stroyed him to leave all that he loved. He'd built a
wall so nothing could ever touch him again, nothing could ever harm him.

He was his own man: independent, strong.

Yet this mere slip of a woman was working to
find a crack in his defenses. He couldn't allow it
to happen. Never again would he be vulnerable.
Never again would he open himself up to hurt.
She, of all people, should understand how easily
the heart bruised.

Together they could share passion, their bodies . . .
but beyond that, he had nothing else to give.

It was nearing dawn when Anne found herself
again in the carriage, hurtling through the London
streets. The curtains were drawn at the windows so
no one could see her, but she picked up the sounds
of morning activity, people beginning their day. If
fortune were smiling on her, her father and brothers would already be home and abed in a liquor-
induced haze.

As for herself, her haze was pleasure induced.
She was nestled against Tristan, his arm around
her shoulders, his hand absently stroking the side
of her breast while he nuzzled her ear.

"We can't continue on with these trysts," she
said quietly.

"Mmm," he murmured. "I'll change your mind
tonight."

"No, Tristan." Moving away, she turned and
faced him. She saw mostly shadows and yet she

was familiar enough with him now to sense his gaze on her. "I am determined to find a husband this Season, to please my father, to see to my duty. It was the reason behind my trip to Scutari, so I could say good-bye to Walter and accept another man's attentions with a clear conscience."

"I would say you accomplished your goal since you're accepting my attentions easily enough."

She heard the fissure of irritation in his voice. Unfortunately, a spark of annoyance was riffling through her as well. She'd not have him toss into her face what they'd shared. "But we both know it comes with no permanence. It would be unfair to any gentleman who might be courting me if I were to continue with these . . . encounters—as lovely as they are."

"Lovely? Princess, you can no more keep your hands from me than I can keep mine from you. Hot, torrid, wild, yes. But lovely indicates a tameness that doesn't exist between us."

Oh, yes, he was getting angry, addressing her as Princess rather than her name. But she knew it was his pride talking now, not any deep feelings that might be wounded with her departure. "Please, let's not squabble. There can never be anything more between us than what we've shared."

"Oh, I think there could be much more between us. We've only had a few nights when we could have a thousand."

"But nothing permanent. You'll grow bored and sail away—"

"Then keep me from becoming bored."

She laughed at the ludicrousness of it. "Answer me truthfully. If you were not to lose interest in me, would you stay in England . . . forever?"

"It's not that simple. I'm the captain of a ship."

"So you'll leave?"

"Of course I'll leave."

"So I can't hold you here—even if I'm perpetually entertaining."

He cursed harshly. "I need the sea. I can only stand being landlocked for so long and then I'll go mad. But you could come with me—"

"No, I can't. I'm not an adventurer. I want security, children, a home. Tristan, I want what you can't give me."

"You want what I can give you in my bed. You're mad for it."

"No. Yes, all right. I do want it, but we cannot always have what we want. Sometimes we must say no, no matter how difficult. It is what is proper. It is our duty. When a gentleman calls on me, I must be able to look him in the eye, face him squarely, and not suffer from guilt because when he leaves I'll be sneaking off with someone else."

"Don't feel guilty. Men don't."

"Women are held to a higher standard. Doesn't make it fair, but that's the way of it. I can't encourage a man to seek my affections when I'm giving them to someone else. Perhaps you have the ability to hold your heart separate when joined in intimacy with another, but I can't."

It was as close as she dared come to admitting that she was beginning to have strong feelings for him. As her words seemed to have left him mute, she could only assume that what he shared with her never went beyond the physical. She had suspected it of course, but a part of her had held out hope that she might be wrong.

On the other hand it made severing things between them so much easier. She settled back against the seat but not against him. He didn't move to hold her or to take her hand. With each clop of horses' hooves, she felt the chasm widening between them.

She'd been a distraction, an evening's entertainment.

She'd not regret what they'd shared. But that didn't mean that she didn't find herself wishing she could have more.

When the carriage came to a halt, he stepped out and handed her down. She drew the hood of her pelisse over her head, hoping no one would spot and recognize her. He walked beside her until they were almost to the house.

"I can go on my own from here," she said quietly.

"Anne, I want to see you again."

Swallowing hard, she turned to face him. "Not in my bedchamber or on your ship. I'm quite determined that from this moment forward I shall behave properly. If you care for me at all, you'll honor my wishes."

"I've never liked a woman as much as I like you," he said.

"Such poetic words. Careful, you'll have me swooning."

A corner of his mouth hitched up, then settled back into a firm line. "Meet me in Hyde Park this afternoon. Ride with me, as we'd planned before Chetwyn interfered."

How she dearly wanted to. "He didn't realize he was interfering. Besides, I can't. Not today. I have a garden party to attend." Then before she thought things through, she added, "You should come."

"I doubt an invitation has been extended to me."

"It's being held by Lady Fayrehaven—whom you correctly identified as my dearest friend. She won't mind that I invited you. Besides, I can't see you as being a man waiting for something as paltry as an invitation if you want to be somewhere. Belgrave Square." She gave him the address. "At two. Unless of course you're afraid."

"Whatever would I have to fear—an attack by the roses?"

"Then you'll be there. Splendid."

Before he could correct her assumption, she turned, skipped up the steps, and entered the house through the servant's quarters. She knew it un-likely that he would be there. Still she could hope.

Chapter 20

"**Y**ou did what? Have you lost your mind?" Sarah asked.

Anne wondered if perhaps she had. "I doubt he'll come."

They were standing just off the terrace so Sarah could greet her guests as they arrived.

"But if he does, Fayrehaven will have an absolute cow."

"Are there un-absolute cows, I wonder?" Anne asked. "Might he have one of those instead?"

"Anne, honestly. You don't understand what you've done."

"Relax, Sarah. He might not even be here any longer. He keeps saying that he's going to sail away. Perhaps he has by now." She wouldn't put it past him in order to make a point that he wouldn't be bullied into doing something that he didn't want to do.

"I heard he approached you and Chetwyn at the park."

"Are we all the gossip then?"

"Apparently so, yes."

Anne sighed. "I'd arranged to meet Tristan at the park but then Father arranged for me to go with Chetwyn. One could hardly blame Tristan for approaching and voicing some disappointment."

"Tristan? Such informality. You'd best take care that others don't hear you referring to him in that manner."

"Oh, Sarah, we seem to care about such trivial things."

"Yes, well, those trivial things lead to a good marriage, and speaking of, I see that Lord Chetwyn has just arrived. And look at how he smiles now that he's spotted you. I daresay, I think he *has* set his cap for you. Come with me to welcome him. I'm fairly certain he can take your mind off this Lord Tristan."

Unfortunately, Anne very much doubted it.

The very last thing that Lord Tristan Easton thought he would ever be doing was attending a garden party. Yet there he was, standing by the rhododendrons, feeling very much out of his element. Give him a ferocious storm on the high seas any day compared with this maze of etiquette and proper behavior.

He'd been forced to ask Mary what to wear to such an event, which had resulted in her arching a brow in speculation. He'd been halfway tempted to tell her about Anne, to hear her advice on dealing with a troublesome woman, but what was Anne's crime? Denying him her bed. If he was planning to marry her, he'd admire her for it. As it was, he was merely frustrated—or he would be by night's end. So he'd held his tongue, left Mary none the wiser, and prodded her again for assistance on his attire. Having spent a good part of her youth in a convent, she'd been of little help and suggested only that he not be too formal. "What you might wear to the park."

At least he'd gotten that part right.

He'd arrived late because he wasn't certain he wanted to come. What he was certain of was that he wanted to see Anne again, and she'd issued her blasted challenge, one similar to the one he'd delivered when he wanted to entice her into climbing the mast. She'd implied he was a coward. Blast her to hell. The woman stood toe-to-toe with him, never backing down—something no other female of his acquaintance had ever done. His other partners had been content to romp about in bed. Anne wanted to romp elsewhere.

He'd spied her as soon as the butler had shown him into the garden. She was holding a mallet, attempting to strike a ball so it went through a metal archway. She wore a lilac dress with a high neck that was buttoned all the way to her chin. He understood why that shade was her favorite. It went well with her fair complexion. The dress had long sleeves that ballooned out from shoulder to elbow, then narrowed down into a snug fit against her skin. Gloves covered her hands. She wore a small hat, brim down on one side, up on the other.

He wanted to march over and tell the three gents standing around her that he knew what she looked like with all those buttons undone. He knew the silkiness of her skin that all that clothing hid. He had peeled off her gloves, peeled off her dress, peeled off everything.

Without even bothering to glance around, he knew she was the most beautiful lady here. It didn't matter what anyone else looked like. To him, she was exquisite. The way the sun lightly danced over her face, trying to chase off the shadows provided by her hat. The way she moved with such lithesome grace. He'd experienced her elegance when they'd clambered to the crow's nest and when he had her in his bed. But here with an audience, she was poised. She belonged here, and he wished to hell that she didn't.

She gave one of the gents—Chetwyn, he recalled—a playful slap before directing her attention to the blue ball at her feet. She lightly tapped it. It rolled along the green grass, hit the side of the arch, and came to a stop without going through. She craned back her head and laughed, the sweet trilling traveling across the garden to touch him as though she were right beside him. She was more comfortable today, here in the garden, than she'd been at the ball. Perhaps because that night had been her first public event since going into mourning. She was settling in now, and he could see that this was her world. She moved about it with the same ease that he swaggered over his ship.

She said something to Chetwyn. With a slight bow he moved in behind her—

Tristan clenched his back teeth, tightened his hands into fists, and growled low. He didn't think he'd been loud, but she suddenly jerked up her head and looked in his direction. With a soft smile to Chetwyn, a word to the other gents, mallet in hand, she began striding across the green and he wondered briefly if she was coming to deliver a blow to his head for disturbing her game.

Then she smiled brightly at him as though she was truly happy to see him, and he felt a sharp stab of pain in his chest. He would do anything to keep that smile on her face, and that made him want to leave because he'd never cared so much in his life about the ridiculous parting of the lips, revealing of the teeth.

"You came," she said softly.

"You are quite astute, Princess."

Her smile diminished and he wanted to kick himself for the harshness in his tone. Could he sound any less charming? Maybe she should hit him with the mallet. Good and hard.

"You're not comfortable," she said.

"You seem to have quite the round of admirers."

"Jealous, then."

Why should he be jealous? He'd tasted what they hadn't and would again if he so desired. He so desired, dammit. Two minutes after leaving her company, he wanted to be back with her. He didn't know what to make of this strange obsession. "I think coming here was a mistake. I should probably go."

"Turning cowardly, already?"

He gave her a look that normally quelled rambunctious men—men much heftier than she—into behaving. She merely angled her chin defiantly.

"It's only because you don't know everyone," she said patiently. "Let me introduce you around." Gliding over, she slipped her arm around his.

"Keeping the mallet?" he asked.

"Never know when I might have to use it on a hard head. In particular, yours."

He couldn't help the grin that tugged up the corners of his mouth. Her eyes were sparkling with teasing. She nudged her shoulder against his arm. "I'm glad you're here."

He realized with a sudden unequivocal certainty that he would walk through hell for her. No doubt he was about to do just that.

Anne began with Chetwyn because she knew that, like Walter, he possessed a kindness and wasn't likely to give a cut direct. That she couldn't rely on her brothers to be charming was a sad state of affairs. She was quite aware of the two who had come—Jameson and Stephan—shooting daggers at Tristan. Based on his cocky grin and swagger, she was rather certain he was mindful of it as well.

She supposed she couldn't blame them for keeping their distance. Confidence radiated off him, and his command of himself and those around him was evident in his mien. In his presence, everything—everyone—dwarfed. Just as they had on his ship, as they did in her bedchamber. It wasn't because he was a lumbering giant. Because he wasn't. It was quite simply that he was so self-possessed. He'd been on his own since he was fourteen. In years, he was no older than Jameson, but in life's experiences, her brother had no hope of ever catching up.

Until this moment she wasn't quite certain she'd realized all that. What could he possibly talk to these men about that he wouldn't find trivial? The weather? When they complained of the light drizzle while he had survived nature's fury? A trip to the seaside when he had walked along shores that possibly weren't even marked on a map?

She wanted to tell her brothers to stand at his side, that he possessed a goodness. But her brothers would only accuse her of becoming starry-eyed. Perhaps she had. She knew only that her heart had soared when she spotted him lurking beside the rhododendrons. He'd come when she knew he didn't want to, so perhaps she meant a tad more than a bit of bed sport to him.

"I remember my father speaking of a visit he made to Pembrook," Chetwyn said, sipping on the champagne that the footmen were serving. "I seem to recall he had a jolly good time fishing while there."

If she hadn't spent so much time in Tristan's company, she wasn't certain she would have noticed the subtle start of surprise that appeared in his eyes and was gone in a blink. She wondered if it was because he hadn't expected Chetwyn to be so cordial or if he was remembering a happier time.

"Yes," he finally said. "We have a pond. It was once well stocked with fish. I spent many an hour sitting with father, waiting for them to bite."

"Is that why you love being out on the water?" she asked, striving to keep the conversation on an even keel.

"I love the sea because it provided me with a safe haven when mine was taken from me." Although she had been the one to ask the question, he directed a challenging glare to Chetwyn as though he expected him to argue against the claim.

"I never much cared for Lord David," Chetwyn said. "He seemed to be rather too full of himself."

For the second time Tristan seemed taken aback. But before he could respond, Chetwyn added, "If you'll excuse me, I need to have a word with Fayrehaven. Lady Anne, don't think I've forgotten that we've yet to finish our game."

She smiled. "You were giving me such a sound thrashing that I was hoping you would forget."

He winked at her, brushing her elbow lightly and quickly with his fingers. "Later, m'dear."

He strolled away as though he had no cares, and she wondered if Tristan would ever be as at ease. Even that first night when he'd been slouched in his chair at the tavern, he'd possessed an alertness, as though he could enter into the thick of a brawl with a second's notice.

"I didn't think to ask earlier, but how is your head?" she asked.

A wicked gleam came into his pale eyes and she suspected he was going to say something bawdy. Perhaps he thought better of it, because his words were innocent enough. "Much improved."

He shifted his attention back to where Chetwyn had departed. "Was your fiancé like him?"

Now she was the one startled. "Like Chetwyn? Very much so, yes. They were brothers after all."

"I'm nothing at all like my brothers."

"At your core, I suspect you are. Did you all fish with your father?"

"We did. God, I haven't thought of that in years. Father was a large man—or at least he seemed so when I was small. His presence diminished everything around him. He was bold, strong, invincible. As grand as Pembrook. But at the pond, I would stand beside him and . . ."

She watched his throat work as he swallowed. "And what?" she prodded.

"Suppose you teach me to play croquet."

She'd rather pursue what had brought the melancholy to his eyes. She hoped it was tender memories, knew that even the fondest of reminiscences could bring a hint of sadness for the moments remembered, and those lost. He had lost so much. She was rather certain he'd share no more with her. Besides, it was best to move back into the fray of the party before her brothers decided they needed to interfere.

"It's quite easy. I suspect you'll be rather good at it. Come along."

She retrieved two balls, told him to select a
mallet.

"I'll share yours."

She gave him a pointed look. "You need one
with a longer handle."

"I'll make do."

"But you'll have to hunch—"

"I'll be fine, Princess."

"You are quite the stubborn man." Grateful
others were farther along in the game, she trooped
over to the first stake, well aware of his long strides
keeping pace. "The object, of course, is to run the
course, passing the ball through the wickets until
we reach the other stake. Like so." She positioned
herself, concentrated on placing her mallet in align-
ment with the ball so that a smart tap—

She felt his arms come around her, his hands
close over hers.

"What are you doing?" She hated that she
squeaked, sounded breathless, was frozen.

"Learning to play croquet."

"You could by *watching* my movements."

"And such lovely moments they are, but where's
the fun in merely watching? Much better to learn
by experiencing. You see, this way, I know precisely how to hold the mallet, how much my body
should tremble—"

"Tristan!" Her voice was low and sharp.

"You *are* trembling, Princess."

"In anger. You're making a spectacle of us."

"You didn't seem to mind my being behind you
last night."

Oh, dear Lord, she hadn't. She'd been on her knees, he on his, when he entered her. "We didn't have an audience."

"I want you, Anne. Where can we go for a few moments alone?"

"You're going to ruin my reputation. Then who shall have me?"

"I'm not doing anything improper."

"You're doing everything improper."

"I thought the whole point with these games was to offer an opportunity for flirtation."

"But not an opportunity to hold, to—" *To be acutely aware of your warmth, to inhale your earthy orangy scent, to imagine those hands that are now tightened around mine luxuriously caressing my body.* "You go too far."

"I could go farther and well you know it. Why did you invite me here if not to flirt?"

"I thought—"

"My Lord Tristan!" Lady Hermione called out.

"Dear God," he grumbled, "that girl is as tenacious as a barnacle."

He released her, stepped back, and while Anne knew she should be grateful—had she not been advocating for just such a move?—she was sorry that he was no longer holding her. As she spun around to greet Lady Hermione, she noticed that Jameson was much nearer and she had no doubt that he'd been charging over to rescue her. That would not have gone well at all.

"Had I known you were going to be here, I'd have not delayed my arrival," Lady Hermione gushed, her cheeks flushed, her smile so wide that it filled half her face.

Oh, what a nasty thought. Normally, Anne was not one to think unkindly of others. She wasn't jealous. Absolutely not. She understood that Tristan was a temporary fixture in her life. One did not become attached to things that had no permanence.

"Lady Anne was just teaching me to play croquet," Tristan said.

"Oh, is that what she was doing?" Lady Hermione gave her a once-over. "I wasn't quite sure."

"You look lovely today, Lady Hermione," Anne said, wanting to get the attention off of herself.

"Why thank you. It's a new gown. The color of Lord Tristan's eyes." She batted her pale lashes up at him.

"Yes, I have eyes of my own so I can quite see that," Anne said. Oh, she was in an ungracious mood. She couldn't very well claim Tristan, could she? That would bring about an entire host of complications.

Lady Hermione apparently was not to be deterred from her quest. "Oh, I say, Lord Tristan, I would so love a turn about the garden. Will you accompany me?"

"Lady Anne and I are engaged in a game of croquet."

"But surely it will keep. With English weather, you never know about the sun. It could rain at any moment."

The argument made no sense for if it rained,

how would they play croquet? Besides, there wasn't a dark cloud in the sky. It was a lovely day. If it rained, Anne would eat her hat.

"Please, just a quick turn."

Anne could tell that he was debating between telling her to take a jump into shark-infested waters and offering kindness. When he turned to her, she wasn't surprised to see the regret in his eyes because kindness had won out. "Not to worry," she offered, before he could say anything. "Jameson is lurking nearby. I'm of a mind to entice him into playing me and then beating him soundly."

With a wink he took her mallet, and holding it with only one hand, let loose a negligent swing that sent the ball rolling through the first two wickets.

"You cad! You know how to play."

He grinned. "Before you spotted me, I'd watched you long enough to figure it out." He leaned near. "Later, perhaps," he said quietly, and she could do no more than nod, certain he wasn't referring to catching up to her later *here*.

She tried not to feel a spark of envy when he offered Lady Hermione his arm and escorted her toward the roses. She wished she was walking in the girl's place. No one would fault her for talking and laughing with him as they strolled about the garden. How simple—

"Well, that was an embarrassing display," Jameson said tartly as he came to stand beside her.

"Yes, I daresay, Lady Hermione seems intent on garnering his attention."

"I was referring to you and that man."

Her blood boiled. "That *lord*." She moved in front of her brother and even though he was a head taller, she still managed to meet his gaze levelly. "He is a lord, Jameson, however much you may wish he wasn't."

"A *lord* does not wrap himself around a woman—"

"I was instructing him on how to properly hold the mallet."

His jaw dropped. "You honestly expect me to believe that you were responsible for that charade?"

"I don't expect anything of you except to be civil. Why will you not give him a chance to prove himself? It's not his fault that Lady Hermione traipses after him like she's transformed into his shadow. Would you rather he rebuffed her, hurt her tender heart?"

"She has nothing—"

"She has everything to do with it and well you know it. As do I. Now do you wish to play a game of croquet or not?"

"I don't like him."

She took a deep breath. "That's a pity. Because I do."

Resisting the urge to *accidently* swing the mallet into his shin, she held tightly to it and marched away.

"He's absurdly handsome, isn't he?" Sarah asked.

Anne was sitting at a small round table with her, eating a scone, sipping a cup of tea. She knew she should be out enjoying the company of the other guests, but she seemed only capable of watching Tristan as he played croquet with Lady Hermione. "I hadn't noticed."

"Of course, you have, silly girl. I suppose the duke would be so if not for the scars that mar his face."

"Why didn't you invite him?"

"Lord Tristan? I should think it's obvious."

She gave Sarah a pointed look. "No, Keswick."

Sarah seemed to become interested in her clotted cream. "Well, I don't really know him or his wife."

"How can they become known if everyone ignores them?"

Sarah looked up indignantly. "What would you have me do?"

"Call on the duchess."

"What if the duke is there?"

Anne smiled. "He's not going to bite."

"He's quite frightening."

"At the ball I thought his wife looked to be madly in love with him, so how bad can he be?"

"I suppose we could go together."

Anne's smile grew. "I think that's a lovely idea."

Sarah glanced toward the guests. "I didn't invite her, you know."

"Who?"

"Lady Hermione. She prattles on so, drives Fayrehaven to distraction. One of her friends must have sent word that Lord Tristan was here. She is making quite the fool of herself."

"I feel for her. He won't settle down. He won't give up the sea."

"Not for her, but he might for you."

Anne jerked her head around. "Don't be ridiculous."

Sarah scoffed. "Anne! I fully expected at any moment that he would toss you over his shoulder and cart you away. The man is clearly intrigued by you."

"It's all a game, Sarah. Just a game."

No matter how much she might have wished otherwise.

Brooding, Tristan sat alone in Sebastian's study, slowly sipping good whiskey and staring at the portrait above the fireplace. It was late. The house was quiet. He supposed he should go to Rafe's for a bit of sport, but he'd had enough of games for the day.

Once Lady Hermione had latched onto him, he'd been unable to shake her. He didn't want to hurt her but she was becoming quite the nuisance. Not that he'd listened much to what she'd had to say. Instead his mind had drifted off to a lazy afternoon when he'd been fishing with his father. He'd been happy. That's what he'd been unable to tell Anne. Standing beside his father, he'd known contentment. A month later he'd been running for his life, and he'd not experienced that sort of contentment again until he'd been standing beside Anne on his ship.

What was it about her that made her different from every other woman?

Hearing the door open he glanced over and watched as Sebastian strode toward him with the confidence of a duke. He'd once used Sebastian as a mirror, but now they were far too different, and it had little to do with the scars that puckered their flesh.

His brother was settled with a wife and son. He had his estates. He was again in possession of his titles. He was where he would have been had they never been forced to leave everything behind. Yet it wasn't the same. It occurred to him only now that Sebastian and Mary should have been at that blasted and utterly boring garden party.

Sebastian stopped by the cherrywood cabinet and generously filled a tumbler with whiskey before taking the chair across from Tristan. "You were awfully quiet during dinner."

"Did Mary send you down to prod me for answers?"

"She was a bit concerned."

Tristan ran his finger around the lip of his glass. "I attended an affair at Fayrehaven's this afternoon. Croquet, little pastry delicacies that would hardly fill a boy much less a man, and nothing stronger than champagne."

Sebastian arched a brow. "Are you courting Lady Hermione?"

"God no! Can you truly see me with such a flighty chit?"

Sebastian studied him intently for a moment. It

was disconcerting to realize that even with his solitary eye he could probably see more clearly than Tristan. "Someone, though. Do you want to talk about her?"

Tristan shook his head. "No."

What he had with Anne was between them, and while he knew his brother wasn't one to gossip, Tristan wasn't ready to give voice to his thoughts where she was concerned. He couldn't quite sort them out. He should be back at sea by now, and yet here he remained in dismal London.

"Whoever she is, was she the reason for your lapses into silence during the meal?"

"No, I . . . I spoke with Lord Chetwyn for a bit this afternoon. He mentioned his father fishing at Pembrook. I'd forgotten about that—the fishing." And his father guiding his hands, teaching him how to properly bait the hook, to cast his line . . .

Sebastian's lips rose on one side, the other too burdened with scars. "The pond is still there, the fish still abundant. You should come for an extended visit, longer than it takes to bury a man anyway. Mary is quite pleased with the new residence."

Two years ago he'd ridden by Pembrook on his way to the abbey ruins where he was supposed to meet with his brothers to begin their quest to reclaim their birthright. He'd returned to see his uncle buried at the village church. He'd had no desire to linger. Pembrook was not where he called home.

"Did you tear the old one down?" With cren-

ellated walls and towers, it was more castle than
manor.

"No. I had planned to but Mary convinced me
that it still had a purpose. She is a wise one, my
Mary, so I have a tendency to heed her advice."

"She is also a stubborn one. I suspect she'd make
you pay for not doing so."

Sebastian chuckled softly. "Yes, she would."

Tristan downed his whiskey. "She should have
been at that damned party today."

Sebastian did little more than nod. "Acceptance
will all come about in time. How long do you anticipate being here?"

"Until my business is done."

"Your business with this lady who shall remain
unnamed?"

"I have yet to tire of her."

"That is indeed a strong endorsement for her
qualities."

Tristan heard the sarcasm in his brother's voice,
but he wasn't offended by it. He suspected it spoke
more to what was lacking in himself. "It truly
is, Keswick. I've never had much trouble leaving before, which I fear doesn't say much for my
character."

"Do you love her?"

"One needs a heart to love. I admire her. I certainly desire her. I even have a fondness for her.
But love and I are strangers, and I suspect it will
always be so."

"The trouble with love, Brother, is that it isn't
always polite enough to introduce itself. It simply

settles in and takes up residence without even bothering to wait on an invitation. I loved Mary for years, but it wasn't until I thought I would lose her that I finally realized just how much she meant to me. Without her, I am but a shell. I would give up everything for her: my titles, my estates, my very life."

"I will never give up the sea."

"Then take care with this lady's heart."

"She is quite practical. She has no illusions regarding where our involvement will lead. She is being courted, and I suspect by Season's end she'll be some man's wife."

"But not yours."

Tristan shook his head, wished he had more whiskey. "No, never mine."

Chapter 21

Anne wondered if inviting Tristan to the garden party had been a mistake. The following day he sent her two dozen roses. The unsigned note accompanying them had simply said, "You were right. Thank you."

Right about what, for pity's sake? That he would enjoy the garden party? That they couldn't continue their trysts?

A week had passed and she'd not seen him. She tried to settle into the life that she had expected: morning calls, balls, dinners, courtship. But it seemed so trite. As though now she was a stranger to it all. She forced herself to carry on as though she'd not changed one whit since the stormy night she'd walked into a haze-filled tavern. Her father and brothers noticed nothing amiss.

Even Chetwyn seemed unable to detect the differences in her. He called upon her often, most

afternoons in fact. This afternoon being no exception. They had abandoned his curricle and were
now promenading through the park, admiring the
foliage and flowers. She couldn't imagine Tristan
occasionally stopping to admire a bloom or inhale
a fragrance.

Two other gentlemen had expressed an interest
in her, but she wasn't as comfortable with either of
them as she was with Chetwyn. He was a solicitous
soul and he fit her very much as an old shoe might.
She grimaced at the image. He was more than that.
He was pleasant, charming, kind. He never spoke
harshly of anyone. He never tried to take advantage of their time together. He didn't sneak her
into dark corners for a kiss. He didn't suggest in a
low sultry voice that perhaps she should leave her
window unlocked.

He made her smile. He brought her carnations.
He read her poetry. But mostly he spoke of the ball
that he and his mother would be hosting in honor
of Walter.

"It's been good to see Mother engaged in something other than weeping. She and Walter were so
close, you know," he said quietly as they strolled
through Regent's Park. They'd taken to visiting
different parks and she wondered if it was in part
because he hoped to avoid running into Tristan.

She considered telling him that Tristan was apparently no longer in her life, but that would be a
tacit confession that he had once been, and she
wasn't quite certain how that would go over.
She heard no rumors of him and Lady Hermione

so she wondered if he was on the sea. She tried so terribly hard not to think of him at all, but he was always there, taunting her with memories.

But if she'd learned anything at all of late, she'd learned that memories did fade, muting the joy or pain associated with them. She had but to be patient and soon all of her remembrances would revolve around Chetwyn.

"I can't imagine the devastation of losing a child," she said, equally quietly. They always spoke as though everything they said was not to be shared with others, was a secret. It created a sense of intimacy, but knowing what true intimacy was, she recognized their habit carried a falsehood with it. She supposed one day that it wouldn't. If he continued to court her. If he ever asked for her hand.

She could only hope that if she did marry, on her wedding night, when her husband discovered she was not . . . untouched, that he'd believe she'd given herself to Walter on the eve of war before he marched off, and hopefully he'd forgive her for such a rash act.

"It was devastating for her," Chetwyn said. "At one point, she even said that she wished it had been me."

"No, Chetwyn." She squeezed his arm. "She didn't mean it. Grief was speaking, not her."

"So I told myself. I wish Father were alive. Sometimes I feel as though I'm a fake, wearing the mantle of marquess."

His father had died nearly ten years ago. He

should be accustomed to it by now, but still she realized that it could not be easy for one so young. Walter would have been twenty-five. Chetwyn was three years older. The same age as Tristan. She couldn't imagine Tristan bemoaning his responsibilities. But then his life had been very different. The two could not be compared.

"You are an exceptional marquess," she assured him.

"My mother might stop harping once I've seen to my duty of acquiring a wife."

Her breath caught. He grimaced. "Sorry. I am here with you because I wish to be. I enjoy your company."

"Parents are troublesome, though, aren't they? Father is desperate for me to find a husband. But it is such a permanent thing that I don't think the decision should be made in haste."

"Quite right." He sighed. "The ball. I was discussing the ball. May I confess something?"

"Without question."

"Mother and I fought this morning. I'm of a mind to invite the Duke of Keswick. He fought in the Crimea. It seems appropriate."

"Your mother disagrees."

"Wholeheartedly. I understand he's a bit rough around the edges, but he behaved exemplary at the last ball he attended. I thought perhaps he could even speak of the need to not forget those who fought and returned with challenges."

"I believe he would be a wonderful addition to what you have planned."

He smiled. "I quite agree. Now if you could help me convince Mother . . ."

"What if I did a bit more than that?"

"What have you in mind?"

"You shouldn't invite him."

"But you just said—"

"I'll invite him. Then your mother can't be mad with you."

"No, she'll be mad with you."

"But I don't live with her."

"But you very well could in the near—" Blushing scarlet, he faced her and took her hands. Her heart was pounding like a regimental drum. "You must know that my interest in you goes beyond poetry and walks in the park."

Her mouth suddenly dry, she nodded.

"If my interest is not wanted, you have but to say and I shall leave you be."

So polite, so damned polite. He would never anger her; he would never challenge her; he would quite possibly never fight for her. She wanted more, but even as she thought it, only one man came to mind: Tristan. He brought with him thousands of lonely nights. With Chetwyn, she would have no loneliness. She would quite possibly have no passion, but perhaps she'd had enough to last a lifetime. Her aunt thought love was rare, and Anne had possessed it for a short while. Surely passion such as she'd known was even rarer. But the price to keep it was too high.

"Your attention is welcomed, Chetwyn."

Smiling, he lifted her gloved hands and pressed a

kiss to her knuckles. "You've made me very happy, Anne, and I shall do all in my power to see that you are happy as well."

"But first you must please your mother."

He chuckled lightly. "Yes, quite. At least until I can move her into the dower house." He turned and they began walking again. "So about this invitation to Keswick . . ."

Living a good bit of his youth on the streets of London, Rafe Easton had developed a keen instinct when it came to judging men. Not all hands offered in assistance were harmless. Not all smiles led to laughter. Not all friendship was true.

So it was—as he stood in the shadows of the balcony of his gaming hell and watched his brother tossing dice—that he knew Tristan was in an unusually foul mood. Oh, he was quick to smile and jest but it was a performance, although Rafe was fairly certain his brother always performed when in London. Only tonight it reflected a harder edge. Tristan wasn't enjoying the role he'd chosen for himself.

Rafe truly didn't care if his brother wasn't happy, but he could see his temper roiling to the forefront, and the last thing with which he wanted to deal was a brawl in his establishment. He'd worked hard to get where he was, made sacrifices, done things he'd have rather not done.

So he'd be damned if he'd allow one of the brothers who'd left him at a workhouse to tarnish what he'd accomplished.

"Mick, tell my brother that I wish to have a word."

"Yes, sir," the young man standing behind him said before skittering off to do Rafe's bidding. Those who worked for him were loyal, but still he didn't trust them much farther than he could see them. He certainly didn't banter it about that he was a lord. Shortly after he and his brothers had made their return to Society, a few of his members recognized him, but because he kept to the shadows, many ceased to associate him with Pembrook. In time, for him, it was as though nothing in his life had changed.

He watched as Mick approached Tristan, leaned over, and whispered in his ear. Tristan paused midcourse in a throw and jerked up his gaze toward the balcony. Their eyes met, and Rafe knew that his held a challenge equal to the one that Tristan was sending. Rafe had no doubt that he could hold his own. He'd stopped being the baby brother the moment they'd cruelly abandoned him. He'd certainly never sniveled or wept since that night. No, since then he felt nothing at all.

The same couldn't be said of Tristan. It seemed he felt a great deal too much.

Tristan sent the dice flying and turned away from the table without waiting to see how they might have landed. Mick stepped in to retrieve the winnings about which Tristan obviously didn't care.

Rafe headed for his office, regretting that he knew what Tristan needed was a brother to stand beside him, but Rafe had long ago stopped being a brother to anyone.

The nerve of the pup! Summoning Tristan as though he were a mere member of the club to be brought to task because he was playing a bit too hard, drinking a bit too much, and swearing a bit too loudly. Granted, he didn't pay the yearly fee so he supposed technically he wasn't a member, but Rafe had never denied him the pleasures of his gaming hell. Tristan flexed his hands, contemplating how nicely his fist would fit into his brother's face.

Tristan strode into the office in time to see Rafe fill two glasses with whiskey and shove one across the desk until it came to rest on the far side near a chair that faced him. Rafe took his seat, snatched up his glass, and lifted it in a silent salute before downing its contents.

Tristan supposed all that counted as an invitation.

"Why do you collect the damned globes?" he asked.

Rafe's jaw clenched before he poured himself more whiskey. "Why are you acting as though someone took your favorite toy?"

"It was you, wasn't it?" Tristan asked as he stepped farther into the room. "When we were boys. You were the one who stole my wooden horse." His father had bought it for him at a fair. It was beautifully made, painted black, with a small decorated leather saddle. Tristan had carried it in his pocket everywhere he went. He'd even slept with the silly thing until he was eight.

"Of course it was," Rafe replied laconically with no indication of remorse.

"Bastard. Do you still have it?" Since leaving Pembrook, he'd never longed for anything from there. He didn't know why he suddenly wanted the blasted horse, but he did dammit.

"No. Sorry, old boy, but it got left behind with my childhood dreams." Rafe grimaced and downed his whiskey.

Tristan realized he'd revealed more than he'd intended. The brothers had shared little of their paths since that awful night, as though they didn't wish to burden the others. He still loved his brothers, wished them well, but he hardly knew them. But then they barely knew him. He wanted it that way. It made him feel . . . safer. Not that they would wish him harm, but he didn't like feeling vulnerable. Talk of the past always made him feel as though he were fourteen again and facing demons. He could hardly countenance that he'd revealed as much as he had to Anne.

Damn but he missed her. She'd been right, of course. He couldn't continue climbing in through her window when she wanted the sort of life that she did so badly. Being at Fayrehaven's garden party had shown him that.

He took the offered seat, lifted the glass, studied the amber liquid, and turned his attention back to his brother. "It was hard on you when we left."

"I see no point in discussing what is too late to change."

"Sebastian's face is half gone. My back was torn asunder more than once. What scars do you bear?"

"None that concern you, but I won't tolerate you causing trouble in my establishment."

Not tolerate? Tristan wondered how Rafe thought he was going to bloody well stop him from doing any damned thing he wanted. "I was rolling dice."

"You were looking for a fight."

"Going to give me one?"

"If you like. I have a boxing room."

Tristan tossed back the whiskey, relished the burning, and studied his brother. He'd never noticed how broad-shouldered Rafe was or how large and capable his hands seemed. He usually saw him going through ledgers like a bookworm. Although he recalled that Rafe—gravely injured—had fought off some ruffians when the brothers had first made themselves known in London.

Tristan grinned. "I'd just beat you, easily no doubt, and then you'd have another reason to despise me."

Rafe shrugged, poured more whiskey into both their glasses. "So who is the woman who's causing you trouble tonight?"

Tristan couldn't help the look of surprise he directed his brother's way. "What makes you think it's a woman?"

"Because if it was a man, you'd take your fists to him and be done with it. But a woman must be handled a bit more delicately."

Tristan couldn't argue with that. "The lady is none of your business."

"Suit yourself. Just don't cause trouble in my

place." Rafe opened a ledger and began to study the entries.

Tristan sipped his whiskey. He didn't need to discuss his personal life. He didn't need anyone to help him sort it out.

"Lady Anne Hayworth," he heard himself blurt out, then wished he could take a cat-o-nine to his tongue.

Rafe looked up. "The Earl of Blackwood's daughter?"

"Yes."

"Did she not pay for the passage on your ship?"

"She paid." A thousand times over. That was part of the problem. Having tasted the payment, he wasn't of a mind to do without. But the time had come. He was rather sure of it. She tried to entice him to move about in her world, but he fit as easily as a fox in the midst of hounds.

"Then you want more from her."

He wanted everything. He couldn't stomach the thought of Chetwyn, of any man, running his hands over her flesh, burying himself deeply inside her—

Damnation. A possessive fury he'd never known shot through him.

"Lord Chetwyn has an interest in her." It hadn't helped matters that he'd seen her in the park with the blasted lord that very afternoon. She'd looked happy, had been smiling up at him. She'd laughed. Her arm had been wrapped around his as though she'd turned into a clinging vine. And damn them both to hell, they looked right together. Proper. Chetwyn was everything he wasn't. People ap-

proached them, spoke with them. They didn't
stand warily back wondering what to expect.

"And you want to marry her?"

"Good God, no." He couldn't contain his alarm
at the notion. How the hell did his brother come
to that conclusion from this bit of conversation?
"Marriage is not for me."

"You just want to bed her then."

There was no "just" when it came to bedding
Anne. Her in his bed brought him more pleasure,
more . . . joy than he'd ever known.

"I don't want Chetwyn sniffing about her."
Which wasn't fair to her if she liked the fellow, but
dammit all, life wasn't fair.

"Suppose you could abduct Chetwyn, drop him
into the ocean somewhere."

"Don't think I haven't considered it. But someone would take his place in her affections quickly
enough. She's a beautiful woman. Charming.
Feisty. She can hold her own in an argument,
doesn't back down easily. When her temper flares,
my God, she's something to behold."

"You're in love with her."

"What? No, absolutely not. She's simply interesting and I appreciate interesting things." Love
certainly wasn't an emotion with which he was familiar or had any desire with which to become familiar. It weakened a man. He'd loved his mother
and she'd died in childbirth. He'd loved his father
and he'd died. He'd loved his uncle and the blighter
had led them to the tower. No, love wasn't for him.

Rafe studied his refilled glass of whiskey. Tristan

had a difficult time believing that the self-assured man sitting before him was the sniveling brat he'd known as a child. As the youngest, he'd been pampered and spoiled. But there was no softness in him now. *What paths did you traverse, Brother?*

If he weren't more interested in solving the dilemma he faced with Anne, he might work at getting Rafe drunk and questioning him about the past. Instead he watched the wheels turn in his brother's eyes.

Finally, Rafe said quietly, "The most powerful weapon among the aristocracy is gossip."

Tristan was well aware of that. It had forced Sebastian to marry Mary. "As I mentioned, I don't wish to marry her."

"You don't have to, but I thought you were striving to ensure that Chetwyn—or any other lord for that matter—didn't."

Tristan cared for her too much to hurt her in that way: to bring her public scorn and not marry her. But then things had turned out well enough for Sebastian and Mary. Anne would always be here waiting for him. He might actually begin to look forward to returning to England.

The suggestion began to have merit. Tristan wanted her. He never denied himself anything he wanted. He knew she desired him. It would be unfair for her to marry Chetwyn when she yearned for another. He'd be doing Chetwyn a favor.

Her as well, truth be told. She just needed to realize it.

Chapter 22

In the end, Chetwyn delivered the invitation to Keswick himself. A bit of rebelliousness on his part, Anne supposed, or perhaps he wanted her to view him as a man's man. "Ladies tend to prefer a gentleman with a backbone," he'd joked during one of their outings to the park.

So she determined he was striving to impress her, to press his suit, to stake his claim.

"You and Chetwyn are all the talk," Sarah said now as they stood off to the side in the ballroom at Chetwyn's residence. "I rather like him."

"So does my family."

Her father and brothers couldn't have been happier with all the attention Chetwyn was lavishing on her. They sang his praises to her whenever they crossed her path in the hallways of their residence. It was very much like living in an opera. Although she could hardly fault them.

He was akin to them. He had attended the same

schools, belonged to the same clubs, shared the same interests. He didn't jump into shark-infested waters to save a child from gaping maws.

He had traveled to Europe and Egypt. He wanted to journey to America someday, perhaps after he was married. Of late he spoke often of a future that included a lady, and she knew that in his mind, that lady was she. She tried to envision a future with Chetwyn. But she seemed unable to see anything beyond parks, balls, and theater.

She wanted to gaze into his eyes and long for his kiss. She wanted to grow warm with the possibility of him touching her.

"Do you like him?" Sarah asked.

"He's pleasant, yes. More than pleasant, really. He makes me smile."

"But does he make you laugh?"

She turned to her dear friend. "What sort of question is that?"

"An odd one, I'm sure, but I've discovered that for true happiness one must laugh. Fayrehaven makes me laugh on occasion."

"I'm certain I've laughed with Chetwyn." Although she couldn't remember a moment when she had. Not truly. A small laugh here and there she supposed. Was she being unfair to him to want for more?

"What about Lord Tristan? Have you seen him of late?"

"No. I told him that we couldn't continue on as we'd been. I think he took my words to heart." More than she'd wished for, truth be told. She

hadn't meant that she never wanted to set eyes on
him again. She just wouldn't serve as a convenient
mistress or lover.

"And how was that?" Sarah asked.

"Pardon?"

"How had you been?"

"Oh, you know, passing here and there, knowing all along there would be nothing permanent.
A good strong wind would have him back on the
sea."

"Do you miss him?"

Terribly, but she fought not to dwell on it because she would not sink into despair. This Season
was about pleasing her father and finding a husband. "I hardly give him any thought."

"Liar. I'm married and I give him thought. He's
a remarkable specimen."

"Sarah, you're not helping matters."

"Apologies. I daresay, it's wonderful what Chetwyn and his mother are doing for the soldiers."

A change in topic, thank God.

"Yes, they're exceedingly generous." She suspected this would be but the beginning of Chetwyn's efforts. He had a kindness in him that wanted
to protect and shelter. He would make an excellent
husband. If he were hers, she would strive to be
an exceptional wife. But then she wondered if she
should have to strive. Shouldn't it come naturally?

The orchestra struck a chord, the room quieted, and with her son's assistance, Lady Chetwyn
stepped onto a dais. Her hair had gone completely
white since her younger son's passing. A bit of mur-

muring began and she clapped her hands. When silence again reigned, she said, "As you all know, caring for our soldiers is an endeavor that is near and dear to my heart. Funds are needed to ensure that those who are not yet able to work are cared for. We owe them housing, food, and warmth. We owe them our undying gratitude for going where we did not wish to tread. I hope you will not find offense in how we wish to begin this ball. Consider that it is done with the best of intentions. Unmarried ladies, please come forward."

"That's you," Sarah said, nudging Anne's shoulder with her fan.

"Do you know what this is about?" she asked.

"No. I would think you would, though. You're the one who's been keeping time with Chetwyn."

"He's been quite secretive about the plans." He caught her attention then, winked at her, and jerked his head toward the dais. She had a feeling in the pit of her stomach that she wasn't going to like this.

"There you go. Off with you now," Sarah insisted.

Anne meandered over to where the other ladies were standing about, smiling, and giggling.

"Do you know what they have planned?" one of the ladies whispered.

Anne shook her head.

"I've heard it's going to be scandalous," someone else said sotto voce.

Anne had never associated the word scandal with Chetwyn.

"The first dance with each lady will go to the highest bidder," the marchioness announced.

A couple of ladies squealed. Anne wished she'd stayed with Sarah until she saw that Chetwyn seemed rather pleased with himself, rocking back and forth on his heels, his gaze never straying from her, his mouth tilted upward in a gentle smile. She was beginning to suspect that this little spectacle was as much about him claiming her as it was about raising the needed funds for a soldiers' home. She had expected a moment like this to come. She simply hadn't anticipated that it would be so public, but she was determined to be a good sport about it.

As each of the ladies took the dais, there was an abundance of blushing and a few bids, as though people weren't quite comfortable with the notion. Lady Teresa had received the highest bid so far: twenty-five pounds.

Anne's was the fourth name that Lady Chetwyn called out. As heat warmed her face, she stepped onto the dais and tried not to feel uneasy with all the attention focused on her. Her father, of course, wasn't here tonight, but she caught sight of Jameson grinning and nudging Chetwyn, encouraging him no doubt. It was suddenly obvious how the winds were blowing. She would be betrothed by the end of the Season, married by the end of the year. She would never be lonely again. It was what she wanted.

"Lady Anne Hayworth, gentlemen. What shall you bid to be the first to waltz with this lovely lady this evening?" As she spoke, she smiled at her son.

Anne saw him raise two fingers. "Fifty pounds."

A few gasps resounded. His mother's smile widened, not so much because of the astonishing amount but because she hoped it would get the other gents into the spirit of things. Or perhaps it was because her son was making it clear that he valued Lady Anne Hayworth. Considering the amounts that had gone before, no one was going to challenge—

"One hundred."

Anne felt her breath leaving her body as she recognized the voice. What was he doing here? Surely Chetwyn had not invited him, but the crowd parted to reveal Tristan leaning negligently against a white marbled column. Although he was dressed as a gentleman, he seemed more roguish tonight, more dangerous. If at all possible he'd grown more devilishly handsome in the two weeks since she'd seen him. She'd begun to think he'd left England, and she'd been determined not to mourn his leaving but to carry on. But here he was.

Anne's mouth was so dry that it was as though she'd swallowed sawdust.

"One fifty," Chetwyn challenged.

"Two hundred."

Gasps floated through the room. Someone clapped. Jameson looked on the verge of committing murder. Chetwyn's jaw tightened. "Two hundred and fifty."

She looked at Tristan and tried to convey with

pleading eyes, *Please don't bid any more. Let Chetwyn have this moment.* But either he couldn't read or he didn't care.

"Five."

"Two hundred and sixty," Chetwyn announced.

"My apologies, my lord, for not being clearer," Tristan said, his voice booming to the far corners. Anne suspected it was communicating through storms that gave him such a command of the room. "I wasn't bidding two hundred and fifty-five, but rather five hundred."

Let it stop here, dear God, let it stop here. She could see Chetwyn hesitate and then he seemed to straighten himself up. "Six hundred."

"One thousand," Tristan responded with no hesitation. He was not a man accustomed to losing, and she knew he had no intention of losing here.

Chetwyn acknowledged the bid with a slight nod as he stepped back. Anne's heart went out to him. She wanted to leap from the dais, rush over to him, and assure him that everything was all right. She was his. But duty forced her to stand and bear the humiliation of having all eyes on her filled with speculation. First the garden party, and now this. Her reputation was likely to be torn to tatters.

"Well, sir," Lady Chetwyn said, her smile sickly, "you certainly got into the spirit of things and your generosity is much appreciated. Next, we have Lady Hermione."

If looks could kill, the glare Lady Hermione bestowed upon Anne as they passed each other would have surely seen her on her way to the grave.

In long strides Tristan ate up the distance separating them and offered Anne his hand as she
stepped off the dais. Her embarrassment for Chetwyn had her ignoring it. She walked to an empty
spot near the wall to await the end of the bidding
and the beginning of the music. Tristan took up his
place beside her.

"You purposely sought to humiliate him," she
said, her voice low and seething.

"I promise you that was not my intention. I
merely wanted to dance with you."

"A thousand pounds?"

"For a good cause. Surely you can't fault me for
that."

Perhaps not. If she thought his intentions were
honorable, rather than simply a means to gain
something that he wanted. If only Chetwyn hadn't
looked so disappointed, so defeated.

"You can't always have what you want, especially when it hurts others," she admonished.

"Trust me, Princess, I spent a good deal of my
life not having what I wanted. If I'm in a position
to take, I take. Besides it's only a dance. He can
have the next and it won't cost him a ha'penny."

She watched as Jameson escorted Lady Hermione off the dais. So her brother had bid on her. She
wondered for what amount. Certainly not the ex-
orbitant amount of a thousand pounds. "I thought
you understood that my purpose in this Season
was to secure a husband."

"Which is the reason that I've stayed away, but I
missed you, dammit."

She could have sworn she heard longing in his voice, longing that would mirror hers if she said the same words. She had missed him as well. Dreadfully. But admitting it would serve no purpose except to prolong an inevitable separation. "I wasn't aware you were invited."

"My brother and his wife were. I tagged along. Are there rules that say I shouldn't have?"

Chetwyn was no doubt wishing at this moment that he had been precise with his invitation. She was grateful that in the end he had delivered it. Otherwise he might be under the impression that she had invited Tristan.

"I thought perhaps you'd left England."

"Not yet." He grinned. "Obviously."

"What are you doing here, Tristan?"

"I told you. I missed you. I wanted to dance with you."

"Did you have to draw so much attention?"

"I'll leave if it's what you want, and he can have the damned dance."

"The home can use the thousand pounds."

"I'll still pay it. I honor my debts. Tell me to go and I will."

Closing her eyes, she took a deep cleansing breath. Then she opened them to find him watching her. His gaze dropped to her lips before lifting back to her eyes. She saw the yearning there and it matched a similar longing in her. Whatever was wrong with her? "I suppose I should be flattered that you would pay so much for a single waltz with me."

"Most women would be, I should think. But

then I learned very quickly that you are not most women."

"People are watching us."

"Perhaps because the music is starting." He extended his arm. "Do I escort you onto the dance floor or to Chetwyn?"

"To Chetwyn."

She saw the flash of irritation before he wiped all emotion from his face. "As you wish."

She placed her hand on his arm and he turned away from the dance area to the corner where Chetwyn was talking with his mother. He was going to do it. Deliver her to another man.

"The dance floor, damn you," she whispered.

When they were moving among the other couples, he said, "Tell me that you missed me as well."

She shouldn't, but she did. "Dreadfully."

He grinned, even as his eyes promised she'd not be lonely later tonight.

"Don't look so smug. It only reinforces how difficult a relationship with you is."

"Doesn't it make it worthwhile when we're together?"

She laughed lightly. "Oh, you are arrogant."

"Only if I claim what I can't deliver. What do you see in him?"

"Who? Chetwyn?"

He nodded. "He seems rather uninteresting to me."

"Little you know. He is a man of many facets. He's working to better those less fortunate."

"Well then, he's a saint, isn't he?"

"Don't mock him. At least he's doing something larger than himself."

"You admire that."

"I do. Rather a lot actually."

"We should discuss this further. Meet me in the garden three dances from now."

Glancing around, she saw her brother dancing with Lady Hermione. They were both watching her and Tristan rather than each other. She was surprised they didn't crash into someone. "Now that my brothers know you're here they'll be watching my every move."

"Then I'll make certain they see me leave through the front door."

"You're very good at these games. I don't want to think about how often you've played them."

"You're not a game to me."

"What am I then, Tristan?"

"I don't bloody well know. I only know that I have a desperate desire to be on the sea, but my ship remains in port and I am where I would rather not be."

She couldn't help but smile. "You sound so terribly unhappy about it."

"Disgusted actually. I'm accustomed to going where I want to go when I want to go. Yet here I am, floundering in indecision. So meet me in the garden. Or would you rather I crawl in through your window?"

Both, she thought. Whatever was wrong with her? Prolonging their time together would only cause heartache. Still, she heard herself say, "The third dance from now."

Tristan was in the hallway headed for the door when he heard, "Why did you bid on her and not on me?"

With a deep sigh he came to an abrupt halt and turned around. "Hermione."

The disappointment in her eyes was enough to make him regret that he wasn't the man she wished he was.

"I sent word to you about this affair because I wanted you to come and bid on me. Lady Chetwyn had told my mother what she planned."

And he had come hoping Anne would be here. Not so much to stake a claim, but to ensure that no one else did. It was the reason he'd remained in the shadows until he knew for certain that she was in attendance. If she hadn't been, he'd planned to slip quietly away.

"Lord Jameson bid on you."

"Thirty pounds. Not a thousand. A thousand for *her*? Why?"

That was the question, wasn't it? The one he couldn't answer, even to himself.

She took a step nearer, tears welling in her eyes. "I love you."

"You can't love me, Hermione. You don't know me."

"I would do anything for you."

Then leave me be.

"Then find your happiness with someone else. I'll be setting sail soon, and God knows when I'll be back. You would have a lot of lonely nights, sweetheart." Why would he use that argument with her, yet deny it as consequential when Anne made the same point?

"I don't care. I'll wait faithfully just as I've done these two years."

"I don't want to hurt you, Hermione. You're a lovely girl, but you're not for me."

"But Lady Anne is? I don't understand. She's not even pretty."

"Not pretty? She's the most beautiful woman I've ever seen."

"Her nose is too small and her lips too plump."

Chuckling, he shook his head. "Go back to the ball, sweetheart, and set your cap for someone else. Lord Jameson if you're smart, but I'm not for you."

Rather than continuing to argue with her, he turned on his heel and strode from the residence. He didn't want to be cruel, but he could think of no other way to get his message across.

He hadn't said where in the garden they were to meet, but Anne was fairly certain that the farther from the residence the better. She didn't doubt for a minute that Tristan would find her—wherever she was. She didn't give any thought to why she felt that way or why she had such confidence in him. Nor did she want to acknowledge how much she was anticipating this little tryst.

The couple of weeks that had passed since she'd last seen him had left her wanting. Dancing with him earlier, meeting with him now was only serving to reignite a flame she had been working to douse. He had to leave her be. They could no longer have any association. Because it only made things more difficult all the way around. It threatened her resolve to carry on. She had moved past Walter. Now she needed to move beyond Tristan.

But when a strong arm snaked around her waist and drew her into the darker shadows of the garden, when a mouth covered hers with purpose, when her curves were pressed against the familiar hard lines and planes, she sank into him with nary a protest. It was marvelous to be surrounded by his unique fragrance, to have his taste teasing her tongue, to have his hands stroking her shoulders, cupping her breasts, to hear his groans mingling with her sighs.

"Damn, but I've missed you," he rasped as he dragged his mouth along her throat and lower, where the swells of her breasts awaited his questing lips.

Heat spiraled through her and her knees weakened. Why did she have so little control when he was near? Why did she have to yearn for what she could never fully hold? She didn't want to not have moments of passion like this, but they would be too few and far between. Loneliness was a bitter companion. It wouldn't hold her on cold nights. It wouldn't comfort her when sorrows struck. It wouldn't celebrate with her moments worth remembering.

Tristan had left the ballroom and Chetwyn had taken his place: talking with her, dancing with her, fetching her some refreshment. He would be there until she left. That it was his home barely signified. What mattered was that he would always be within easy reach. She wouldn't be sitting somewhere wondering where he was. She would always know. She wouldn't be worrying that he was brawling with some ruffians or fighting some tempest that might break the ship apart. With Tristan she would spend her life in uncertainty.

She had done that once with Walter. She knew the strain that the constant not knowing placed on her. It aged her. It killed her spirit. It left her in perpetual mourning.

"Chetwyn is advancing his suit."

Tristan stilled, his mouth pressed to the hollow at her throat, one hand cupping her backside, the other her breast. She felt the bulge in his trousers nudging against her belly. She listened to his harsh breathing in the stillness of the night.

"You're going to marry him?" he asked flatly.

"Perhaps, if he asks. I don't know."

"But we can have tonight."

"No. Having decided my course, it wouldn't be fair to him for me to stray from it. Even for another night with you."

Even though he did little more than release her, she staggered back. She hadn't realized how much she'd been leaning on him.

"Yet here you are with me in the garden."

"To explain—"

He snagged her waist, brought her back in, and captured her mouth with unerring accuracy. She heard a moan, realized it came from her as she met his questing tongue with hers. Her arms were entwined around his neck, her fingers tangled in his hair, her body straining to be even nearer.

"You can't resist me," he said.

It was the triumph in his voice that had her shoving away from him. Arrogant cad. She was weak where he was concerned. She wanted to shriek. She wanted to pound her fists against his chest. She wanted to tell him that he held the power to destroy her.

"I can't deny that there is an attraction and that you are extremely skilled when it comes to delivering pleasure, but my future is with Chetwyn."

"Give me tonight, Anne. Give *us* tonight. On the ship."

Even knowing what her answer should be, she succumbed to what it would be. "I'll go to the mews after my brother takes me home. If you're there—"

"I'll be there."

Chapter 23

They'd not stayed in harbor. Instead Tristan had ordered the ship taken out to sea. Not far. Just enough so the wind toyed with Anne's hair while she stood on the deck, just enough so all the stars were visible. Just enough so she heard a whale in the distance.

She couldn't deny that she understood why he had an appreciation for the sea, but she didn't want to spend her life competing with a mistress who would always come first in his heart. Nor could she blame him for wanting it when it had always been there for him. When he had needed a place to run, it had provided sanctuary.

Tristan stood behind her, his legs braced, holding her near while the ship rocked gently, the sails now furled until they were ready to return to shore.

"I can understand why you love it out here," she said quietly.

"I think you love it as well."

"I appreciate it. That's a very different thing."

"I've never shared any of this with another lady."

She turned in his arms until she was facing him. "And I've shared with you far more than I've ever shared with anyone."

"Regrets?"

"Nary a one."

Rising up on her toes, she kissed him with all the hunger, the yearning—and yes, even the love—that she held for him. She would never utter the words that might hold him to her because she cared for him too much to deny him the sea.

Or perhaps she feared her love wouldn't be enough to hold him.

It didn't matter. What she felt was not to be shared or examined. They would have tonight, and then she would lock it away.

With her nestled securely against his side, they made their way to his quarters. It was not what she would want for a home, but it was his home. She was glad he'd brought her here again.

Then she had no time to reflect on anything because his mouth was on her and his hands were working quickly to divest her of her clothing. She was just as eager, grateful that he'd come to her in only boots, shirt, and trousers. She'd have him bared in no time at all.

"You're not wearing a corset," he said as he jerked her dress down.

"No."

"Good girl."

"If you dare pat my head—"

"Your head is not what I intend to pat."

She laughed as they scattered their clothes about the floor before falling into the bed. She didn't want to acknowledge that she didn't sleep nearly as deeply when she wasn't snuggled up against him. Perhaps, though, it was only that when she was with him she always went to bed sated.

She wanted a long, slow, leisurely sojourn into lovemaking, but they had been apart too long for anything remotely tame. It was as though neither of them could get enough of the other.

His tongue swirled and danced with hers. Arching against him, she ran her hands along the familiar flesh. She didn't want to consider how right it felt to have his body bearing down on hers. She wanted to lose herself in the sensations that he was drawing to life.

Everywhere he caressed mourned when he moved on to someplace else, and he left nothing untouched. From her crown to her toes, he stroked and tasted, he kissed and nipped, he suckled and licked.

She did the same with a boldness that astounded her. He was hers—completely and absolutely. For tonight anyway. Eventually he would drift away, and she would let him go without tears or a scene. She would be grateful for what they had tonight.

Then she would settle into being a proper lady. But tonight she intended to be decidedly improper.

Shoving on his chest, angling her hips, she rolled him onto his back. "My turn," she breathed.

Breathing harshly, he asked, "What's this?"

"You'll see."

He threaded his fingers through her hair and brought her down for a kiss. She would give him that, let him have control for a moment. As though she had any choice in the matter. She enjoyed his kisses too much to give one up freely so she straddled him and sank into it, allowed their mouths to seek and claim. But when he came up for air, she slid down, kissing his neck, tasting the salty dew that was already beginning to coat his skin.

She eased down farther, trailing her tongue over his chest.

"Where are you going, sweetheart?"

She lifted her gaze to his. "On an adventure."

Tristan stared at the heat in her eyes and was surprised he didn't ignite. Although he was hot enough to do it on his own without any further prompting from her.

From the beginning he had wanted her, but nothing had prepared him for the urgency and the desire that propelled him tonight. Perhaps it was because he knew what she offered, perhaps it was because he had been denied her for so long—

Or perhaps it was because he knew he would never again have her.

He had decided this would be their final parting, and he hated the thought of it almost as much as he hated the idea of staying in England. Of being shackled to the land.

He'd been surprised when she'd not objected to

his taking the ship from the harbor, to bringing them out on the sea. He had fully intended to sail through the night, to keep her with him until he was done with her. She might think she didn't want to see the world, but she did. How could she not? Especially when it involved being in his arms every night.

But she trusted him, dammit. Believed him to be a better man than he was, a man who kept promises even when they didn't benefit him. He'd hoped his bidding so outrageously on her this evening would provide enough gossip to discourage Chetwyn's suit, but now he realized the selfishness of it. He couldn't have her forever. He was a bastard to deny her a chance at the sort of life she craved.

Yet she seemed not to comprehend what an absolute blackguard he was, because wedged between his legs, she moved even lower. His breath stuttered, his hands fisted in the sheets. "Anne," he croaked.

Once more she lifted her gaze and he saw triumph there. Then she gave him a saucy look before lowering her mouth—

He bucked as the heat of her mouth enveloped him.

"Christ!" He plowed one hand into her hair while the other kept him anchored to the bed. Pressing his head back against the pillow, he watched her working her magic. Only one thing felt better and that was being buried deeply inside of her. He wanted to beg, plead with her to never do this to another man. It would drive him to madness to envision her with someone else.

Damnation, he should order the sails hoisted. He should set a course to the far side of the world. He should keep her with him—

But she would hate him and her sweet mouth would never do such naughty things again.

Pleasure and pain rippled through him. Pleasure brought on by her energetic ministrations; pain because he didn't deserve what she was so willing to give. He'd wanted to deny her a future with another man.

And now he knew he had to let her go.

"Anne." Reaching down, he brought her up until she straddled his hips. He guided himself into her before urging her down for a kiss. He thought he tasted himself on her lips. No one had ever given him as much as she had. In such a short time, she'd given him everything.

She rode him as though her very life depended on it. He knew his did. Straightening, she skimmed her hands over his chest while her hips rocked in tandem to his. He cupped her breasts, stroked and massaged—

She dropped her head back. Sweet sighs echoed around them, and then she was crying out—

Her body spasmed around him and fierce pleasure ripped through him, tearing asunder his world, leaving him sated and devastated as she collapsed on top of him. He didn't know where he found the strength to wrap his arms around her and hold her tightly against him. Selfish bastard that he was, he never wanted her to leave.

But as he heard her drift off to sleep, he knew the minutes were ticking away and soon, very soon, she would no longer be in his life.

Never again would he hold her, know the joy of her.

He had traversed his path for too long to detour from it now. Sadly, it was a path that didn't include her.

Wrapped in Tristan's arms, Anne stood in the darkened shadows of the garden. She didn't know why she'd thought he would sail in a direction that would take them away from England instead of toward it. She might not have objected. When she was with him, lost in the haze of pleasure, she seemed to have little common sense.

But it was here with her now. She had a thousand things to say to him. But only a few truly mattered.

"No more, no more midnight trysts. The window to my bedchamber will be locked. I will never again set foot on your ship. But if you attend a ball, you may ask me to dance."

"I may just do that. And we still haven't had our ride through Hyde Park."

"No, we haven't."

Leaning back she looked up into his face. She wished she could wait for the dawn to light it but the longer she dallied, the greater the chance of her family discovering that she had been quite improper. "Good night, Tristan."

Before he could say anything, she spun away from him and raced up the garden path. She didn't want to acknowledge the disappointment that swamped her because he didn't snatch her back into his arms.

Chapter 24

Anne very much remembered the joy that had spiraled through her when Walter had asked for her hand in marriage. When Chetwyn asked, what she felt was a sense of stepping onto a path that wasn't quite steady. But sitting in the parlor with him on bended knee in front of her, wariness in his eyes as though he expected rejection, what could she say other than, "Yes, of course, it will be my honor to become your wife."

Honor? Good God. It sounded so dreadfully trite and dull.

He pressed her hands to his warm lips, lips that would soon be pressed to other parts of her. It would be pleasant, she was sure of it, and she would be happy.

"You have made me the most joyous man in all of London today."

"I couldn't be more delighted myself."

Delighted? What was wrong with her? She would never be lonely again. It had been only two days since she last saw Tristan and her thoughts were constantly turning to him. The sooner she moved on to becoming a wife, the sooner she would have other matters to distract her.

She heard the front door slam and saw Jameson barreling past the parlor doorway. "Something's up there," she said.

A man just proposed to you, and you're side-tracked by your brother's arrival home? She gave her attention back to Chetwyn. "I'm sorry. That was rude of me."

"No, don't apologize. He did seem to be in a bit of a bother, didn't he? Shall we share our good news with your family? Perhaps that will improve his mood."

"Yes, by all means." *Smile,* she ordered herself. *This is what you wanted.*

She knew he had spoken to her father already because it was her father who had come to her bedchamber a half hour earlier to inform her that the Marquess of Chetwyn wished to speak with her. She'd suspected of what he wished to speak so she'd changed into a pale lilac gown, one she'd been saving for a special occasion.

He helped her to her feet, wound her arm about his, and patted her hand where it rested in the crook of his elbow. "I shouldn't like to wait too long," he said.

"I see no reason why we should. I should think that Society would understand that a woman who has spent two years in mourning would be anxious to get on with her life."

"My thoughts exactly." They turned down the hallway. "I know there are things that must be tended to. A wedding gown, a trousseau, of course. Perhaps you could let me know tomorrow what date would work well for you."

"I'll visit Sarah this afternoon. As she's gone through a wedding, she can help me determine a time frame."

"Wonderful."

Could their conversation be any less rife with excitement? They reached her father's study and she heard loud voices coming from within.

"Jameson seems to be in top form," Chetwyn said quietly.

"Indeed."

"Perhaps we should wait—"

"I think not. My family can use some good news."

The servant opened the door. They walked in. Jameson, pacing about, came to an abrupt halt. Her father was sitting behind his desk, scowling. Her other brothers were standing about looking none too happy.

"Is everything all right?" Anne asked. A silly question because obviously something was amiss. Jameson looked as though he wanted to put his fist through a wall—or worse, into someone's face.

She wasn't certain now was the proper time to share her news.

"Hardly," Jameson barked. "It's that scapegrace, Lord Tristan."

Anne's heart pounded so hard against her ribs that she was surprised it didn't knock Chetwyn aside. He did, however, separate himself from her. "What of him?" she asked.

Jameson puffed up like an irate rooster. He shot his gaze to Chetwyn as though he were somehow at fault. "After the charity ball . . . Lord Tristan Easton secreted Lady Hermione away. Spent the night with her. She returned home with her hair tumbled, and her gown ripped. Now he refuses to marry her. When I confronted him, he said she was lying."

She was! Anne bit back the words. Oh, God, she couldn't do this to dear, unsuspecting Chetwyn.

"Pity those ruffians you hired didn't do a better job of putting him in his place," Stephan muttered.

She felt as though the earth had shifted beneath her and she was in danger of losing her balance. "You hired the ruffians who attacked him at the docks?"

Jameson straightened to his full height. "They were to deliver a message to him to stay away from you. I suppose you know of it because he told you."

She looked at Chetwyn, discovered him studying her intently, and wondered what he suspected. "Forgive me, Chetwyn," she whispered before turning back to a brother she suddenly immensely disliked. "He didn't have to tell me of it. I was there . . . on the docks . . . with him when the four of them attacked."

"Christ!" Edward blurted, while Stephan's eyes bugged and Phillip's mouth dropped open. Her father's face turned a mottled red.

"Anne—" Jameson began, his voice seething.

"I can also assure you," she cut in, "that he was not with Lady Hermione following the charity ball. He was with me. Until dawn. Did he not tell you that?"

Appearing horrified, Jameson shook his head, opened his mouth, closed it.

"So perhaps he's a gentleman after all, striving to protect my reputation."

"Good God," her father barked as though he'd finally found his voice. "But Chetwyn—"

"Yes, Chetwyn," she said softly, turning to him. "I'm so sorry. Shall we simply pretend that you never asked and I never said yes?"

"Will Lord Tristan marry you?" Chetwyn asked.

She released a choked laugh. "I doubt it."

"He bloody well will," Stephan said.

No, she thought, he bloody well won't.

"She's lying?" Sebastian barked.

"She's lying," Tristan repeated for the third time.

Sitting in a nearby chair, Mary watched as the two brothers faced off.

"I warned you to take care with her, that this would happen," Sebastian said.

Lounging back in a chair, Tristan laughed. "I'm not sure what more care I could have taken than not leaving the ball with her. I can't help it if she's lying through her teeth."

"If you weren't with her, then where were you?"

"That, Brother, is none of your business."

Ah, Mary thought. He was with someone, and she suspected she knew who the lady was.

"It's going to be all of London's business—"

"It's nobody's damn business. But if you must know I was on my ship. My men will vouch for me. I was feeling claustrophobic after the ball so I went for a sail."

"Only your men can vouch for you?"

Mary hid her surprise. It seemed her husband was more aware of the situation than she thought. He knew another lady was involved.

"Only my men."

"I doubt they will hold much sway. People will think you've bribed them to lie for you. Lady Hermione comes from a powerful family. Not to mention that they are much more well liked than we are."

"I'll speak with her."

"I'm not sure that's wise."

"I'm not going to marry her."

"I'm not sure you'll have a choice."

"I was forced once before to do something that I didn't want to do. It'll be a cold day in hell before I'm forced again."

Mary watched as her husband paled.

"I had no choice. I had to get you away from England. You were second in line."

"I'm not blaming you. I blame Uncle. But I will not marry Lady Hermione. I can speak with her or I can simply set sail tonight."

"If you leave, you'll never be able to return."

"Tell me, Brother, what the hell am I returning to?"

Mary watched as Tristan stormed from the room and her husband sank into a chair. She thought he'd moved beyond the guilt from what happened all those years ago but it still lingered. It probably always would, until his brothers were happy.

She rose, walked over to him, knelt before him, and took his hands. "Did you not once tell me that we must let him travel his own path?"

"But he's lost, Mary. I can see that now and he has been since he was fourteen. Maybe marriage to the chit would help settle him."

"Not when he loves someone else."

Sebastian studied her. "Do you know who was on the ship with him?"

"I don't *know* but I have a good idea."

"Then why doesn't he announce it and marry her?"

"Because just as he doesn't want to be forced, my love, I suspect he doesn't want to force her."

"It makes no sense."

"He'll find his way."

He sighed. "At fourteen, I thought we would be able to step back into our roles so easily. I should have kept us all together."

"You made the best decision you could at the time."

"You're not going to let me feel guilty about this are you?"

"No. Come upstairs and I'll distract you."

Standing, he drew her to her feet and kissed her. She would never tire of his kisses, never tire of—

A knock on the door brought their prelude to lovemaking to an end.

The butler stepped inside and announced, "Your Grace, Lords Blackwood and Jameson would like a word."

"Ah." Sebastian exchanged a glance with her. "Would you care to wager that it was Lady Anne Hayworth on the ship with him?"

Smiling softly, she shook her head. It was whom she'd suspected all along.

Under the circumstances, Tristan supposed that he could have come in through the front door. Her brothers wouldn't be happy to see him, but considering that they had confronted him at Sebastian's this afternoon and informed him that he would marry their sister, he expected they would begrudgingly allow him to speak with her in the parlor. But quite honestly he felt a need to see her without anyone knowing.

So he was perched on the sill of her window watching her. She sat on a sofa before the fireplace. In spite of the warmer weather, tonight a fire burned in the hearth and he wondered if revealing their little trysts had chilled her. But what struck him the most was the loneliness he sensed coming from her. How often she had spoken of the lonely nights that awaited her if he remained in her life. Until this moment he wasn't certain that he'd quite comprehended the full extent of what being with him would cost her.

He slipped into the room and walked over to the fireplace. She barely moved a muscle. Simply lifted her gaze from the fire to his eyes as he pressed a shoulder against the mantel.

"Why did you tell them that you were with me?" he asked quietly.

Looking lost, she shook her head. "Because they thought you were a man without honor. She was lying, yet all of London would believe her over you. I suppose my father and brothers paid you a call."

"They did."

"Did you tell them to go to the devil?"

He'd wanted to. "No, I told them that I'd marry you if it was what you wanted."

She released a brittle laugh. "How many ladies receive two proposals in one day? Yours isn't quite as charming as Chetwyn's."

A fissure of something dark and possessive shot through him. "He asked?"

"Yes, just before we discovered the trouble that Lady Hermione was stirring up."

"What did you tell him?"

"I told him yes, and then I had to apologize for being less than a lady."

His hand began to ache and he realized he was gripping the mantel so hard that his knuckles were in danger of pushing through the skin. He loosened his grip. "Did you want to marry him?"

"It's all moot now. He'd not have me. Besides, he deserves someone who is above reproach."

"But did you *want* to marry him?"

"I don't want to be lonely. I've had two years of that. And Chetwyn is kind, generous. He would have been an exemplary husband. Life would have been good I think but—" She offered him a small smile and shifted her gaze to his hand that was once again gripping the mantel. "You can relax; I'm not going to marry you either."

Strangely her words served only to heighten his tension. "Why not?"

"Do you love me?"

"Does Chetwyn?"

"That's not the point." She rose to her feet and joined him by the fire. He could see the sadness in her eyes so much more clearly now. He hated it. "Your life is obviously on the sea. Mine is here. If I'm unmarried then I'm free to make choices."

"To take a lover without guilt," he said, each word biting.

"Would you deny me what comfort I might find with another?"

He touched her cheek, but she refused to be quieted.

"Can you promise me that you'll not take comfort with other women when you'll spend months from home—"

Home for him was the sea. The majority of the time he would be there.

"—in places with exotic women? Would you not be tempted to stray? What would our marriage vows be but a farce?"

"And when you get with child?"

"If I'm not with you, it won't be yours, will

it? Who knows? In time, perhaps I'll meet a man who'll forgive my sins."

In the meantime she would be alone, sitting on a sofa, staring at the writhing flames of a crackling fire.

He guided his thumb along the corner of her mouth. "It was never my intention to cause you any pain."

"I know. Still unintended consequences are rather troublesome and must be dealt with."

"Your family won't be happy if I don't marry you."

She gave him a sad smile. "They won't be happy if you do. They don't like you and I find that rather a shame—that they don't appreciate the man you are."

A blackguard? He'd torn her reputation asunder. He couldn't give her what she deserved. A home, husband, children. Permanence. A life without loneliness. But he almost broke out in a sweat at the mere thought of not getting back out on the sea. Perhaps if he'd never known anything different—

"Will they send you away?"

"I shall send myself. I still have the money from Walter. I shall be a lady of independent means." She cradled his jaw. "I'll be fine, but you must let me go completely."

"I won't stay away from England forever."

"But when you return you mustn't seek me out. It would be unfair to us both, to have continual joinings and partings. It's too hard, Tristan. It's too damned hard."

"I won't leave until I know for certain that you're not with child."

"I'm not. My courses began rather fortuitously this morning. I'd have not accepted Chetwyn's offer otherwise."

He didn't understand the disappointment he experienced at her reassurance that she wasn't carrying his child. He didn't want children. His life wasn't suited to them. He was completely unencumbered, free to do as he desired. And what he desired was to leave, to be back out on the water.

"I'll never forget you," he said as he lowered his mouth to hers to taste her for the final time. She was right, of course. Walking away from her was one of the most difficult things he'd ever done. But she wouldn't be happy on his ship and he wouldn't be happy off it. Nor would she be happy waiting for him to return. No matter how glorious the reunions might be, there would always be the bitter knowledge that they would come to an end.

With Rafe's assistance, Tristan was able to learn that Chetwyn's favorite club was Dodger's Drawing Room. With a letter of introduction from his brother, he was allowed into the hallowed gentlemen's domain. With some well-placed coins in the proper palm, he quickly located Chetwyn in the smoking salon, sitting in a plush chair in a seating area near a fireplace. He was smoking a cigar and sipping brandy. He was also flanked by all four of Anne's brothers. They were no doubt consoling him.

Tristan was actually grateful for their presence. It would ensure they all heard what he had to say.

He could feel eyes coming to bear on him, attention being diverted to him. He'd always given the impression that he savored being the center of things, but the truth was that he abhorred it. Perhaps it was the remnants of having his uncle's attentions focused on him and his brothers. When he was shivering in the tower, he'd wished that he'd been invisible, that his uncle had ignored him, that he was insignificant. Maybe that was part of the reason he hated being in London, where every aspect of a person was scrutinized and commented on. Anne relished this life and he couldn't wait to leave it.

As he approached the seating area, Tristan watched as Anne's brothers came menacingly to their feet while Chetwyn did little more than study him with a speculative gleam. It seemed the man was always observing, seeing things that Tristan rather wished he didn't.

He came to a halt before Chetwyn. "Gentlemen."

"You haven't been to see my sister," Jameson said.

"Actually I've just left her."

"You bastard," one of the younger pups groused, his hands balling into fists.

Tristan ignored him. "Chetwyn, I thought you should know that I'm not going to marry Anne because nothing happened between she and I."

"She said—"

He cut Jameson off. "That she was with me. Yes. On my ship. On the deck with the smell of the sea around her and the wind blowing her hair. I did my best to convince her that she'd have a more enjoyable time below in my quarters, but she was having none of it. She simply wanted to be on the water for a bit. Fewer cares out there, she said. As a gentleman, I swear to you that nothing untoward happened, certainly nothing that demands she spend the remainder of her life shackled to a rogue such as myself. I'm not giving up the sea, not even for her." He shrugged. "Which will leave her very lonely indeed."

Chetwyn slowly came to his feet. "You did attempt to seduce her."

"Without question. But she's made of stern stuff, your Anne." He nearly gagged on the last two words.

"I believe we need to take this conversation into the alleyway," Jameson said, rage evident in his eyes.

Tristan held Chetwyn's gaze. "Yes, I believe we do."

The conversation was fairly brief, a few harsh curses uttered as fists were flailing. He had no doubt that the more brutal of the blows came from Jameson—not for Anne's sake, but for Lady Hermione's.

They left Tristan in a crumpled heap, with a battered face and a couple of broken ribs. He groaned as Rafe gently turned him over.

"Did you enjoy watching that?" he asked through a puffed-up tender mouth, tonguing a loose tooth.

"Not as much as I thought I would. How did you know that they'd want to pummel you?"

"It's what I'd do if we'd had a sister and some blackguard treated her the way I treated Anne. Help me up."

Oh, he hurt, dammit, as he staggered with a great deal of help to his feet. He couldn't straighten, not completely. He wasn't even certain he could walk.

Rafe slipped beneath Tristan's arm to give him support. "They gave me hope."

Through eyes half closed with swelling, Tristan squinted at his brother. *"What?"*

"The globes. I collected them because they gave me hope that there was someplace out there better than where I was."

"But you have new ones. You're still collecting them."

Rafe didn't respond as he helped Tristan hobble to the waiting carriage, and Tristan couldn't help but wonder if his brother was still searching for someplace better. It occurred to him that he and Rafe weren't so very different after all. Wasn't that the reason he stayed on the sea: searching for what he'd lost?

Chapter 25

Anne stood in the grand entry hallway waiting for the butler to inform Tristan that he had a caller. The London residence was one befitting a duke. She'd never visited before, but it was her understanding that it was during a ball held here that Tristan and his brothers had made their notorious entrance back into London Society.

Anne was not prone to snooping and while she knew she should wait where the butler had left her, she found herself drawn to the portrait depicting two boys that was hanging above a table adorned with flowers at the edge of the entryway. The boys couldn't have been any older than twelve. They were of the same height with the same build and matching features, and yet they were remarkably different. They stood with their backs to each other, looking out, one incredibly serious, the other with a bit of deviltry in his eyes and the start of a smile that promised mischief.

"Can you tell them apart?" a soft voice asked.

Anne spun around and curtsied. "Your Grace, my apologies. I didn't mean to pry—"

"Don't be silly. I'd have not placed the portrait there if I didn't mean for it to be viewed." She wore a pale green dress that made her upswept red hair seem more vibrant. But her emerald eyes spoke of harsh wisdom. "I wanted people who came here to see them as they were, to perhaps understand how life changed them. For a while we thought the portrait had been destroyed, but a servant recently discovered it hidden behind some furniture in an attic. It's been here for only a couple of weeks. But I digress. You didn't answer my question, Lady Anne. Can you tell them apart?"

Nibbling on her lower lip, Anne looked back at the portrait that represented youth lost. "The one on the left is Lord Tristan."

"You know few could ever see the difference in them. I never understood that. It seemed easy to me, but I thought perhaps it was because I always loved Sebastian."

Anne jerked her head around, met the duchess's speculative look. She didn't love Tristan. "The artist managed to capture Lord Tristan's teasing nature, I think. That's all."

"He did have a bit of the devil in him. Still does, truth be told, but it's not quite as innocent as it once was."

"Are any of us as we grow up?"

"I suppose not. I understand you've come to see Lord Tristan, but unfortunately, he's not here."

"Do you know when he might be returning?"

The duchess shook her head. "They set sail last night, from what I understand. My husband saw them off at the docks."

"I see. It could be years then."

"I suspect it will be, yes." She studied Anne, and Anne wondered what her face revealed. "Will you join me for a spot of tea in the garden?"

"I would be delighted." And perhaps, just perhaps, some of her melancholy would lift. As she followed the duchess through the house and into the garden, she wished now that she and Sarah had come to call as they'd spoken of doing.

Anne sat at the lace-covered table that the duchess indicated. As they sipped tea, Anne glanced around. The garden was awash in color and fragrances. "You have a very talented gardener."

"I stole him from my father, but is it really my roses you wish to discuss?"

Anne set aside her cup. The duchess waited patiently, her expression open and inviting. Anne thought under different circumstances that they might have been friends. She released a small self-conscious laugh. "I'm not quite sure what I'm doing here. As I understand it, Tristan announced at my brother's club that our involvement was quite innocent. To staunch any further gossip, Lord Chetwyn and I are to be married in two weeks. I thought he should know that all is right with the world again."

"Is it?" the duchess asked.

Anne nodded, because the affirmation wouldn't pass her lips. If all was right with the world, why was she so remarkably sad? "He needs the sea . . . Lord Tristan."

"I'm not sure he knows what he needs."

"He told me that you rescued him."

"I'm not quite certain of that. I helped him and his brothers escape but that's not quite the same as rescuing, is it?"

"You were incredibly brave to do what you did."

"Unlock a door? Hardly. They were much braver—to ride off into the unknown."

She made her part seem insignificant, but Anne didn't see how it could have been. It seemed everyone in this family fought to make light of an event that had changed all their lives.

"You should come to Pembrook sometime," the duchess said. "I think it would help you to understand Lord Tristan better. The original Pembrook was a castle, with a dungeon where people were tortured and a tower where prisoners awaited their fate. After our marriage, Keswick spent many an hour pounding a hammer against the walls of the tower, striving to destroy it. But it still stands. He decided to leave it in case his brothers needed to take part in its destruction. But his brothers haven't returned there since they laid their uncle to rest."

"Do *you* think he meant to kill them as they believe?"

"Without a doubt. I heard him plotting their murders. I try to imagine how terrifying it must have been for them in the tower—without light, warmth, or comfort. Waiting. Waiting to be murdered, by their own blood. You would think having shared the same experience in the tower that they would be very similar. It shaped them. There can be no denying that. But it is what happened after they left the tower that made them the men they are today."

Anne couldn't help but wonder if Tristan needed the sea because he was still trying to escape the horror of what he'd learned in that tower: that someone he may have loved would kill him, that the brothers he loved would be ripped from him, that the only one he could ever truly rely on was himself.

She wanted to weep for the lad he'd been when an artist had painted his portrait. She wanted to weep for the man who, she was beginning to realize, would never return home because it had been stolen from him when he was a lad, and he no longer knew how to find it.

It was sometime after midnight when Tristan brought his horse to a halt near Pembrook. He had a bright moon. In the distance he could see the silhouette of the manor house that Sebastian had built on a rise. He had yet to visit there. He wondered if it would feel like home. He doubted it.

Home had always been the looming castlelike structure that cast night shadows over him now.

Two days earlier he'd docked his ship in the port from which he'd escaped when he was a terrified lad on his own, running for his life. Twice he'd returned to Pembrook, but neither time had he come by water. He was a man now, fearful of nothing, yet he hadn't relished the notion of docking his ship in the same harbor from which he'd escaped. Still he had given the order and watched from the quarterdeck as the *Revenge* glided silently into place. From Marlow, he learned many of the skills that made him a good captain.

But there had been no one to teach him how to be a lord. Not teach him perhaps—so much as remind him. His father had certainly drilled particular behaviors into him. He pressed a gloved fist to his tightening chest as another memory with his father took hold. They'd all been banished until lately. He'd had so little time to think of anything beyond surviving and revenge.

God forgive him, but he'd actually initially resented Sebastian because he'd handled their uncle's demise single-handedly. Tristan had been denied any satisfaction in it. By the time he received word from Sebastian, and made his way with Rafe to Pembrook, the vicious swine was already cold and closed in his coffin. Twelve years of plotting revenge—stolen from Tristan.

With every strike of the lash against his back he'd wished his uncle dead. With every storm, with every bout of hunger when food was scarce, with every absence of wind, with every mile that separated him from his brothers and left him feeling so wretchedly alone—

Reaching into his pocket, stroking the kidskin glove he'd acquired the night he met Anne, he acknowledged that was the reason that he'd been blessedly relieved she hadn't wanted to marry him, the reason he hadn't fought her on it. He understood her loneliness. He hadn't wanted to admit it, but he did. He knew the abstract sense of it, the concrete pain of it. He would leave her and forget her. Go on with his life. He wouldn't love because love tied one down. Love bound. Love and everything that accompanied it terrified him.

Dismounting from his horse, he tethered it to a small scraggly bush and walked through the abandoned courtyard. He knew that Sebastian had plans to destroy this monstrosity, but he had yet to carry through on them. He was too busy striving to keep his wife happy. Love altered a man's course. It was as unpredictable as a storm.

He strode to the tower. As a lad he'd always thought it so damned tall. Even now it dwarfed him. Wrapping his hand around the latch, he pulled open the door, listened to the hideous screeching of hinges. They'd squealed that night when their uncle's henchman had escorted them to the tower.

"We didn't fight," he whispered. They went like trusting lambs. It was only once they were locked inside the uppermost room that they'd realized something was amiss.

Why would they suspect anything? No one had ever hurt them. They were the lords of Pembrook, idolized and protected by their father.

In the grayness, Tristan made out the lantern hanging on the wall. Taking the matches from his pocket, he struck one and lit the lantern. The shadows wavered around him. He began trudging up the stairs. The old wood moaned. He could smell the must and the odor of disuse.

Finally he reached it. The room. The heavy wooden door stood ajar. Inside was the small table and two stools, one of them overturned. He considered righting it but his attention was arrested by the huge hole on the other side of the room. He set the lantern on the table and examined what remained of the wall.

He remembered Sebastian telling him that he'd taken a sledgehammer to it, that he'd vented his anger there. Through that hole their uncle had eventually fallen to his death.

"Damn you," he rasped. "Damn you! You stole everything of importance. I don't care about the titles or the properties. You stole my brothers from me. You stole the opportunity for me to be the sort of man who was content to live in one place, the sort of man who would be worthy of Anne until the day he died."

He spotted the sledgehammer in the corner, hefted it up, and slammed it into the stone. "Damn you! You made me what I am. My own needs, my own desires, they always come first. There is a wall around my heart as thick—"

He hit the wall again.

"—as formidable—"

Slam.

"—as strong—"

A portion of the wall crumbled, broke apart, went flying away from him and into the darkened abyss of the night. Breathing heavily he stared at the damage he'd done. He could tear down the wall. It had been strong enough to hold them when they were boys, but it wasn't strong enough now to hurt him.

Dropping to his knees he did what he'd wanted to do that long-ago dreadful night, but feared that once he started, he'd be unable to stop.

He wept.

For the boy he'd been.

For the man he was.

For the lord he wished he might have become.

And he screamed out because in the end, his uncle had won. He'd destroyed Lord Tristan Easton. And Captain Crimson Jack didn't know how to find him again.

Chapter 26

In two hours Anne would be married, yet as she stood in front of the cheval glass in her gown of satin, lace, and tiny beaded pearls, she felt no measure of excitement. She liked Chetwyn. She surely did. Marriage to him would be proper. She would be proper. She adjusted the veil that fell from a wreath of orange blossoms and wished she'd chosen some other sort of blossom because oranges always reminded her of Tristan. And she didn't want to think of him today. She didn't want to think of him ever again.

She was wrapping about her finger the strip of leather that he had once used to bind his hair, to bind hers. She needed to toss it away, but she knew, instead, she would return it to her jewelry box before she left for the church.

"Don't you look lovely, my lady," Martha said. "Lord Chetwyn is such a fortunate man."

"It is I who am fortunate." The words were

the proper thing to say, so why were her eyes burning? "I think you'll be happy in Chetwyn's household."

"Ew."

Anne turned to find her maid's brow furrowed so deeply that she was surprised the woman didn't yelp in pain. "Ew?"

Martha released a deep sigh. "I was going to tell you after the wedding—"

"Tell me what?"

She smiled brightly. "Mr. Peterson has asked me to marry him. I've said yes."

Anne took Martha's hands. "Oh, that's wonderful. Congratulations. Although I don't understand why that should make you dread Chetwyn's household."

"Oh, I don't dread his house, but telling you, m'lady, that I won't be going. I'm giving my notice."

Releasing her hold on Martha, Anne scoffed. "That's a silly thing to do. It'll be years before he returns—"

"No, he came back last night. Said he missed me too much and had the captain turn the ship about."

Anne's heart slammed against her ribs. "They're in port?"

Martha nodded. "Yes, miss."

Anne's gaze shot to the window. What was she expecting for God's sake? To see Tristan clambering into her bedchamber?

"But they're setting sail again this afternoon," Martha continued. "Just not with Mr. Peterson.

He's given up the sea. He's going to work in a shipping office or some such. He's saved his money so we can purchase a home. I don't have to work any more."

"Oh, Martha, I'm so happy for you."

"I'm happy for myself." Her smile grew. "I never thought to find love. He's a good man."

"I've no doubt of that."

A brisk knock sounded on her door. Martha hurried over to open it. Stiff and clearly unhappy, Jameson stood beside Chetwyn. "Leave us, Martha," her brother ordered.

Martha gave Anne a quick look before scampering into the hallway.

"Chetwyn wishes to speak with you before the nuptials. Highly unusual, but I've granted him permission. However, the door is to remain op—"

Chetwyn stepped into the bedchamber and slammed the door shut in her brother's face. Anne pressed a hand to her mouth to stifle her laughter. She could only imagine Jameson's startled expression. She'd never seen Chetwyn so forceful. It was a bit disconcerting to realize that it excited her to see him this way.

He strode to the fireplace, raised his arm, pressed it against the mantel, and stared into the cold empty hearth. "Do wish I'd stopped by your father's study for a bit of spirits."

"I have some brandy."

Looking over his shoulder at her, he grinned. "Do you?"

"Yes, would you like some?"

He shook his head. "No, I suppose not. You should know, Anne, that I will treat you kindly."

"I never doubted that."

"You will never want for anything. I am convinced and believe with all my heart that I can provide you with a satisfactory life. But I daresay that I believe you deserve more."

"I don't understand."

"I think Lord Tristan is a rotten bastard," he continued. "But be that as it may, I've seen the way he looks at you and more, I've seen the way you look at him."

"How is that, my lord?" she dared to ask.

"As though you are the only two people who exist in the world." He faced her completely. "Do you love me, Anne?"

She dreaded answering him. She didn't want to hurt him but she couldn't begin today with a lie.

"I don't love you either," he said as though she had responded. "I asked you to marry me because of Walter's letter. I've come to the unfortunate conclusion at a rather inconvenient time that it's not enough upon which to base a marriage."

"Walter's letter?"

He reached into a pocket inside his jacket and removed a yellowed crumpled piece of paper. "He was ill when he wrote it. I suspect he knew he would die. He asked me to see that you were happy, and I thought that I could ensure that best if you were my wife. I thought I owed him that at least. I pushed him into joining a regiment, into making his own way. Our coffers are thin, you see, and I didn't want

to give him an allowance. Then we declared war on
Russia and I told him to sell his commission. Marriage to you would bring him a dowry; he could
make do with that. But he didn't want to be seen as
a coward. It's my fault he's dead."

"No, Chetwyn." Her heart going out to him,
she crossed over and placed her hand on his cheek.
She had yet to put on her gloves and she was grateful she could offer him a warm touch of comfort.
"He always liked playing soldier as a lad. You
know that. Nothing you could have said would
have swayed him from going. His heart was set on
it. You can't hold yourself responsible. We all have
to make our choices and live with them."

"Is that what *we're* doing, Anne? Making
choices with which we must live?"

"Are you crying off?" she asked, halfway teasing, halfway serious, not quite sure what she
wanted his answer to be.

"We beat him up you know."

"Who? Walter?"

"No. Lord Tristan."

Her stomach tightening, she stepped away.

"The night he came to the club," Chetwyn explained. "After he told us that he had attempted to
seduce you but that nothing occurred between you
and he. We escorted him outside and pummeled
him. Rather badly, actually. He didn't lift a hand
to stop us."

"No, he wouldn't have."

"I thought he'd have been a better fighter, that
he would have held his own against us."

"He certainly could have if he'd chosen. I saw him beat off the ruffians that my idiot brother hired while barely mussing his clothes."

"So why didn't he resist?"

"I suspect because he thought he deserved the beating. Or maybe he wouldn't hurt those I care for. Probably the latter," she said after a bit more thought.

"Do you love him, Anne?"

Tears burning her eyes, she shook her head. "It doesn't matter. The sea is his home . . . and what sort of life would that be for a lady?"

"If it includes love, I should think it would be a very wonderful life, indeed."

"Oh, Chetwyn." A sob broke free, and he enfolded her in his arms. He smelled of tart spices while she longed for the fragrance of oranges.

"I vowed that I would honor Walter's request and see you happy, but I don't believe your happiness lies with me."

"According to my maid, he's sailing off today."

"Then it seems to me that you should tell him how you feel before he goes. My carriage is in the drive if you wish to go somewhere."

"My father and brothers have taken to watching me like a hawk."

"I shall entice them into the library to drink a toast to my happiness."

Leaning back, she studied his strong features and thought it was quite possible that in time she would have come to love him. "I hope someday you find a woman who deserves you."

"Meanwhile, darling Anne, let's stop Walter's ghost from coming to haunt us, shall we?"

Laughing, she wiped the tears from her cheeks. "By all means."

Tristan read the words a third and final time. He'd never been a man of indecision and he wasn't one now. He knew what he wanted, and while he wasn't quite certain he'd acquire it, he did know that he'd live with regret for the remainder of his life if he didn't at least try.

With a deep sigh, he dipped the pen into the inkwell and scrawled his name on the designated line. Dropping the pen on his desk, he headed for the doorway.

"Just like that and you're done?" Jenkins asked.

Tristan paused at the door and glanced back over his shoulder. "I have a church to get to."

"Good luck, Cap'n."

He was going to need a good deal more than luck. Tristan rushed through the door and up the stairs to the deck. His plan had been to get off the ship as quickly as possible, but he needed one more moment. Just one.

He went to the railing, wrapped his hands around the familiar wood that had become worn over the years—

"Tristan! Tristan!"

He jerked his attention to the docks and watched as Anne, dressed in ivory, with a veil and a swath of skirts billowing out behind her, ran along the warped planks, dodging this way and that to avoid the working men. His heart lurched, tightened, threatened to stop. What the devil was she doing here?

"Anne!"

"Tristan!" She began frantically waving her arm as though he couldn't see her.

But even a heavy fog wouldn't have kept him from seeing her. And certainly nothing was going to keep him from her. He leaped over the railing and jogged down the gangway. He reached the dock in time to gather her in his arms. "Anne."

Damnation but it felt so good to hold her again, as though he'd finally come home.

"I'm going with you," she said, clinging to him. "I don't care if it's improper. I don't care if my reputation will be ruined or no gent will want me after you're done with me—"

Leaning back, he pressed his thumb to her lips before she could utter any more nonsensical words. "Why in God's name would I ever be done with you?"

"Because I'm not a proper lady. Because I've lain with you without benefit of marriage. I know it makes me the sort of woman that a man doesn't want forever. But I don't care. I don't care if you never marry me. I don't care if I live in sin and my family refuses to acknowledge me. I'll travel the world with you. I'll swim naked in ponds and—"

"You don't swim."

"I'll learn. Just please. Take me with you to the far side of the world."

"I can't, sweetheart."

He saw the devastation of rejection fill her eyes and he wanted to kick himself for the words he'd spoken and the ones he hadn't. "I've sold my ship, Anne."

She blinked, the shock of his words apparent. "Why ever would you do that?"

"So you'd have no doubt that I was committed to living a life on land. I was on my way to the church, to embarrass you in front of all of London. I was going to charge to the front of the sanctuary, kneel down, and ask you to become my wife before you had a chance to exchange vows with Chetwyn."

Smiling brightly, she laughed. "Were you really?"

"I love you, Anne, so damned much that it terrifies me. But a life without you terrifies me more. I don't need the sea. All I need is you. We'll find a posh house here in London and one in the country and I'll be a gentleman that you can be proud of."

Tears welled in her eyes. "Oh, my darling, I am proud of you. And you are a gentleman and a gentle man in spite of the hardships of your life. I love you, Tristan. I didn't want to. I didn't think I ever wanted to love again because the potential for hurt is so great, but so is the potential for happiness. With you I'm happy. With Chetwyn, I would be only content. I don't care if we live in London or the country or a cottage by the sea. I only care that I'm in your arms."

"That, my darling, is where you shall always be."

Chapter 27

Chetwyn stood off to the side of the vestry. He'd told Anne that he would keep the guests waiting some fifteen moments before announcing that no wedding would take place—on the off chance that Lord Tristan broke her heart and she still wanted to marry Chetwyn.

"I can't believe you sent her to him," Jameson grumbled. He was beside Chetwyn while her father stood at the window, also not terribly pleased with Chetwyn at the moment.

"She loves him and well you know it. I daresay she loves him more than she loved Walter."

"He's not a proper lord."

"I suspect his father, if he were still alive, would disagree."

Jameson scoffed.

Chetwyn heard a commotion at the front of the church and stepped toward the doors. Anne strolled in with Lord Tristan at her side. Behind them were the Duke and Duchess of Keswick and Lord Rafe Easton. Taking a deep breath, he went to greet them.

"Well, it seems I shall announce that a wedding will not be taking place this morning."

"Not necessarily," Lord Tristan said. "I already obtained a special license."

Chetwyn fought not to be taken aback. He knew it was something that couldn't be done in a day, so apparently marriage to Anne was something Lord Tristan had been planning. "Cheeky bugger. What if she'd say no?"

"But I didn't," Anne said. Leaning up, she kissed his cheek. "Thank you, Chetwyn."

He thought she'd never looked more beautiful. Her eyes were filled with such joy, joy he didn't think would be there if she was going to be marrying him.

"You're very welcome."

Then Lord Tristan turned to Anne's father, Lord Blackwood. "My lord, I know having me in your family is probably the last thing you would ever wish for, but I treasure Anne with all my heart. She will never want for anything that is within my realm to provide. But I cannot give her your blessing. That must come from you. I hope you will bestow it."

Lord Blackwood approached his daughter. "Are you sure about this, Anne?"

"I love him, Father. With or without your blessing, I intend to spend the remainder of my life with him. It would be easier with your blessing."

"Then God help me, you have it."

With tears in her eyes, Anne hugged her father. "Thank you."

"Lord Jameson—" Tristan began.

"I won't give my blessing."

"I'm not fool enough to ask for it, but I thought if Lady Hermione were here—"

"She is."

"Perhaps you would ensure she doesn't create a fuss."

Jameson straightened his shoulders. "I'll do it for Anne. Not for you."

Chetwyn wondered if Jameson realized he was also doing it for himself.

"I say, Chetwyn, I was wondering if you might stand with me," Lord Tristan said.

Chetwyn could not have been more surprised if the man had asked for *his* hand in marriage. "Surely your brother—"

"If you would honor this request, I think it would go a long way to smoothing things over for Anne and the scandal we've stirred up. I also have an additional request."

As Chetwyn listened, he couldn't help but think that Walter was smiling down on them with approval.

Lady Hermione could hardly countenance that Lord Tristan was standing at the altar slightly behind Lord Chetwyn. She wondered what that was about. But it didn't matter. What mattered was that Lord Tristan had returned and he would no doubt be at the reception. She could apologize to him for her deception and work to convince him that he belonged with her.

It had been difficult to come here today, to suffer the stares and speculative looks, but she had wanted to witness Lady Anne's marriage, to see her nemesis permanently removed as a threat. Surely Lord Tristan was standing beside Lord Chetwyn as a symbol that he was glad the lady would no longer be available to him. For she had lied as well, saying that she'd been intimate with him, when all she'd done was sail on his ship.

Perhaps later this afternoon, Lord Tristan would take Hermione aboard his ship. They could sail the world—even if she got dreadfully sick in a row-boat. A ship would be different. His ship would be different. Perhaps they would even kiss. It wasn't fair that he'd never even tried to steal a kiss from her.

She was startled from her reverie as Lord Jameson edged onto the pew beside her.

Organ music floated toward the rafters and everyone stood as Lady Anne glided down the aisle, her hand on her father's arm. As she neared the altar, Lord Tristan stepped out from behind Lord Chetwyn and took his place beside her.

"No," she whispered and started to move past Lord Jameson.

"Let my sister have her moment."

She jerked her gaze up to Lord Jameson. His eyes held pity—no, sadness. For her. She wanted to weep. Lord Tristan would forever be beyond her reach if she didn't stop it. But then she realized he had always been so. She simply had been too foolish to admit it.

As everyone took their seats, Lady Hermione sank onto the hard pew.

Lord Jameson leaned near her and whispered, "At the reception at my father's house there will be dancing. Perhaps you would honor me with your first dance."

She looked at him then, really looked at him. Hadn't Lord Tristan told her that Lord Jameson was for her? Hadn't he bid on her at that awful charity ball when no one else had?

In answer to his question, she simply wrapped her hand around his. He gave her a small smile before turning his attention to the ceremony.

Something in her shifted and she saw him quite differently. He was far more handsome than Lord Tristan. More polished. And someday he would be an earl. Lord Tristan, well, he would always be merely a second son.

She realized something else as well. Lord Jameson had always been there for her. How could she have overlooked him with such ease? What a silly chit she'd been.

Anne watched as Tristan stepped around Chetwyn to take his place beside her. The favor he had asked of Chetwyn was to stand in the groom's place until Anne arrived at the altar. He feared if he was initially standing there that the speculation and gossip would create a stir that would detract from her entrance.

Based on the sharp intakes of breath, gasps, murmurings, and whispers, she suspected he'd been right. She imagined the loudest of all was Lady Hermione's but Jameson was with her now, and he would keep her from ruining this moment, even if it meant carrying the barnacle out of the church.

Then Anne was no longer thinking of Lady Hermione or the people in the pews. All her attention was focused on the strong handsome man standing in front of her. She didn't know what had possessed her to think she could have married anyone else, that she would have been content with him off sailing the world without her at his side.

She loved him so much, wounded soul and all. They were each broken in their own way, but somehow the cracks and fissures allowed them to fit together perfectly.

He looked so deeply into her eyes that she felt as though he touched the very core of her. In his improper way, he'd managed to do everything right. He'd asked her father for his blessing. He'd included Chetwyn so he wouldn't feel completely cast aside.

As words about love and devotion echoed around her, she slid her gaze to Chetwyn. With a smile, he winked at her. She did hope he would find someone worthy of him. She was glad that he didn't hold it against her for not being that person.

He was so remarkably good. She would always be grateful to him.

As she exchanged vows with Tristan, she knew Chetwyn was correct: she was on the path to having a very wonderful life, indeed.

With the moon turning the water to silver, Anne stood on the deck of the *Revenge* with Tristan's arms wrapped tightly around her. It seemed an appropriate place to be for their first night together as husband and wife. He'd paid Jenkins to take them to Yorkshire. They planned to stay at the ancestral estate at Pembrook, in his brother's new residence, while they searched for a home of their own.

She didn't think she'd ever known such happiness.

He pressed his lips to the nape of her neck. "Had enough of the sea, my love?"

She leaned back against him. "Will you truly be able to stay away from it?"

"Bit late to be questioning me about it now."

"Tristan, I'm serious."

"I thought it was the traveling I loved, the exploration, the adventure. But I came to realize it was simply that I was lost. I thought my home was the sea, and instead, I finally realized that my home was with you."

She turned about in his arms and cradled his face between her hands. "Poetic words, Tristan, but not an answer."

"I might need the sea from time to time, but not the far side of the world. We'll get a smaller ship, perhaps. We'll sail around Great Britain. Picnic on an island. I can be content with a piece of the sea as long as I have you."

"You shall always have me."

Rising up on her toes, she pressed her body to his as she kissed him. She could hardly countenance now that she had thought she could not endure the loneliness if she married him. A bit of time with him was preferable to none at all. She would always have a tender regard for Chetwyn for his forcing her to face that fact. Walter had taught her that life was short, could be snatched away at any moment. Chetwyn had shown her that it was not enough to be content. Tristan had revealed to her that love was based on choices, sacrifices, and passion. A passion that was not limited to bedchambers.

She had loved Walter. She truly had. But what she felt for Tristan went beyond anything she'd ever experienced.

As his mouth moved expertly over hers, she heard the distant lowing of a whale. It didn't sound quite as lonely as it had before. Perhaps because now her heart and soul were filled to overflowing with love for this man who held her as though she were his anchor, his mooring.

He lifted her into his arms, and she nestled her head into the crook of his shoulder. The curious had been at the reception her father had held for her following the marriage ceremony. While there was some tension in the air—she wasn't certain if her brothers would ever fully embrace Tristan— she'd been too happy to give it much credence.

The Duke of Keswick had been the one to raise his glass in a toast to them. "To my brother and the lovely lady who brought him home."

It had seemed simple enough, but she suspected there were undercurrents in his words. Tristan had returned home two years ago, but she knew he had still been adrift. They'd both lost their moorings, had been floundering about with no tether.

But now her life again had purpose, her feet were sturdy on the path. She, too, was home.

Once locked inside the cabin, they took their time removing each other's clothes, building the anticipation when they would once again come together after what had seemed ages. He had new scars: a small one above his left brow, a tiny one on his chin. Gifts from her brothers, no doubt. She gently touched the faint, fading bruising on his ribs.

"You shouldn't have let them beat you," she said.

"I didn't think you'd much like it if I tore into them. Besides I deserved it." He cupped her face. "I'd hurt you, Anne. I'll never hurt you again."

His mouth covered hers, and she couldn't help but think that she would have this taste, this heat, this passion for the remainder of her life. Anytime she wanted it. He would be there. Yet even knowing she would have no lonely nights without him, she was greedy for tonight.

It was she who deepened the kiss. She who stroked. She who led them to the bed.

When his weight came down on her, she curled around him, held him near. Happy. So gloriously happy. Had she truly thought she could live the remainder of her life without this, without him?

What a silly goose.

"Hmm?" he murmured as he swirled his tongue over the shell of her ear.

She hadn't realized she'd spoken aloud. "I was just thinking what a silly goose I was to think I could be content with anyone other than you."

Lifting himself up, he gazed down into her eyes and she couldn't help but remember that first night. His crystal blue eyes held a tenderness now that they hadn't then. Oh, there was still the deviltry in them, there always would be. She knew that it was a lingering piece from his youth—something in him that his uncle had failed to destroy, something that lashings couldn't dim, something that Society couldn't tame. She wished he'd suffered none of the hardships that had plagued his life, but she also knew they had brought him to her. This remarkable man, whom she loved so deeply.

"I'm glad you came to your senses," he said.

"Me? *My* senses?" She laughed. "You sold your ship."

"Glad I came to my senses as well. Dear God, but I love you, Anne. I would have had a wretched lonely life if you hadn't married me."

"How could I refuse to marry you when I love you so desperately? I love everything that comprises you—the sea captain and the lord. They're so intertwined. You may think they're different aspects to you, but they're not. Even when I knew you only as a captain, I always thought there was a certain nobility in you, in your deportment. When I discovered you were a lord, I could still see the courageous and commanding sea captain. And always, there was the wicked man you were."

"Wicked in a good way?"

Her grin widened. "Definitely in a good way. Be wicked now, my love."

"Only if you'll join me in the wickedness."

She did. Wholeheartedly. Touching, stroking, tasting.

They explored each other as though it were their first coupling, as though they'd arrived on an uncharted island and were carefully making their way around it. Yet laced throughout was the familiarity that they had traveled here before.

When he joined his body to hers, she wanted to cry out with the wonder of it. He was hers, absolutely, completely. And she was his.

When the pleasure soared through her, she did cry out—his name—and she heard her name forced through clenched teeth. Their voices mingled, become one just as their bodies had.

Rolling to the side, he brought her up against him, tucked her in close.

"I'm not lost anymore, Anne," he said quietly. "After fourteen years of wandering, I've finally found home. You are my safe harbor."

"And you are mine, my love."

She didn't delude herself into thinking that their life would be without storms, but they would weather them, because they would have each other. Always.

Epilogue

Off the Yorkshire Coast
Some Years Later

"**M**ummy, look! I'm steering the *Princess* all by myself!"

Anne glanced up from the two-year-old daughter on her lap to the six-year-old one standing at the helm, her father protectively behind her, his legs braced, his hands covering hers. The sturdy yacht, its sails filled with wind, sliced through the open water without a care. At least once a week Tristan brought the family out on the sea.

"I can see that, darling. You're doing a marvelous job."

"I'm going to be a ship captain when I grow up."

"I have no doubt."

Tristan laughed, before signaling to Mouse—

who more often than not went by Martin these days—to keep watch over his eldest girl. He crossed the deck and scooped up his four-year-old daughter from where she was playing with the wooden blocks he'd carved for her. "You'll be sailing the ship next, Princess."

"Papa! I'm the princess," their eldest shouted.

"You're all princesses," he assured her, before sinking into the chair beside Anne. He leaned over toward her and whispered, "You're my favorite."

Laughing softly, she said, "Don't let them hear that. You'll have a mutiny on your hands."

They'd purchased a lovely house near the sea. They went to bed every night with the sound of the waves crashing against the shore. At first after he acquired the yacht, he often took it out for the day. But over the years, his solitary sojourns had become fewer. He designed luxury yachts. Mr. Peterson oversaw the craftsmen hired to build them. They sold them for a princely sum. The *Princess* had been the first. Below deck were comfortable accommodations that rivaled many homes.

Once or twice a year, they would travel to a distant port. Their three daughters were seeing small portions of the world and feared nothing. She suspected that someday they would provide quite a challenge to any young man who wished to court them.

Of course any such young man would have to be brave enough to face their father first. He would be far worse than her brothers when it came to protecting his princesses.

"Why don't we leave the girls with the nannies and go below?" he suggested.

"Are you really going to leave your daughter at the helm?"

"Mouse will guide her. He won't let anything happen to them."

"He's almost their big brother, isn't he?" Tristan had hired him to care for the boat, to keep it in top shape. He lived in a small cottage near theirs. For a child who had been deemed worthless, he had a good life. As a young man now, he charmed the ladies. A talent Anne knew he'd picked up from Tristan.

She signaled for the nannies and when their two youngest were safely in their care, she rose and walked to the railing with Tristan.

"The sea doesn't call to you as much anymore, does it?" she asked.

"No. An hour here or there suits me just fine."

"Do you ever miss it, the life of adventure you led?"

He turned her in his arms, and she gazed into the pale blue eyes that she'd loved for so long now.

"You're all the adventure I need," he told her before lowering his mouth to hers, sweeping her away on the tide of his love.